JUST HOW BIG *IS* ODELIA GREY?

What reviewers are saying...

"Odelia Grey is a keeper."—*Library Journal*

"Jaffarian plays the formula with finesse, keeping love problems firmly in the background while giving her heroine room to use her ample wit and grit."—*Kirkus Reviews*

"[Odelia Grey] is an intriguing character, a true counter against stereotype, who demonstrates that life can be good, even in a world where thin is always in."—*Booklist*

"A sharp, snappy mystery novel...This is a fast and furious read that should be fun to see as a series with Odelia as the lead character."—*AmaZe Magazine*

What fellow authors are saying...

"More fun than a lunch pail full of plump paralegals, *The Curse of the Holy Pail* is a tale as bouncy as its bodacious protagonist." —*Bill Fitzhugh, author of* Highway 61 Resurfaced *and* Pest Control

"[*Curse of the Holy Pail* is] even better than her first...a major hoot!"—*Thomas B. Sawyer, author of* The Sixteenth Man *and former head writer/producer of* Murder, She Wrote

"Sue Ann Jaffarian does a masterful job. Once you get to know Odelia Grey, you'll love her. I know I do."—*Naomi Hirahara, author of* Summer of the Big Bachi *and* Gasa-Gasa Girl

"A plus-sized thumbs up. Jaffarian's a new sharpshooter in crime fiction."—*Brian M. Wiprud, author of* Stuffed *and* Pipsqueak, *winner of Lefty Award for Most Humorous Novel*

ALSO IN THE ODELIA GREY SERIES

Too Big to Miss
(Midnight Ink, 2006)

The Curse of the Holy Pail
(Midnight Ink, 2007)

Epitaph Envy
(coming in 2009)

SUE ANN
JAFFARIAN

AN ODELIA GREY MYSTERY

THUGS
AND
KISSES

MIDNIGHT INK
WOODBURY, MINNESOTA

MIDNIGHT
INK

FIRST EDITION
First Printing, 2008

Book design by Donna Burch
Cover design by Ellen L. Dahl
Editing and layout by Rebecca Zins

Midnight Ink, an imprint of Llewellyn Publications

Library of Congress Cataloging-in-Publication Data
Jaffarian, Sue Ann, 1952–
    Thugs and kisses / Sue Ann Jaffarian.—1st ed.
        p.   cm.—(An Odelia Grey Mystery)
    ISBN 978-0-7387-1089-1
    1. Grey, Odelia (Fictitious character)—Fiction. 2. Overweight women—
Fiction. 3. Legal assistants—Fiction. 4. Women detectives—California—
Fiction. 5. California—Fiction. I. Title.
PS3610.A359T48 2008
813'.6—dc22

                                                                    2007033884

Midnight Ink
2143 Wooddale Drive, Dept. 978-0-7387-1089-1
Woodbury, MN 55125-2989

www.midnightinkbooks.com

Printed in the United States of America

DEDICATION

To the 2007 winners of the American Beauties Plus Pageant—making a difference, one woman at a time:

Natisha Webb
American Beauties Ambassador Elite

Dora-Lee Durham
American Beauties Plus Woman

Chauna Howard
Mrs. American Beauties Plus

Robin Gaines
Ms. American Beauties Plus

Joi Bannister
Miss American Beauties Plus

ACKNOWLEDGMENTS

Thank you from the bottom of my heart to:

Whitney Lee, my incredible agent; Diana James, my high-energy, always-thinking manager; Barbara Moore, my patient and encouraging editor at Midnight Ink, and all the other wonderful folks at Llewellyn Worldwide/Midnight Ink who continue to help me make my dreams come true;

Author and friend Jane DiLucchio, for her insight into the character of Sally Kipman;

Julie Bauer and Marilyn Tarvin, for being my "focus group" and providing helpful comments;

Attorney Jay Hartz, for sharing his opinion and knowledge for some of the legal background needed for this novel;

My many friends and family who cheer me on and keep my feet on the ground; and

To the many readers who take time from their lives to tell me how much they enjoy my books.

SPECIAL ACKNOWLEDGMENT

To the members of the Los Angeles Chapter of Sisters In Crime: it has been a privilege and an honor to have served you as president for the past four years.

ONE

"WHY AM I NOT surprised?"

The question, phrased more like a long-suffering supplication to a supreme being, was accompanied by a copy of this morning's *Orange County Register* being tossed onto my small, cluttered desk like an under-thrown Frisbee.

When it slid to a stop, just short of smacking my almost-full coffee mug, I saw that the paper was open to the front page of the local news section and folded in such a way as to show off a photo of me—yes, *moi*, Odelia Patience Grey. The caption above the photo blazed: *Food Fight Erupts at Local Market.*

A resigned sigh escaped my lips. I had hoped that no one would recognize me. After all, in the caption under the grainy photo, I was merely referred to as an unidentified woman.

The question had come from Mike Steele, my boss. He stood in front of me, waiting for an answer to what I felt was not a question deserving of a response. In my opinion, it had sounded purely rhetorical in nature. I continued to stare down at the fuzzy

1

photo in the paper, my lips tighter than a pair of size 6 shoes on size 9 feet.

Michael Steele is a partner at Wallace, Boer, Brown and Yates, the law firm in Orange County, California, at which I am employed as a paralegal. I've been with Woobie (the nickname given the firm by its employees) for about eighteen years, and I would be looking forward to the next eighteen years, if it were not for the man standing in front of me.

I didn't need to raise my face to know that Steele would be immaculately groomed from his *GQ*-handsome, close-shaven face right down to his fingertips, which would be professionally buffed and shining like dew in the morning sun. And I didn't need to glance in his direction to know that he was wearing an expensive and beautifully tailored suit. It was also unnecessary to look up to know that he was peeved at me. The sarcasm in his voice hung in the air, waiting to be admired, round and bright, like ornaments on a Christmas tree.

A few years ago, when my old boss, Wendell Wallace, retired, I somehow fell within Steele's grasp. Steele had requested that I be assigned to him, and the firm agreed. They had even sweetened the pot for me with a nice raise and a private office.

They assigned me to him with an apology, claiming they trusted me to keep Steele and his law practice in line. In other words, I became his professional keeper so the firm's founding partners could sleep at night.

Now, don't get me wrong—Mike Steele is an incredible lawyer. He's brilliant, focused, and ethical, which in this day and age is an accomplishment all on its own. He brings in a ton of new business and is the firm's top attorney in generating billable hours. He's Midas with a law degree.

It's just that sometimes he needs to be beaten about the head with the people-skills bat.

Without raising my face to look at Steele, I gave in and broke my silence. I pushed the newspaper back in his direction. "Not exactly my best side, is it?"

In the photo, my two-hundred-plus-pound bulk was being squeezed from either side by two angry women. I looked like a pesky pimple ready to pop. The young woman on my right was cute, twenty-something and, like me, plus size. The other woman, who turned out to be her aunt, was trim and looked a lot like her niece, just older and smaller. Both women towered over my five-foot-one-inch frame.

Steele cleared his throat. Peeking up through the hair that slightly hid my face, I saw him cross his arms in front of his chest. He wanted an explanation and would wait all day for one, if necessary. I didn't owe him any details, and I could be just as stubborn. However, today I decided to go for bonus points with shock value.

Lifting my chin in his direction, I shook my head and tossed my almost-shoulder-length medium brown hair away from my face.

"Jesus, Grey!" In a flash, Steele's arms uncrossed and he was leaning toward me, both hands flat on my desk. He angled his head to get a better view. "What the hell happened to you?"

"I was slugged by a leg of lamb," I explained, trying to be non-chalant about it, pretending that assaults by butchered meat happened every day.

At that moment, Kelsey Cavendish, the firm's librarian, strolled into my small office. With three people, it now reached capacity under the local fire code.

"Hey, Odelia, any plans for lun—" She stopped mid-sentence, then exclaimed in a folksy accent, "Damn, that's one helluva shiner!"

Kelsey immediately pointed an accusatory finger at Steele. "Did he give you that?"

"What?" Steele half-shouted, turning an indignant, flushed face her way.

"Well, Greg certainly didn't give it to her," Kelsey shot back.

"Actually," I said, interrupting, "I believe my assailant came from New Zealand."

"Cavendish," Steele snarled in Kelsey's direction, "you don't really believe that I'd strike Grey, do you?" He glanced at me. "No matter how tempting."

Kelsey coolly looked him up and down. She was one of the few people at Woobie who didn't shrink in his presence. My guess is that if I ever left the firm, she'd be next in line for the keeper position.

"Nah, Steele, I don't."

A woman in her mid-thirties, Kelsey Cavendish was tall, slim, and angular, with a plain, friendly face. She was Olive Oyl in the flesh, but with a bigger clothing budget. She gave Steele a wide grin, slipped past him, and plopped herself down in the small chair across from my desk.

"Though I'll bet you lunch at Morton's that Odelia's thought about clobbering you a few times."

I couldn't help myself. Like a rude belch, a short, loud guffaw escaped my lips. Kelsey was right, I *had* thought about clobbering him, and on more than just a few occasions. In fact, I know dozens of people who would like to gather in the parking lot and beat the living crap out of him, starting with his last twenty secretaries.

Michael Steele went through secretaries like I buzzed through Thin Mint Girl Scout cookies. Our office manager, Tina Swanson, had given up on keeping the secretarial bay outside his office filled and now the placement job fell to yours truly. Lucky me. Currently, we were trying out a very talented temp named Rachel Keyo. She had just completed her third week with us and so far, so good. At least she didn't show signs of bolting -yet. And even though Rachel was a drop-dead gorgeous woman with long, sculpted legs and the face of a Nubian princess, Steele didn't show signs of seducing her—yet. Of course, Rachel was also in a very advanced state of pregnancy. This latter situation seemed to have a good, yet strange, effect on Steele. Instead of his usual behavior toward secretaries, which could swing between charming, sexual scamp and overbearing, demanding ass, Steele treated Rachel with unchar-acteristic tenderness, even reverence. Kelsey, who never misses a trick, referred to it as his Madonna fixation. Personally, I don't care what it's called, as long as he keeps treating Rachel with respect and the work keeps flowing out the door.

Jolene McHugh, another attorney at Woobie who shares secre-tarial services with Steele and me, loves working with Rachel, and no wonder. Rachel's legal skills extend far beyond typing and dicta-tion. Her last job had been in the legal department of a large corpo-ration, but several months ago she was laid off when that company downsized. She came to us on a trial basis through a friend of one of the attorneys, and if everything continues smoothly, Jolene and I will recommend that Tina hire the woman permanently after her maternity leave, providing, of course, Rachel was equally excited about the idea. But Jolene had already expressed her concern to me that somehow Steele would screw things up for everyone.

Kelsey looked down at the newspaper still on my desk, and her smile grew wider. "Is that really you?"

I nodded slowly, suddenly wishing I had called in sick.

Kelsey leaned in closer. "So, just how did you get that shiner?"

Steele, who was now leaning against the doorjamb, also moved in closer. You would have thought no one had work to do.

With a deep sigh that swelled my hefty bosom like a rolling wave, I began the saga of the leg of lamb, only to be interrupted by my phone ringing. A look at the display told me that the caller was Zenobia Washington, my best friend. No doubt she had also seen the morning newspaper. I ignored the phone. I would call Zee back later. I returned my attention to Kelsey and Steele and sighed again.

"It's nothing, really," I continued. "I was simply in the market last night—just popped in to pick up some food for Seamus and dinner for myself—when these two women started arguing next to me at the meat counter. Rose, the older one, who turned out to be the younger one's aunt, began chiding her niece about her weight. In fact, she was being kind of mean about it."

"Oh, no," Steele groaned, shaking his head. "Odelia Grey, champion of chubbettes, to the rescue."

Steele was sarcastically referring to Reality Check, a local support group started several years ago by my late friend Sophie London. Now I lead it, together with Zee. Originally, Reality Check was

6

formed to help large people emotionally cope in a weight-obsessed society. Now it included others facing similar bigotry over other issues, such as physical disabilities.

I curled my lip at Steele before continuing. "Anyway, the niece—her name's Manuela, Manuela Collado, I believe—started crying and snapping at Rose, and pretty soon the scene escalated into a full-blown family feud."

"And you couldn't keep your freckled nose out of it, could you, Grey?" Steele gave another shake of his perfect head. "You couldn't just walk away? Maybe head to the frozen section and grab a carton of Ben and Jerry's?"

"Steele!" Kelsey snapped. Turning to me, she said, "Go ahead, Odelia, clobber him. I won't tell."

"You want to hear this or not?" I asked with annoyance. "If not, I have work to do."

"Sure, Grey," Steele said, supporting himself once more against the doorjamb, hands casually shoved into his pockets. "Sing us a stanza of 'Odelia Had a Little Lamb.'"

Rolling my eyes, I continued. "By the time I tried to break Manuela and Rose apart, it had turned quite nasty and a crowd had gathered, including, I later found out, a photographer from the *Register* who just happened to be in the store and had his camera bag with him." I stopped to take a drink of lukewarm coffee from the mug on my desk.

"Anyway, Manuela was calling her aunt some pretty colorful names, and Rose was getting in some good, sound slaps. I had almost succeeded in pulling them apart when, out of nowhere, Manuela picked up that darn leg of lamb and swung it like Babe

Ruth, hitting a homer with my left eye." I looked from Kelsey to Steele. "Satisfied?"

Kelsey looked at me, then at Steele, then back to me. "Did you at least get to keep the leg of lamb?" Both of them cracked up with laughter.

"Just for that," I said to Kelsey, "you're buying lunch."

It was then we noticed Fran Evans, a senior associate, standing just outside my door. She was tall and willowy, with a long mane of thick, blond hair and a very attractive face that would be down-right stunning if she smiled more. As usual, she was all business and wore an air of disdain like a heavy fragrance. Around the firm, she was getting the reputation of being the female counterpart of Mike Steele. Once she had our attention, Fran indicated she needed to speak with Steele.

Steele told her he'd be with her shortly, then continued our conversation. Fran, her jaw set tight, glared at him. When Steele didn't make a move to acknowledge her further, Fran tossed her hair in a little fit and took her leave. Once she was gone, he pulled his hands out of his pockets, stood straight, and looked me in the eye.

"I repeat myself, Grey. Why am I not surprised?" He shook his head yet again. "You're the only person I know for whom it seems perfectly natural to go into a market for cat food and end up being KO'd by a roast." He laughed. "Only you, Grey."

"Too bad about the shiner, Odelia," Kelsey told me, ignoring him, "especially with your big reunion this weekend. But maybe it won't be that bad; it might change from plum purple to puke yellow by then—much easier to cover with makeup."

Steele raised an eyebrow in curiosity. "Reunion?"

Crap, I thought, *something else for him to bug me about. He'll probably come up with a weekend full of work just to spite me.*

"Odelia's thirtieth high-school reunion is this Saturday," Kelsey cheerfully informed Steele.

"Damn, Grey, didn't know you were that old." Steele appeared to be calculating something. He finally said, "I was … what … about eight years old then." He paused for what I'm sure he thought was dramatic effect. "Were you an actual flower child? Did you trip the light fantastic to Joplin and Morrison? Do any streakin'? Heh, heh, heh."

My future with Woobie was looking more like being sentenced to death row.

When he didn't get a rise out of me, due to an amazing amount of self-control on my part, Steele gave a *humph* and started to leave. Partway out the door, he stopped and turned back around.

"Don't forget, Grey, I'll be out of town the beginning of next week."

"Where ya goin'?" Kelsey asked eagerly. "And how long can we count on you being gone?"

Steele gave her a chilly smile. "If you're a good girl, Cavendish, maybe I won't come back." Then he strode down the hall to join Fran.

"Why," I asked Kelsey, as I retrieved my purse from a file drawer in preparation for lunch, "do men always make promises they never intend to keep?"

TWO

Whoa! was my immediate reaction as I walked into my thirtieth high-school reunion. My palms grew clammy. My legs threatened to buckle. *Please, please, please tell me I'm hallucinating.*

As soon as we entered the hotel ballroom, my eyes were assaulted by an explosion of soft blue and seafoam green crepe paper. The ballroom was decked out in an exact replica of our senior prom—20,000 Leagues Under the Sea—right down to the real fish tanks positioned throughout the room and the *blub-blub-blubbing* of waterlogged air bubbles piped in over the sound system. I didn't know which would happen to me first—passing out from shock or wetting myself; maybe the two would happen simultaneously. Talk about multi-tasking.

The invitation to the reunion had only said that the reunion committee was cooking up a big surprise. Some surprise. My heart rate increased notably. If I had known in advance that one of the worst nights of my life was going to be revisited, I would not have come. Needless to say, my prom night had not been warm, fuzzy, or romantic, although I must admit, it could have been worse. After all, I hadn't been doused in pig's blood like Stephen King's Carrie. Yet it was definitely not one of those evenings I discussed wistfully with middle-aged girlfriends over a glass of wine. Nor was there any decaying corsage lovingly pressed into a scrapbook anywhere in my house. I had attended the prom, true, but it was one of those memories I've spent thirty years trying to erase, like a magnet continuously passed over a hard drive.

My thoughts of bolting were disrupted by a commotion near the entrance. I turned toward the noise to see Donny Oliver entering the ballroom on the shoulders of several former members of the football team. He was waving and cheering, making his way through the fake sea creatures and his former classmates like a conquering hero returning from war.

I couldn't move. My feet felt encased in cement blocks instead of my new black suede pumps. Donny Oliver was the very worst of my high-school memories—the bogeyman in a quarterback uniform. I watched warily as he slid to the floor from the shoulders of his high-school comrades and started shaking hands. Someone handed him a beer. Someone else gave him a cigar. I half expected Donny to announce he was running for public office.

I prayed for early senility.

"Odelia?" I heard a female voice tentatively ask. "Odelia Grey, is that really you?"

I turned toward the melodic and kind-sounding voice to find a woman looking at me with happy curiosity. She was of medium height, with bobbed dark hair and a long, lean face with deep crow's feet nestled around the eyes. She beamed at me, displaying a mouth of slightly crowded teeth.

"Johnette? Johnette Spencer?" I inquired, answering her question with a question. She nodded enthusiastically, and we hugged.

Johnette Spencer had been in most of my classes during our four years in high school. She had been tragically shy, painfully thin, and sported thick, black-rimmed glasses. Over the years, we had eaten lunch together often. Like me, she had been a loner, not belonging to any specific clique.

The glasses had been replaced by contacts, or maybe laser surgery—who knew these days. But Johnette was still thin and bony. She had not succumbed over the years to middle-age spread and a losing battle with the bulge. Glancing around at many of our former classmates, I comforted myself with the knowledge that I hadn't really been the fattest kid in my class, merely a woman ahead of her time.

Johnette continued beaming her high-watt smile. "Well, it's Johnette Morales now. Has been for quite some time. Twenty-seven years, to be exact."

Johnette tugged on the shirt sleeve of the man standing behind her, urging him to come forward. He looked vaguely familiar. I tried to subtract three decades. He was bald, just under six feet tall, and built like a weightlifter gone slightly to seed. Football and the name Victor Morales came to mind.

"Of course," I said to Johnette, still trying to shake off the initial shock of the reunion theme and Donny's entrance. "You married Victor. I remember hearing about that."

"Funny how things work out," she said. "Victor and I hardly knew each other in high school. It wasn't until college that we became friends and eventually fell in love." Johnette blushed. Victor smiled broadly.

Victor Morales had been on the football team. He had been a quiet boy, not given to rowdiness like so many of the guys on the various sports teams. He had been popular but not stuck-up. His only flaw, I recalled as I stood looking at him and his wife, had been his friendship with Donny Oliver, big man on campus and school bully. Nice boys like Victor had circled around Donny like moths to a flame because of Donny's prowess on the football field. Under Donny's influence in high school, Victor would never have dated a wallflower like Johnette. Yes, funny how things work out.

"Isn't this amazing?" Johnette said, sweeping her hand in an expansive gesture as if spreading pixie dust over the room.

"Swell," I responded in a voice cold enough to keep the ice caps from melting.

"But it's just like our senior prom, Odelia," she said with enthusiasm. "Remember?" Suddenly, it was Johnette who remembered. Her smile vanished and she reddened. Victor studied the wall behind me.

Remembering my manners and eager to change the subject, I indicated my date and introduced him. "Johnette, Victor, this is Dev Frye."

Devin Frye is a homicide detective in Newport Beach. I met him when he was assigned to the murder investigation of my friend Sophie London a couple of years ago. He has curly blond hair flecked with gray and compelling blue eyes. He also stands well over six feet tall and is built like a moose on steroids. Dev is a football team all by himself and makes me feel downright petite despite my size 20 body. The two men shook hands amiably.

Johnette quickly surveyed Dev, then looked to me with an eager smile. "So, is it Odelia Frye now?"

Taken aback, I shot a glance at Dev. He was blushing and studying, or pretending to study, a five-foot-long cardboard sea horse that dangled near his head. A thought came to mind, and I glanced down at Dev's left hand. Sure enough. Dev, a widower of just a couple years, still wore his wedding band. Johnette had made a natural assumption.

"No," I answered with a slight chuckle. "Dev and I are just good friends."

Johnette looked at the two of us with suspicion, and her face lost some of its friendliness. Victor, on the other hand, looked at us with renewed interest.

"Oh look, there's Sally Kipman," Johnette said with forced cheer. She tugged at Victor. "Let's go say hello." And with a slight nod, they were gone.

"That went well," I said to Dev.

Dev bent down so his mouth was near my ear. "So what happened at your prom?"

"Nothing."

"Give me a break, Odelia. I'm a cop. 'Nothing' doesn't make people *that* uncomfortable."

"Nothing, Dev, really; just childish pranks long forgotten." I aimed my eyes at Dev's wedding ring and shamelessly used it to get his attention off my senior prom. "I think Johnette thinks you're married ... and I'm not."

I scanned the crowd in the direction Johnette and Victor had headed. Sure enough, there was Sally Kipman, another personal annoyance from my past. This was turning out to be a reunion of my worst nightmares. A glance at my watch told me we had only been here seventeen minutes. That was long enough to bond with old schoolmates, wasn't it? After all, the fiftieth reunion was just twenty years away. Why do it all in one night?

I turned to Dev. He had stopped scrutinizing the sea horse and was now staring sheepishly down at his shoes, no doubt wishing he had worn sneakers so he could make a quick getaway should the need arise. I sighed and gave him a small, warm smile. It was hard to believe this very same man could make a hardened criminal shake in his socks.

He shook his head slowly. "I should have told them I was a widower. Or at least taken off my ring."

"Why?" I asked. "It's no one's business who you are." I guided him over to the registration table, where more former classmates waited to hand us our name tags.

My official boyfriend, Greg Stevens, was supposed to accompany me to the reunion. But a few days ago, he woke up with a cold that turned nastier with each day. Greg's illness gave me mixed feelings. On one hand, I was worried about him being ill. But on the other, it gave me an excuse not to attend the reunion. Why he had to be his usual gallant self and insist on my going anyway, I'll never know. He had suggested that I take Zee, but instead, at the last moment, I changed my mind and asked Dev Frye to be my escort. There was no way in hell I was going to go to this clambake alone or without a proper date.

Dev and I made our way into the main seating area and snagged ourselves a couple of chairs at one of the tables set for ten. Several chairs had napkins on them, letting all newcomers know they were already taken. After placing napkins on two chairs, Dev disappeared into the crowd to wrangle us a couple of drinks while I blazed a trail to the ladies' room.

I had checked my black eye—not a bad cover-up job, if I do say so—and was reapplying a fresh coat of lipstick when Johnette Spencer, now Morales, came into the large restroom. She looked quickly down when she saw me and started for a stall, but stopped short before entering. She just stood there, frozen. I watched her slim back reflected in the mirror in front of me. It seemed like she wanted to say something but wasn't sure how to go about it.

As teenagers, we had been good friends, and I had spent a lot of time with her. Many afternoons after school we had studied together at her house while her mother, in true June Cleaver form, plied us with Cokes and snacks. When I was sixteen, my own mother abandoned me and disappeared, and I went to live with my father and stepmother. Johnette and I had become especially close during that turbulent time in my life. It bothered me now that a possible misunderstanding had tainted what should have been a happy renewal of friendship. It bothered me that she had been so quick to judge. And it bothered me that I had been so quick to cut her off about the prom. After all, our senior prom had been a happy night for many people. I just wasn't one of them.

Without preamble, I explained Dev. "Dev's a recent widower. His wife died of cancer."

Johnette glanced quickly over her shoulder, catching my eye in the mirror. "Oh," she said softly. "I'm sorry. About his wife, I mean."

She turned her face back to the stall, but instead of entering, she abruptly turned on her heel like a soldier doing an about-face.

"Odelia," she began, still speaking softly. "I'm also sorry about being so rude out there. And I'm very sorry I brought up the prom." She took a couple of steps toward me. I glanced down and noticed that she was wringing her hands slightly. "I really am so very glad to see you."

"It's okay, Johnette," I told her. "I'm very happy to see you, too. And the prom is ancient history—really." Before another heartbeat passed, I took a step toward her and reached out my arms for a hug, not so much because I wanted to, but because instinct told me she needed a hug—badly. And she did. She fell into my arms, burying her small frame into my ample bulk. I could feel her shoulders slightly shaking. When we parted, I saw that she was weeping.

"It's okay, Johnette," I assured her again. "No harm done."

"It's not that, Odelia." She started to cry in earnest.

There was a small sitting area just inside the ladies' room door with a small padded bench. Grabbing some tissues from a dispenser, I handed them to Johnette and steered her toward the bench.

"What's the matter, Johnette?"

She looked down at the tissue that was quickly being mangled in her grasp. I had one arm around her shoulders and could feel her take a deep, lung-expanding breath before answering.

"Victor's having an affair."

Now it was my turn to give a soft "Oh."

"That's why I was so upset when I saw you with that man. I thought he was married and you were cheating with him." She looked up at me. "Stupid, isn't it? You having a fling with a married man?"

Her remark confused me. I didn't know whether she thought that highly of my ethics or if she thought I couldn't find a man with whom to have an affair. But this wasn't about me.

17

I gave her shoulder a squeeze. "Are you sure Victor's having an affair?"

She nodded. "I followed him one afternoon. He was supposed to be playing golf, but instead he went to some woman's house." She started weeping again. "Oh, Odelia, she was young—and very pretty." She blew her nose. "I saw them embrace."

I found myself speechless, not a natural state for me. I continued to squeeze my arm around her shoulders and pulled her close. Occasionally, a woman would come into the restroom, glance our way, and keep going toward the stall area. In due time, Johnette stopped crying, blew her nose, and straightened her shoulders.

"You go ahead, Odelia," she told me, taking one of my hands and giving it a little squeeze. "You go on out there and keep that nice man company. I'll be along very shortly."

"You sure?" I asked skeptically.

She nodded. "I'm just going to freshen up before going out myself."

Still not convinced she should be left alone, I did as she asked and started to leave the bathroom, only to be stopped by bony fingers clutching my arm.

"Please don't tell anyone about this, Odelia. I don't want anyone's pity."

Assuring her of my discretion, I said, "I'm sure you and Victor can work this out. You've been together a long time."

"Yes, we have." Johnette contorted her thin lips into a forced smile. "I'm sure it'll be all right in time. Lots of men have a mid-life crisis and return to the nest once it's out of their system." She looked to me to validate the statement.

"So I've heard," I responded automatically, all the while thinking that if Greg ever cheated on me, he'd be going from paraplegic to quadriplegic in no time flat.

Back again in the main ballroom, I made my way to our table to find Dev and Victor deep in sports talk. The Moraleses were going to join us at our table, Dev informed me. I smiled tightly at the alleged cheater as I took the seat Dev offered. A much younger woman, huh? The cheating would have been bad enough, but as a middle-aged woman, I took it somewhat personally that he might be straying with a newer and shinier model.

I was telling the men that Johnette would be along shortly when movement caught my eye. Approaching our table was Donny Oliver. Grr.

"Hey, Vic, great to see you," Donny boomed as he made his way to Victor's side. The two men shook hands. With Donny was another former football player whose face was familiar but remained nameless to me. Victor shook his hand, too.

Then Donny saw me.

"What?" He looked at me in exaggerated surprise. "This can't be Odelia—Odelia Grey?"

In high school, Donny Oliver had been a commanding sight. Ruggedly handsome with wavy brown hair, a dimpled chin, and deep-set, dark eyes, he stood just over six feet tall with a trim, hard body and wide shoulders. He didn't look all that different now, except that his dark hair was laced with gray at the temples, and his face was marked with slight lines around his eyes and mouth. A boozy smell emanated from him. Yep, just like in high school.

Memories as rancid as week-old tuna invaded my brain, and anger gurgled inside me. I felt ready to blow, like a shaken soft drink. *Let it go, Odelia,* I cautioned myself. *Control. Control. Control. You can do it.*

"Hello, Donny," I said through teeth clenched hard enough to worry me about cracking a crown.

Donny looked at me with amusement, then opened his arms wide. "Ah, come on, Odelia. Give your old friend a hug."

I glanced at Victor, who was looking embarrassed, then at Dev, who was looking both puzzled and concerned. I searched my brain for something glib and funny to say, something that would ease my tension and put Donny in his place.

"Eat shit and die, Donny." The comment may not have been original, but it was heartfelt.

He laughed. So did the guy with him. They were the only two amused. On my other side, I felt Dev start to rise.

"Is Tommy Bledsoe with you tonight?" Donny asked, looking around. He turned to the guy with him. "How about it, Steve? Wouldn't that be perfect? Odelia, Bledsoe, and this damn Sea Hunt shit, together again. Now *that* would be a reunion." They both laughed.

I said nothing. Dev stood up, but Donny took no notice.

"Come on, Odelia," Donny said, still with his arms spread. "Give me some of that heavyweight lovin' like you used to."

"Leave her alone, Donny."

It was a woman's voice. I turned to see Sally Kipman standing near the table with her hands on her hips, looking rather formidable. Johnette stood behind her, doing a great imitation of a frightened rabbit. I could have sworn I even saw her long, bony nose twitch. Geez, could this get any worse?

20

I continued my quest for the very elusive self-control. My jaw, still clenched, was starting to ache. What I really wanted to do was to push Donny's head into one of the nearby fish tanks until it became one of the bubbling tank ornaments alongside the toy pirate ship. Without much effort, I could picture little multi-colored fish swimming in and out of his nose. Entertaining this thought, I could feel control within my grasp.

Donny started to say something to Sally when another voice chimed in. "Yes, leave the lady alone." This command came from Dev as he moved to stand by my chair in front of Donny.

"Who the hell are you?" Donny asked Dev. I was pleased to see Donny flinch at Dev's size. My jaw relaxed a tad at the sight.

"Detective Devin Frye of the Newport Beach police. And this lady's date."

"Let's get out of here, Donny," his buddy said, putting a hand on his arm. Suddenly, I remembered his name—Steve Davis.

Donny looked down at me, then up at Dev, seeming to make up his mind about something. He turned to Victor. "Come on, Vic, let's go get a beer."

Victor looked at the people gathered around the table, including his wife. "Sorry, Donny, have to pass."

Donny looked surprised at Victor's insubordination.

"Leave it alone, Donny," Steve said, trying to steer him away from the table.

After glancing once more at me, then at Dev, Donny Oliver strode away. In seconds, he was shaking hands and slapping backs in another crowd of people.

"Some people just never grow up," Johnette said. She moved to Victor's side. Her husband slipped a protective arm around her waist.

Dev sat back down in his chair and looked at me. "Okay, *now* are you going to tell me what this is all about?"

I didn't look at him when I answered. "Maybe someday."

"Sally's going to join us," chirped Johnette, trying to move the mood of the table along to happier thoughts.

Oh boy. Although, I reminded myself quickly, Sally did just come to my assistance with Donny.

"Hello, Odelia," Sally said as she took a chair across from me and Dev. "Nice to see you again." Her voice was clear but clipped.

In high school, Sally Kipman and I got on each other's nerves on a daily basis. Thinking back, I can't remember why. Maybe it was because our personalities mixed like oil and water. Or maybe it was because we were too much alike.

Sally Kipman transferred to our school after her mother and father divorced and her mother relocated the two of them to Southern California from New Jersey. Sally wasn't happy to be in California and was even less happy to find herself from a broken home, a status that was still fairly new in the early '70s.

Until Sally came on the scene in our sophomore year, I was one of the only kids in school whose parents were divorced. While I retreated into boxes of cookies, Sally took a different approach in expressing her emotions. She was surly and belligerent to everyone, including teachers, and quick to start a fight. She quickly embraced youthful rebelliousness and her right to freedom of speech, no matter what was said or who got hurt by her machine-gun tongue. Like Johnette and me, Sally was a loner. At first, we invited her to have lunch with us. But she responded to our invitations with such verbal abuse that we finally stopped asking.

For reasons unknown, Sally's hackles would rise whenever she saw me. And, I must admit, the feeling was mutual. In our junior year, she told everyone I was fat because I was pregnant. I retaliated by telling everyone Sally was a lesbian. Shortly after that, following two weeks of detention and an order from Mrs. Zolnekoff, the school principal, we called an uneasy truce and made it to graduation without assaulting each other.

I looked across the table at Sally Kipman. Like Donny, she still looked very much as she had thirty years ago. Maybe mean people don't age; maybe all their natural vileness acts like embalming fluid. It seemed like a plausible explanation to me.

As in high school, Sally's body was tall, slim, and athletic. Her hair was dark blond and cropped short in a becoming tousled cut. She wore no makeup that I could see, and never did that I could remember. She was tan and fit and very attractive in a no-frills way. She no longer had an air of pent-up anger, but she still definitely had one of no-nonsense. Seeing me looking at her, she flashed me a non hostile lukewarm smile, and I returned it. It looked like the truce would hold.

With Donny staying on the other side of the room, no doubt avoiding Dev like he was my personal junkyard dog, the reunion turned out to be much better than I had expected—meaning I actually had fun once my jaw unlocked. During a lovely dinner, the people around the table caught up on each other's lives and passed around photos of children and grandchildren. I was the only one at the table who didn't have either. Even Sally Kipman had a grown son and one young grandson. I showed off a photo of Seamus, my ill-tempered, antisocial, champagne-colored cat.

During dessert, the DJ started playing dance music, and Dev coaxed me onto the floor.

"I'm glad to see you're finally having a good time," he said while we danced to a slow tune. Dev Frye is way over six feet tall, and I top out at five foot one. He had to almost bend in half to whisper in my ear.

"Yes," I answered, "I am. Thanks for coming with me."

"You're welcome. Thank you for asking." He smiled down at me and pulled me closer to him. My nose hit somewhere in the middle of his chest. Suddenly, I was overcome with guilt.

I have always known that Dev Frye likes me a lot, and the feeling is mutual. I also know that he would be actively pursuing me if not for Greg Stevens. And, if not for my love for Greg, I would be encouraging this mountain of a man in his pursuit. When I called Dev about escorting me tonight, I had made it clear that it was a friendship date, and that he would be filling in for an ill Greg. Dev had said no problem, but questions peppered my mind. Was I leading this kind, decent man on with my selfish need to prove something to someone? To who? To Donny Oliver? If that was true, I wasn't playing fair with Dev's feelings.

And Greg—therein lay the bulk of my guilt. Greg was at home right now suffering with a head cold and thinking I was with Zee. He had no idea that I had changed my mind and asked Dev instead. I know that if he knew I was dancing in the arms of Devin Frye, he would be upset. Although Greg likes Dev, he's not in the dark about Dev's feelings for me. In fact, it was Greg who first brought them to my attention shortly after we met the man. And Dev is always there, ready to lend a hand or look out for me whenever I manage to get myself into a jam. Or stumble upon a body. Which are really one and the same since I never seem to be in a jam that doesn't involve a dead body in the mix.

Simply put, Dev, Greg, and I are engaged in an emotional yet polite ménage à trois.

Thanks to me, Greg and I are not engaged, though he has asked and even has a gorgeous ring waiting for when I'm ready. We were engaged for a whole day just over a year ago, but I gave the ring back until I could sort out some personal issues.

I giggled. Dev looked down. I shrugged, not wanting to share my secret. I had decided that on Thanksgiving, just over four weeks away, I would ask Greg to marry me. I would let him know that I'm ready to accept his ring, to be his wife, to formally begin our life together. No one knew of my decision yet, not even Zee.

I shook myself out of my girlish daydreams. Here I was, forty-eight years old, dancing with one man among cheesy, fake sea creatures and make-believe waves while being dreamy-eyed about another. He loves me, he loves me not. All I need is a bunch of daisies to pluck, petal by petal. But I really don't need the daisies; I know without a doubt that Greg Stevens loves me.

By the way, I'm blaming this thirty-year regression on crepe-paper fumes. That's all there is to it.

Another slow song started, and Dev showed no sign of loosening his grip. We continued swaying and gently moving to the music. I closed my eyes and lost myself in thoughts of a white gown and altar flowers ... Greg sitting in his wheelchair, dressed to kill in a tux ... Zee in a gawd-awful taffeta bridesmaid's dress ... people screaming ...

What? People screaming? At my wedding?

My eyes popped open, returning me to a room of blue and green chaos.

Dev stopped dancing and stood stock-still, as if sniffing the air for the direction of the trouble. More screams. Dev and I turned to face the doorway just as the crowd parted and a man staggered in, his shirt-front soaked with blood. Dev made a dash in his direction just as he collapsed to the floor.

It was Donny Oliver.

THREE

A SAUSAGE, PLUMP, WHITE, and uncooked, was being wiggled in my face. It reminded me of the smoked chicken and apple kind I'm so fond of, except that this one had a fingernail attached. Or was the nail something disgusting left behind by the factory? Either way, I was trying to grab at it with my teeth, like bobbing for apples but without bending over or getting my hair wet. I had almost succeeded when a bell sounded, then stopped. I tried to snag the sausage again. Once more, I heard the short ring of a bell.

On the third ring, I realized that the sound was coming from the phone on my nightstand. I made a half-hearted grab for it, but the caller had either hung up or disappeared into my voice mail. I settled back under the covers and closed my eyes, thinking that if I could only catch the sausage, it would go great with some scrambled eggs.

The phone rang again. This time, I answered on the second ring, but no one said hello back. All I heard was someone breathing. I said hello again, then it hit me. The elusive sausage was a dream. Or rather my subconscious retelling of the night before, when Dev Frye had poked his thick, round index finger in my face and told me to mind my own business. But in my sleepiness, the why and about what still escaped me. I said hello once more into the phone. The caller hung up without saying a word. There was no caller ID on my bedroom phone, so the call would remain a mystery for now. Frankly, I was too exhausted to care.

It was nippy in my bedroom, so I burrowed back under the covers. This time I didn't think about breakfast, but about why Dev would shake a stern finger at me. Not that he needed a reason to tell me to mind my own beeswax—he did that on a regular basis.

I yawned loudly. Seamus hopped up on the bed and rubbed his furry head against my chin. I gathered him up and squeezed him like a teddy bear until he meowed for mercy. Cats are wonderful things on cold mornings.

A glance at the clock on the nightstand told me it was just past nine o'clock. Usually I'm up much earlier than this on a Sunday morning. And usually I wake up next to Greg. Why wasn't I next to Greg?

Oh my gawd!

The reunion.

The screaming.

Donny Oliver.

Dev's admonition to stay out of it.

The events of the night before came crashing into my consciousness like a head-on collision. I sat straight up in bed and covered my face with my hands in horror. Donny Oliver was dead. Someone had shot him in the chest—someone at the reunion.

The phone rang again. This time I grabbed it quickly and said hello. It was Zee.

"Did you call here a minute ago?" I asked her.

"No, I didn't," she told me. "I figured after last night you'd be sleeping in, especially after what happened."

"What happened?"

A deep sigh came from Zee's end. I could almost see her standing there with a hand on one bulky hip. "Did you forget about the murder, Odelia? Or were you hoping no one would notice?"

Yep, dollars to donuts, Zee had one hand on a hip while she spoke to me.

There was a click, and another voice chimed in. "Hey, Aunt Odie." It was Jacob, Zee's teenage son. "Did you really see the guy get whacked?"

"Jacob Ezra Washington!" Zee snapped at him. "You get ready for church. Right now!"

"But Mom," Jacob whined, "I'm not a kid anymore. I want to know what happened."

I heard more commotion and muffled voices from the Washington end.

"You're not too old to obey your mother, Jacob." It was Seth, Zee's husband. His deep, authoritative voice came through the phone loud and clear, even though he wasn't speaking to me. "Besides, I want to talk to your Aunt Odie a minute."

Uh-oh. I thought about hanging up but knew they'd only call back. Donny Oliver had been killed at the reunion last night, and I had been there. It must've been all over the news this morning, both on TV and in the papers. Seth was going to lecture me, just as Dev Frye had.

"Odelia, what the hell is going on?" When I said nothing, Seth continued his rant. "Why is it you can't do anything without attracting killers and dead bodies? You're a corpse magnet."

"Zee," I said, hoping she was still on the other line. Usually she came to my defense when her husband became overprotective of me. "You can jump in anytime."

"Sorry, Odelia, but I'm with Seth on this one."

Zee and Seth Washington are closer to me than my blood family. And, like real family, they could be royal pains in my big fat behind.

"Come on, Seth," I said. "A corpse magnet? Is that really a fair comment?"

"Well, let's examine the facts." Seth was an attorney, and it showed. "The security guy. The woman in the ravine."

"Don't forget the dead guy in the pool, Dad." It was Jacob again. He'd probably picked up another extension.

"What did I tell you, Jacob?" asked Zee.

"Don't make me come up there, son," chimed in Seth. "If I do, you'll be washing the cars instead of driving one over to your friend's later on."

We all heard a phone being put down. I was thankful Hannah, their daughter, was at school at Stanford, or I'm sure it would have been four against one, putting me at a more definite disadvantage.

"Odelia," Seth said from his end, "do you need a lawyer?" Seth always thought of that angle first. "Zee told me that you and this Donny guy had history together, some bad blood."

"What?" I yelled. At my tone, Seamus scooted off the bed and ran for cover. "No, I don't need a lawyer. I didn't do anything to

Donny Oliver." I was getting more awake by the second, and more uppity. "This one I didn't kill."

Silence fell over the conversation like a funeral shroud. No doubt, we were all thinking back over a year ago when I did kill someone.

Seth was the first to speak. Now his voice was gentle. "I'm not saying you did, Odelia. I'm just asking if you need some guidance with the questioning and all."

"No, Seth, but thanks. Dev Frye was there. We were all questioned last night."

"Isn't that out of Frye's jurisdiction?" Seth asked. "Did you call him?"

I hesitated, sensing I might be stepping into a minefield with the truth. "No, I didn't call him. He was with me at the reunion. Greg was home sick."

There was a collective pause on the other end of the phone. I could almost see Seth and Zee mouthing comments and raising eyebrows at each other.

"Does Greg know you invited Detective Frye?" Zee asked.

Boom! The first mine exploded.

"I'm guessing by your silence," Zee continued, "that your answer is no."

"Damn it, Odelia," added Seth.

"Dev was just my escort, nothing more."

"Nothing more?" repeated Zee. "Odelia, shame on you. You know better. Detective Frye has a huge crush on you. It's only because of his decency and respect for Greg that he isn't openly courting you, and you know it."

31

"He knew it wasn't a real date and he was okay with it. We're just friends. It's not a big deal."

Seth cleared his throat. Another *uh-oh* crossed my mind. "If it was no big deal, then why didn't you tell Greg?"

Boom! Another mine went off, this time set off not by Seth's question but by my own understanding that he was right. If taking Dev with me to the reunion wasn't a big deal, I would have told Greg about it.

Seth didn't let up. "What kind of game are you playing, Odelia? I thought you wanted to marry Greg."

"I do." My voice was small when I answered.

I do. Would I ever be able to say those words to Greg? To anyone? Forget legendary male commitment phobia—my own inability to commit was sharp enough to put an eye out.

"I do," I said again with conviction.

"Funny way you have of showing it," Zee said.

"Shit or get off the pot, Odelia," Seth added.

"Seth!" scolded his wife.

"I mean it, Zee." He paused. "Odelia, girl, you know I love you, so I'll say it straight. Greg Stevens is a great guy. He deserves to be treated better. You are not being fair to him or to Dev Frye."

On my end of the phone, I was starting to tear up. What Seth was saying was true, but I had already decided to marry Greg. I just hadn't told anyone. But if that was true, why had I taken Dev to the reunion? Was it just to prove to everyone I could get a date? Was it to prove something to Donny Oliver? Donny, who was now dead.

The conversation was getting out of control. I didn't want to think about how I had screwed up. Better to get back to the dead body, the one I didn't kill.

"Dev said he was only shot once," I said into the phone. "Donny Oliver, I mean, not Dev. Once in the chest."

There was silence on the other end. Either the Washingtons were mulling over this information or they were rolling their eyes at each other about my quick change of subject. I'd bet the scrambled eggs and sausage in my dream it was the latter.

I was about to bridge the silence with another tidbit of police information when my call waiting sounded. I told Seth and Zee to hold on and clicked over with the flash button to answer the other call. As soon as I had, I wished I hadn't.

"It's me," said a flat voice.

I hesitated just long enough to take a deep breath. The Washingtons were the least of my worries.

"Good morning, Greg," I said with forced cheerfulness.

Silence. Another mine exploded, this one silent but more deadly than the others.

"How are you feeling, sweetie?" I asked, praying he hadn't read or heard the news.

"The question is, Odelia, how are *you* feeling?" He wheezed and sniffed. "Especially after last night. Seems your reunion was a real killer."

Ouch.

"Why don't I get dressed and come on over, Greg?" I continued with the forced cheery tone. "I'll stop and pick up some fresh bagels on the way."

"No need. I'm in front of your place right now." His voice was still flat, and I knew it wasn't just because of his cold. And it wasn't lost on me that not once had he called me his usual *sweetheart*. Not a good sign.

"Why don't you just come in? You have a key."

There was pregnant pause. Not a first-trimester pause but a full-blown eight-and-a-half-month hesitation.

"We need to talk, Odelia."

No good conversation ever starts with the words *we need to talk*, especially when that statement comes from a significant other.

As soon as Greg hung up, I clicked the call waiting back to Zee and Seth and told them that Greg was here and I'd call them later in the day.

Zee told me she'd be praying for us.

Seth advised me not to blow it.

FOUR

I JUMPED OUT OF bed and made a dash for the bathroom. By the time I had brushed my teeth and hair, I heard Greg entering downstairs, soon followed by an awkward galloping sound as Wainwright, his enthusiastic golden retriever, bounded up the stairs to greet me. After receiving hugs and kisses from me, the dog bounced into the bedroom, where he found Seamus once again back on the bed.

When Greg and I started dating, Wainwright had fallen in love with Seamus immediately. The affection, however, was not returned, and there had been several one-sided battles between the friendly dog and the irascible feline. Now they get along fine, though I suspect it's more tolerance on the side of Seamus than warm fuzzy feelings. When I returned to my bedroom, Wainwright was standing with his front paws on the bed, licking Seamus's ears. The cat withstood the slobbering with stoic patience.

I was about to head downstairs when I noticed myself in the full-length mirror affixed to the closet door. Yikes! The only things bright and shiny about me were my teeth—not even my hair had improved with the brushing. The old, stained flannel nightshirt I was wearing had one torn shoulder seam, and the bags under my eyes looked like unmatched luggage, what with one eye marked with faded shades of green, yellow, and purple. I didn't know if Greg was going to break up with me in the next few minutes or just lecture me, but either way I could not let him see me like this. I had to take my medicine in style.

I was about to call down to Greg that I'd be just a few more minutes when another thought occurred to me. Maybe I should play the sympathy card. I looked and felt like road kill, so why not let him see that I'd had a bad night? If I cleaned up, he might think I had a high old time the night before and not cut me any slack.

Decisions. Decisions.

I looked to the animals for some assistance. Wainwright had stopped smooching Seamus and was curled up on the floor at the foot of my bed. Seamus was in the same position above him on the bed. Both watched me with expectation, as if waiting to see my next move.

For a minute or so, I paced in front of the mirror while twirling a strand of my greasy hair around my right index finger. What I really wanted to do was crawl back into bed and pretend nothing had happened the night before. Even better, rewind the whole last week, starting with the incident in the grocery store.

I was contemplating tying a note to Wainwright's collar and sending him downstairs to his master with my apologies when I caught a whiff of something wonderful. It was coffee, fresh coffee being brewed in my very own kitchen. The promise of tasty caffeine prompted a decision. I would take the road well traveled, that of compromise.

After calling down the stairwell that I'd be just a few more minutes, I took a very quick shower and shampooed my hair. I combed my clean, wet hair back off my face but didn't put on any makeup. Then I donned a cute and comfortable caftan. I would face Greg clean and tidy, but leave some traces of the stress from the night before.

When I entered the kitchen, with Wainwright and Seamus on my heels, Greg was sitting in his wheelchair at the kitchen table, sipping coffee and reading the Sunday paper. He didn't look up when I came in, letting me know he was really angry. I hesitated, wondering if I should go straight to the coffee pot or say something first. When stressed, I have a bad habit of babbling like an idiot. Right now I wanted to chatter nonstop, declaring my innocence with every mindless word.

Instead, I walked over to Greg and kissed his forehead. It was slightly warm, and his breathing was a little raspy. His cold seemed a bit better than it had been yesterday, but it was still bad. He was dressed in a sweatshirt and jeans and smelled of soap. I was glad I had taken the time to shower myself. Greg tensed under my touch but didn't move away. I poured myself a mug of coffee and returned to sit across from him at the table.

"Thanks for making coffee, Greg."

"No problem." He still didn't look up from the newspaper.

"Is there anything in the paper about Donny Oliver?"

"No, probably too late to make the Sunday edition."

I was about to say something when the phone rang. I didn't want to talk to anyone except Greg right now. In spite of my cowardice, I knew we had to get this out into the open if we were to survive as a couple. The phone rang again.

"You should get that," Greg said. I looked at him, and he raised his face to meet my eyes. His face was pale and his nose slightly red, but his eyes were not hard. I breathed easier. "Go ahead, Odelia. I don't mind."

I gave him a weak smile and reached for the cordless phone, noting at the same time that my message light was blinking.

"Did you call earlier, Greg?"

He nodded but said nothing.

On the fourth ring, I punched the answer button. "Hello."

I listened, said a few words, and told the caller I'd get back to him. Then I ended the call and turned my attention back to Greg.

"That was my father. He saw the news about the reunion on TV and was worried."

"Seems the only one not worried is you." He looked up again. This time his hazel eyes bore into me. "I called Dev Frye this morning."

"You called Dev?"

He nodded. "I first heard about the reunion on the early news. I was worried and called you, both here and on your cell. When I got no answer, I called Dev's cell. According to the news, he was at the reunion. According to him, he was there with you. By the way, he wanted to make sure I looked in on you this morning." Greg made the last comment with a slight *humph*.

I looked down into my coffee mug briefly, then back up at Greg. "I took him instead of Zee to the reunion."

"So it seems."

"I guess I should have told you."

"Bingo!" He slammed his hand down on the table, making our mugs jump. Coffee sloshed out of my full cup onto the table. The animals, curled in a corner, went on alert.

Grabbing a nearby dishcloth, I wiped up the spilled coffee. I kept my eyes down. I didn't know what to say. He was right, I should have told him.

"I thought we were in a serious relationship, Odelia. I thought it was exclusive." His voice was tense, as was his jaw.

I still didn't say anything. I was too busy keeping my tears in check.

"I had hoped that once you put that shooting mess behind you, you would finally want to marry me. But obviously, I was wrong."

"No, Greg," I said in a hurry. "You're not wrong. I do want to marry you. I want that more than anything. I just didn't want to go to that silly reunion without a—" I stopped abruptly, knowing that I was about to set off yet another land mine.

"Without a *date*, Odelia? Is that what you were going to say?" Greg raised his voice a notch more, something he seldom did. "People in exclusive relationships do not date other people. Hence, the definition of *exclusive*."

I looked down at the soggy cloth in my hand, barely able to contain my tears, then back up at him. "Dev wasn't a date, Greg. He knows that. I know that. And you need to understand that. He escorted me to the reunion, nothing more." Suddenly, I thought about Johnette and Victor Morales and wondered if maybe they should be having such a pow-wow.

Greg sighed. "I do believe you, Odelia. I've never doubted your love. I just doubt your decisions from time to time. You seem to make some of them for silly reasons, without thinking about the consequences. Even after all this time, you still think about how something affects you, not how it affects *us*. I need to be in an *us* relationship."

He picked up his coffee mug and turned his chair toward the counter and the coffee maker. I stopped him and got up myself. I retrieved the pot, poured a second cup for him, and placed it on the table on a hot pad.

"You don't understand, Greg. I couldn't go to that reunion alone last night, or with Zee. I know I should have told you, but I didn't want you to feel obligated to go. You were so sick." I took a long drag from my mug, hardly tasting it. "I shouldn't have gone at all."

"Now I wish I hadn't urged you to go." He took a sip of his own coffee. The two of us sat at the table a few minutes, both lost in our thoughts and our mugs. Although Greg had quieted down, I knew he was still very angry. Maybe it was the vein bulging every now and then in his temple, or the way he clutched the mug between both his hands, almost like he wanted them around my neck.

"It's not just Dev Frye, Odelia," Greg finally said, breaking the silence. "It's also your knack for stumbling into danger. I just can't keep worrying about you all the time." His voice started to climb again. "Hell, my family can't keep worrying about you. They love you and care about you. My mother would have been on the phone to me in a panic this morning if the news had mentioned you; which, thankfully, it didn't. The brawl in the grocery store had her troubled enough."

"It wasn't a brawl!" I got up, stomped to the sink, and stared out the window above it into my small patio area. It was going to be a cool but sunny fall day. I felt my heart racing and tried to calm down by thinking about the weather. "I was just trying to help those people."

"I know that, Odelia, but the black eye incident aside, most people go all their lives without becoming involved with murder. You can't seem to go more than a year without tripping over a dead body."

"Corpse magnet."

"What?"

"Corpse magnet," I repeated, still staring out the kitchen window. "That's what Seth called me this morning."

"Well, Odelia, I don't want to marry a corpse magnet!"

I swung my head around and gawked at him. "And just what does *that* mean, Greg?"

He covered his face with both of his hands and scrubbed up and down. "Arggh!" When he removed his hands, his face radiated exasperation and was flushed, both from fever and emotion. "It means ..." He paused, took a deep breath, and looked me square in the eye. "It means I don't want to marry someone I have to worry about constantly."

"It means you don't want to marry *me*, doesn't it?"

"Careful, Odelia, don't put words in my mouth."

After taking several deep breaths, I took a cautious step closer to him. I reached out a hand slightly as I moved, then pulled it back as though touching him would scald me.

"But, Greg, it's normal to worry about the people you love."

"It's not normal," he said with a deep sigh, "to worry about a wife being shot at, chased, or threatened in any way on a regular basis; not unless she's a police officer, which you are not."

"Oh, come on," I said with a nervous chuckle. "This is Southern California. People worry about that stuff every day. They worry about it every time they drive a freeway."

Greg was not amused.

"I mean it, Odelia. I cannot be worrying about you stumbling over bodies and sticking your nose into crimes every time I turn around."

I put both hands on my hips and stood my ground. "Who said I was going to do anything about Donny Oliver's murder?" Greg said nothing. "I couldn't stand the guy. Why would I get involved? In fact, he's lucky I didn't kill him *myself* thirty years ago."

"Dev told me there was something between you and this Oliver guy years ago. Something unpleasant, but he couldn't get you to tell him. He asked if I knew anything, and I don't."

"It's not important, Greg. It was back in high school."

"Dev seems to think it's important. You might even be questioned about it in an official capacity."

My mouth dropped open. "Why? It has nothing to do with Donny's murder. I was dancing with Dev when Donny was killed, and he knows it."

At the mention of dancing and Dev, Greg looked away. I looked at his wheelchair and wanted to smack myself for being such a thoughtless heel. After a few moments of silence, Greg started moving away from the table and toward the front door.

"Come on, Wainwright." The dog got up from the floor and started to follow.

"Greg, please don't go." I stopped him partway through the living room and stood in front of his wheelchair. "I'll tell you about

Donny Oliver and me. It's not pleasant, and it has nothing to do with his murder."

"Save it for Dev Frye, Odelia."

"But I thought you wanted to know."

He closed his eyes a minute, then opened them. They were shiny. "I would like to know. But right now I am much more interested in your future … our future … than I am in your past."

The phone rang. I made no move to get the call, and he didn't invite me to take it. Greg and I looked at each other in silence as the ringing continued several more times, then stopped. Greg was about to break the silence when his cell phone, clipped to his belt, chirped. He looked at the display, shook his head slowly, then answered.

After listening, he said to the caller, "No problem, she's here and she's fine." He listened. "I'm sure she'll want to talk to you about Oliver." He listened a bit more. "No, now's fine. Come on over." Then he hung up.

"That was Dev Frye," he explained. "He called just now and got worried when you didn't answer. He's on his way over to ask you again about Donny Oliver. He said the police want to talk to you, but he wants to hear it first."

He turned his chair and rolled around me, heading for the front door.

"Aren't you going to stay?" Panic rose in my throat like bile.

"No, I'm not."

He paused, and for a minute I thought he was going to change his mind. Silly me. Then the last and most deadly land mine exploded.

"I think we need to take a break from each other, Odelia."

My heart stopped, or at least it felt like it had. Donny Oliver may have been shot in the chest, but I'd just been slammed into, full frontal, by a freight train.

FIVE

"DONNY OLIVER WAS MY first," I began, not looking at him.

"First boyfriend? First kiss? First what?"

"First everything." I hesitated. "Well, maybe not my first kiss. That happened in seventh grade at Patti Newler's birthday party. It was my first boy/girl party, and we played spin the bottle. I think the boy's name was Brian."

He gently cut me off. "Back to Donny Oliver."

"Yes, back to him." I curled my legs up under me and leaned back into the thick upholstery of my sofa. I closed my eyes and dug into the deepest and darkest of my banished memories. It was a lot like excavating on an archeological dig.

"It happened the summer just before our senior year. We were both working a summer job at a local restaurant, just a family place with good, cheap food. I waited tables, and he bussed them and helped with the dishes. It was the first time I'd gotten to know Donny outside of school. He was different, nice and normal—no bravado or cockiness. At the restaurant he wasn't captain of the football team. He was just minimum-wage summer help, like me."

Seamus jumped up on the sofa and settled in next to me. I stroked his soft fur. "Most of his friends were gone for the summer, but his parents and the football coach made him stick around and work and go to summer school. In spite of being quite smart, his grades were low. Too much partying with his friends, probably. He had to get them up if he wanted to play his senior year and be eligible for a college football scholarship."

I picked up my soft drink from the end table and took a long drink. Confessing was dry work. Seated across from me on the floor, with his back against an armchair, was Dev Frye. He took the opportunity to take a bite from the slice of pepperoni pizza he was holding, then washed it down with his own swig of soda. The rest of the pizza was in a box on the coffee table. My own half-eaten slice was on a plate in my lap. I picked at the crust with nervous fingers.

"We knew each other from school," I continued, "but ran in different circles. Or rather, he ran with the popular kids, while I was mostly alone, except for Johnette, of course. But that summer we became friends. At first we just said hello, then we started having lunch together. Soon I was helping him with his summer schoolwork. In time, we went to the movies together and stuff like that. Nothing romantic—we were just two kids hanging out over the summer. It was nice."

I felt tears starting and cleared my throat. "I was a lonely kid. And that was just a year after my mother disappeared, and I had to move in with Gigi and Dad. It was great to have a new friend."

"That doesn't sound too bad."

"No, that summer was very nice. But I was no fool. I knew that once school started, the chance of our friendship continuing was meager. Donny was too driven by peer pressure and popularity. He always had to be the center of attention, even if it meant at other people's expense."

I nibbled a piece of pepperoni and thought about what I was going to say next. Dev didn't rush me, which is good, because my mind kept reverting back to Greg and our fight. Donny and Greg: both painful things to think and talk about, yet here I was, immersed in both. But in spite of Donny being dead and Dev needing answers, the issue with Greg crowded my mind and pushed all other thoughts aside, demanding attention like a crying, angry child.

After Greg declared we needed a break, we stared at each other in shocked silence, neither believing the words that were now out in the open—raw and stinging, like a fresh, jagged wound. Both of us seemed afraid to say anything more, frightened perhaps to make matters worse, worried that even the most carefully uttered comment might pour gasoline onto the already heated blaze of anger and frustration. Over the two years we'd been together, we'd had our share of arguments, but this was a full-blown fight, the kind of blowout that leaves couples changed forever—sometimes for the good, sometimes not. After a few moments of awkward silence, Greg bundled Wainwright into his van and drove off, leaving me in a mixed state of shock, anger, and pain.

When Dev arrived, he found me sitting on the floor in the middle of the living room, sobbing my eyes out into the afghan I kept on the sofa. I don't know how long I'd been there, but when Dev rang my bell and received no response, he'd tried the door and found it unlocked. He got me up and held me until I was cried out. Between hiccups and nose blowing, he managed to understand that Greg and I were no more.

Dev had done the decent thing and said we could talk another time. It had to be soon, but it didn't have to be on the heels of my break up with Greg. I told him it didn't matter; why not get all the pain over at once? But Dev knew I needed some time, even if I didn't. He left, promising to be back around dinnertime.

In between Dev's departure and return, I spent hours pacing, moving from room to room, clutching my favorite photo of Greg, crying, and calling myself a bleeding idiot—and sometimes calling Greg worse. When I was too tired to pace any longer, I crawled into bed and spent time staring at the ceiling. The pain was so acute that even the gunshot to my ass a few years ago couldn't hold a candle to it. I literally thought I was going to die, that my heart was going to stop dead in its tracks just as Donny's had the night before. For a minute, I even envied him: better dead than to feel this way. It was a pain I was sure would never end, not ever, not until the day I did finally die.

The phone beside the bed rang, bringing me out of my stupor of disbelief and agony. I only answered it in the hope it was Greg. Maybe I had pulled a Rip Van Winkle. Maybe a day or two, or maybe a week, had passed, and he was calling to tell me the break was over. Quickly, I snapped out of my wallowing and into a muddled rage. How dare he call the shots! If he wanted an *us* relationship, then *us*, meaning *me*, had better be part of the break up and/or make up decision. I snatched up the phone and barked hello into the receiver.

But the caller wasn't Greg. It was Zee, and as soon as I heard her loving, velvety voice, I melted once again into a soppy, broken-hearted mess. She wanted to come right over and comfort me, but I told her no, that Dev was coming by soon to talk about Donny Oliver. I promised her I'd be fine. I promised her a call when Dev left, if it wasn't too late. She told me to call back no matter what time it was. Then I called my father and assured him everything was fine. No sense worrying him over what was going on with Greg and me. All Dad knew was that there had been a murder at my high-school reunion. It was all he needed to know. And he certainly didn't need to know about my past relationship with the murder victim.

So that's what brought me to be huddled on my sofa, drinking soda, eating pizza, and spilling my guts to Dev Frye about Donny Oliver.

"So he seduced you that summer?"

"Huh?" I turned my attention back to Dev.

"Oliver," he said. "Did he seduce you that summer with his attention?"

I laughed. "No. He was actually quite the gentleman, especially considering what happened later at the prom." I took another drink of soda. "The seduction part was more on my side."

Dev's left eyebrow raised in question.

"Don't be so surprised."

I excused myself and disappeared into the downstairs bathroom. When I returned, I was armed with a fresh box of tissue, and Dev had repositioned himself from the floor to the armchair. Instead of pizza, he was now chewing his signature wad of gum and held his small detective's notebook.

"Is that necessary?" I asked, indicating the notebook. "After all, you're not officially on the case, are you?"

"No, but I want to be able to give the guys working on it as much info as I can, to see if they will leave you out of it." He clicked the top of his pen and readied himself for details.

I settled back onto the sofa and started where I'd left off.

"Like I said, I was the one who did the actual seducing, such as it was. His folks had a nice house with a pool, and often we would go to his house to swim after we finished at the restaurant, which was mid-afternoon. Usually we swam with his younger sister, Amelia, but one week his sister was away at camp and every afternoon his mother played tennis, so we were alone a lot."

I blew my nose and continued. "I never fantasized about Donny being my boyfriend. I was having fun, but I wasn't all that attracted to him romantically. I was an odd creature, a teenage girl without romantic notions, but I was sexually curious, and Donny had a great body. I approached the whole thing rather methodically. I decided I wanted to lose my virginity and that Donny might be the best candidate. My only concern was that he might reject the idea of sleeping with a fat girl, and I didn't want to face that rejection. So I tested the waters the week we were alone. First, I made sure he got many great views of my ample cleavage." I laughed. "Let's face it: at that age, I was one of the few girls at school with big boobs."

Dev quickly looked down at his notebook, but I noted a smile on his face.

"Although I'll admit, the first time I saw him with an erection through his trunks, I almost bolted. Knowledge is one thing, putting it into practice is quite another."

50

Dev laughed and shook his head. "Odelia, you are something else. I wish I had known you then."

I shrugged. "I wasn't much different than I am today, just a bit lighter in the weight department and a lot more naïve. And I was just as thick-skulled and single-minded."

Dev put down his pen and smiled again, this time directly at me. It was a knowing smile, a smile full of tenderness and patience. In that moment, I knew that Zee was right: I wasn't being fair to Dev last night. Maybe after the pain of losing Greg passes, who knows? But that would be a long time, maybe forever, and Dev was far too decent and caring a man to be a consolation prize.

"Anyway," I continued, "I baited the hook, and he bit. Now the question was: did I want to reel him in?"

After laughing, Dev got up and went to the kitchen. He retrieved the bottle of soda from the fridge and refreshed our glasses. I thanked him, noting how comfortable he was in my home.

"I gather you did reel him in?"

"Sure did."

Dev raised his eyebrow again. "Did you use protection?"

"Donny wasn't a virgin and had some condoms hidden in his room. I had some in my bag, but I didn't tell him that. I didn't want it to seem planned."

He chuckled. "Did that change your relationship any?"

"We had sex a lot the rest of that week and through the end of the summer. In a way we became a couple, but in my mind we were still just friends. I broke it off right before school started. Donny wasn't happy about it. But I knew he had no intention of making me his public girlfriend, and I wasn't about to be hidden away like a teenage mistress while he escorted cheerleaders to the dances.

Besides, while our summer fling was fun, I had to pick up my regular routine of studying and getting ready for college."

I took a drink and adjusted my legs. "He was mad at first, but soon he had a regular girlfriend and forgot about me. Then, a couple of months after school started, rumors circulated that I was a slut. For a while, a lot of boys, especially those from the football team, were asking me out, but I turned them all down. I knew that most rumors die if there's no fuel to feed them, and soon the rumors about me did stop, especially after Mary Josephs got pregnant and accused one of the math teachers of being the father. Everyone forgot about me after that."

"I can imagine." Dev paused. "Was it the rumors about you that ruined the prom?"

I took a deep breath and counted to five. We were getting into the ugly territory of my past, the part I had tried to suppress for three decades.

"No, but they did have something to do with it."

I paused again, wondering if I was ready to say what had to be said and knowing it had to come out. Others at the reunion might have already told the police.

"I went to the prom with Tommy Bledsoe, another nerd and loner. We were lab partners our senior year in biology. Johnette's date was a shy boy named Curtis, Curtis Johnson, who was killed a few years later in a car accident."

"I remember Oliver mentioning Bledsoe's name last night." He wrote the name down in his book, then underlined it twice and stared at it. "Is that Thomas W. Bledsoe, the owner of Amazing Games Software?"

"Yes, that's Tommy. He was one of the first of the video game pioneers—made a fortune."

"Wasn't his wife killed a few years back? A botched carjacking, I believe."

I nodded. "Yes, very tragic. I didn't know his wife and had lost touch with him. But after that happened, I sent a condolence card to his office and later received a lovely note from him with an e-mail address. We still correspond once or twice a year, just catch-up stuff."

"He didn't attend the reunion, did he?"

"No. About a month ago, he sent me an e-mail saying he was going to be in Japan on business and was sorry he was going to miss seeing me."

Dev leaned forward in his chair, his notebook forgotten. "So, Odelia, tell me what happened at the prom."

I got off the sofa and started pacing while I spoke. "A few months before the prom, Donny approached me, saying he really missed me and our *special* friendship." I paused and rolled my eyes. "Said he wanted to get together before we graduated."

I stopped dead in my tracks, stung by the sudden remembrance that Greg and I had graduated from the same college, just several years apart.

"What's wrong, Odelia?" Dev asked with great concern.

I shook it off. "Nothing worth mentioning." I started pacing again.

"Anyway, I stupidly figured, why not? I missed having sex with him and wasn't interested in having a boyfriend at that time. All I thought about was going to college and working so I could move out of my dad's house as soon as school ended in June. A little fling was in order."

"You were definitely sophisticated for your age, Odelia."

"Maybe I was just old for my age. Or maybe I was merely a teenage slut." I stopped and looked at him. "Looking back, I probably should have found myself an older and experienced lover. It just never occurred to me then that anyone would really want me in that way, except for a horny high-school senior."

Dev tossed me a frown. "So you started up with Donny again?"

"Yes, but just a couple of times, both times at his house when his family was gone. But frankly, I didn't have much free time, and fun though it was, there didn't seem to be much point since I knew the relationship had no future. So, once again, I told him it'd been swell, but let's move on."

I stopped pacing and dropped back down on the couch.

"This time, though, he didn't get mad. He agreed that we needed to get ready for finals and graduation. We parted friends, and I thought everything was hunky-dory—stupid me.

"The prom was actually a lot of fun … until the last item on the program. The plan was to show slides on a big screen of the senior class in various activities—football games, debates, pep rallies, the usual. Near the end, the photos changed, and suddenly there I was on the screen, naked in all my fat glory on Donny's bed."

Dev gasped.

I fought back tears as I recalled the horror. "The next photo was of my face, another of my boobs, and so forth. Everyone was in such shock that it took several photos before anyone moved to turn the damn projector off. Needless to say, I was totally humiliated and ashamed. I started to run out the door, but Donny grabbed me and held me while the photos played. I still remember him, smelling of beer and whispering in my ear, 'Nobody dumps me, especially a fat bitch like you.'"

Tears were streaming down my face. Dev plucked some tissues from the box and held them out to me. He sat next to me on the sofa and for the second time that day put a comforting arm around me.

"Most people were stunned into silence." I stopped to blow my nose again. "Some were laughing. The few chaperones there were busy trying to get to the projector. Tommy ran up to where Donny held me and demanded that he let me go, but Donny just laughed. Then several of his buddies grabbed Tommy, pulled down his trousers, and dumped him headfirst into one of the fish tanks."

"Some prom."

"Yep, a real humdinger. That's one of the reasons I didn't want to go to the reunion—and why I nearly had a heart attack when I saw the theme for the reunion."

"I'm sure it's also why several people pointed fingers at you when the police asked about suspects, even though you and I were on the dance floor at the time Oliver was shot."

Stunned, I looked at Dev. "People accused *me* of killing Donny Oliver?"

"No, Odelia, no one accused you. It's just that when the police questioned people about who might have a possible axe to grind, your name came up. And you did tell him to 'eat shit and die' in front of a lot of people last night."

"But that's just a silly, vulgar phrase. Lots of people say it."

"Yes, true. But when most people say it, someone doesn't wind up dead."

SIX

Considering the events of the weekend, I was very glad Steele was out of the office for a few days. Between Donny's murder and my split with Greg, the last thing I needed was Steele's usual obnoxious comments. I wasn't, however, so safe from Kelsey Cavendish. She was already waiting in my office when I arrived at work Monday morning.

"Please tell me," she began, even before I had a chance to put my tote bag down, "that the high-school reunion with the murder this weekend wasn't yours."

"Okay, I won't tell you."

I sat down, put my bag away, and switched on my computer—all the normal things I did on a workday morning, trying to pretend that everything in my life was normal. I had even gone walking this morning around the Back Bay with the Reality Check group. There weren't many walkers this morning, for which I was glad. Since the murder took place in Los Angeles County and none of the walkers knew the high-school reunion in the news was *my* high-school reunion, I was spared questions. And no one there but Zee knew about the break up. Zee walked beside me, allowing me my silence as I put one foot in front of the other, pretending everything was normal.

Normal.

What is normal, anyway? Isn't it just a standard, a routine, a conformity that people live by or with? It seems to me that what is normal for one person might seem perverse to another, or silly, or unimportant. One woman's normal is another woman's weird and unusual. If you don't count a murder and a break up, everything in my life was normal, or at least normal for me.

Maybe in my little corner of the world, being a corpse magnet is normal. Who's to say it's not?

On that thought, my eyes traveled against their will to the photo of Greg and me taken one Christmas. It sat proudly on the upper right side of my desk in a lovely frame. The tears I had carefully squelched all morning rose to the surface like a storm-swollen river about to breach its banks.

Kelsey was watching me. "I'm sorry about your friend," she said in a comforting voice.

"My friend?" I choked out.

"The guy at the reunion, the one that was killed. Must've been quite a shock. I mean, an old friend getting shot right there, with all of you around."

My mouth opened in a wail, but nothing came out. Tears followed as if pushed forward by a category 5 hurricane. Kelsey got up and shut my office door.

"Oh, honey," she said to me, rushing to my side.

She bent over and encircled me with her arms. I clung to her and cried, much as Johnette had done to me the night of the reunion.

"Was the guy an old boyfriend?"

I shook my head, first sideways, then up and down, then gave up and just tried to get a grip. Eventually, the crying stopped. I grabbed a wad of tissues from the box I kept next to my computer screen. Just as I was mopping myself up, hiccups set in. Perfect.

"It's … not that … *hic* … guy … *hic* … hated him … Greg …," I tried to get it out.

"Greg? Something's happened to Greg?"

I nodded, keeping my lips sealed tight as I held my breath.

"What? What's happened to him?" Kelsey's eyes were wide open in fear.

I let out the breath I was holding. "He … *hic*." Crap. I took another deep breath, held it a moment, then released it. "*Hic*." I picked up the water bottle on my desk and shook it—empty.

"Stay put," Kelsey ordered. "I'm going to get you something to drink."

She left, closing the door behind her. I hiccupped my way through the few minutes until she returned, but at least the flood gates were dry. When the door opened, Kelsey walked in, holding a mug of coffee and a fresh bottle of water. Behind her was Joan, the firm's litigation paralegal. The three of us were known as the Three Musketeers of Woobie.

"Hope you don't mind," Kelsey said. "I brought reinforcements."

I smiled weakly at Joan, and she tried to smile back. I had no idea what I looked like, but it couldn't be great, judging from the sheer fright in her expressive dark eyes. Reaching into my tote, I pulled out my cosmetic bag and retrieved my compact. Yikes! No wonder Kelsey felt like she needed to rally the troops. I looked like a puffy raccoon who'd tangled with a nasty Mary Kay dropout. Quickly, I administered some damage control with spit and a tissue, then patted powder lightly over everything. I looked at my two office buddies for approval and got nods that I interpreted as *it'll do*. By then, the hiccups were gone.

Picking up the coffee mug Kelsey had placed on my desk, I took a long, deep drink and felt the warm, comforting liquid ooze its way through me. After a second long drink, I finally looked at Kelsey and Joan. Joan was parked in the side chair across from me, and Kelsey was leaning against the tall file cabinet to my left. Both were waiting for me to explain my hysteria.

I put down the mug and grabbed another wad of tissues as a precaution. In a flat voice, I announced, "Greg broke up with me this weekend."

Joan gasped, and her eyes immediately pooled in sympathy. Kelsey crossed her arms over her chest and stood straight.

"And why in the hell would he do a stupid thing like that?" she asked.

"Because," I started to say, then paused to clear my throat. I took another gulp of coffee and straightened my shoulders. I would get the words out if it killed me. "Because I'm a corpse magnet."

"Huh?" they said in unison.

I waved a hand as if to erase what I'd just said. "Actually, there were several reasons, but the central one is he's tired of worrying about me. He said it's not normal for someone to get into the trouble I do and have people trying to kill me all the time."

"Well," Joan said, pausing for diplomatic effect, "he has a point."

"Yeah," Kelsey chimed in. "Especially after that murder at the reunion."

"Oh my gosh!" Joan clapped her hands to her mouth and nearly fell off her chair. "That was *your* reunion on the news this weekend?"

Ignoring Joan's drama, Kelsey cut to the chase. "You said that was the central reason. Were there others?"

I nodded and felt my face grow warm. "Something I did at the reunion, something stupid that set off the whole fight."

Again, the two of them waited for me to say something, this time to confess what had set Greg off. Kelsey still stood with her arms crossed over her chest, but now her eyebrows were raised. Joan sat prim and proper, with her hands clasped demurely in her lap.

I took a deep breath and let the words come out in one big gush of hot air. "Greg was sick so I took Dev Frye to the reunion without telling Greg I know it was wrong but I didn't want to upset Greg but when he found out he was livid and that started the fight and then he told me he was tired of worrying about me all the time and then I told him that Seth Washington called me a corpse magnet and Greg said he didn't want to marry a corpse magnet then Dev called and Greg got even more pissed and announced we needed a break from each other."

When I was done, I felt like I needed a hit of oxygen.

"Wait a minute," Joan said, holding up a delicate hand. "Greg said he thought you needed a break from each other?"

"Yes," I told her, nodding. "That's pretty much it."

"Well, technically, a *break* isn't a *break up*." Joan looked at us, pleased with her theory. Looking over at Kelsey, I could tell she was considering it as plausible.

I threw up my hands in frustration. "Of *course* it's a break up."

Kelsey unfolded her arms and wagged an index finger at me. "Now, now, Odelia, don't be too hasty about dumping this relationship into the ground and throwing dirt over it." She paused and looked over at Joan for backup, getting it in the form of a nod. "It's true, you did do a pretty stupid thing, and you do seem to get into more jams than a bushel of strawberries. But Greg loves you. Hell, he even wants, or wanted, to marry you. Feelings like that just don't die overnight." She moved over to my desk, bent down, and wrapped her arms around me once again. "Just give him time to cool off."

Joan reached forward, took both my hands, and squeezed them. "Yes, Odelia, he'll be back. I'm sure of it."

I sighed deeply. A few days or weeks might prove them right. But at this point in time, it crossed my mind that they'd both been sniffing Wite-Out.

We broke our huddle, and they started to leave. Joan had just opened my office door when Jolene McHugh charged in, almost knocking Joan on her butt.

"Okay," Jolene started to say to me, then, catching herself, she turned to the startled Joan. "Sorry, Joan." Like lightning, she turned her attention back to me. "So, where is the despicable slime ball?"

"Woooeee, that comment has Mike Steele written all over it," Kelsey said, slipping past Jolene. "And on that note, we're outta here." She directed the still-shocked Joan out the door and closed it behind them.

Jolene plopped herself down in the chair Joan had just vacated and leaned forward, resting her elbows on the desktop. She stared at me, her blue eyes hot and piercing, like the flame from a welding torch. Jolene McHugh is a long, lean, and leggy redhead of Irish descent. When she's emotional, like this very minute, the freckles on her pale face look like paprika sprinkled over milk.

I took a minute to clear my throat and mentally shelve my personal issues. "Okay, what has our despicable slime ball done now?"

"You don't know?"

I shrugged. "I just got in. And for that matter, Steele isn't even here today."

"I know that, Odelia." Jolene scrunched up her face and pressed further. "So, where is he, and when is he returning? And how can he be reached? I tried him on his BlackBerry, but there's no answer. I want to scream at him *now*, Odelia. Not later and not in an e-mail. I want my pound of flesh *now!*"

Generally, Jolene McHugh is a sweetheart with a very even temperament. Whatever the slime ball—ahem, Steele—had done, it had to be big. And as much as I'd like to see Jolene go the distance with him, I knew I had to calm her down. After all, Michael Steele is a partner, and Jolene is not. Associates, even brilliant senior associates like Jolene, cannot extract even an ounce of flesh, let alone a pound, from a partner. Not unless said associate was ready to look for work.

"I'm not sure if he's due back tomorrow or Wednesday. I just know he took a few personal days. He didn't tell me why." I picked up my phone and punched in Rachel's extension. "Rachel might know something."

As the extension at Rachel's desk rang, Jolene reached over and punched a button, disconnecting my call. "That's the problem, Odelia. Rachel's gone—*poof*, like the wind."

Still clutching the dead phone, I stared at her. "What?"

"You heard me." Jolene leaned back in the chair and ran a hand through her curly red hair. "The best secretary we've ever had in that spot, and she's gone. She called Tina this morning and said she did not want to come back. Not now, not after the baby, never. And I just know Steele has something to do with it."

I shook my head in disbelief. "But she seemed happy enough on Friday, and she and Steele got along famously. I thought we finally had a winner."

My phone rang. The display said it was Tina Swanson, our office manager. I picked it up and said, without bothering with a greeting, "Jolene's with me right now, Tina. So, it's true?" I listened as Tina repeated what Jolene had just told me. Rachel Keyo, dream temp, was gone. She didn't give a reason—just told Tina she didn't want to work here anymore.

In the past three days, I had lost a high-school classmate, a boyfriend, and a secretary. That had to be some kind of record. My only comfort was that I was sure I had nothing to do with Rachel's leaving. My money for *that* dirty deed was on the slime ball.

SEVEN

WE GOT THROUGH MONDAY with little problem. Tina called an employment agency, and they sent a new temp over. His name was John Warren, a budding musician who needed occasional office work for occasional cash. John had worked in our office before, and while he wasn't suited for the long haul at Woobie, he could type fast and accurately and knew how to follow instructions. Jolene needed help, and Steele had left several dictation tapes before leaving for his mysterious trip. We could deal with a more permanent replacement in a few days.

When the Monday workday was over, I looked at the clock with dread. I didn't want to go home. Even though Greg and I didn't see each other that much during the week, I knew my evening would be empty without his nightly call. Zee had called earlier to invite me to dinner, but I had declined. I didn't want to be with well-meaning friends, either. It was almost seven o'clock when Joan Nuñez stopped by to say good night.

"I was afraid you'd still be here," she said from the doorway.

I looked up from the document I was reading, or trying to read. "Well, so are you."

"Yes, but I'm working on trial prep, not avoiding a painful situation."

"Sweetie, I've done trial prep," I told her. "It is a painful situation."

We both laughed, then I stopped short. Something I just said had jarred a rock loose in my thick skull: trial prep. There was a possible trial brewing, and it was a matter that Steele was involved with.

"Joan, Steele didn't call in all day today, at least not to me. Did he call you?"

She shook her head. "Maybe he's embarrassed about Rachel. Maybe he did do something to make her quit."

"Oh, please." I rolled my eyes. "When have you ever known Steele to be embarrassed about anything? Remember that incident with Trudie? He wasn't embarrassed about that in the least, and that was a 9.5 on the shame scale."

Joan blushed as she remembered the short-lived Woobie career of Trudie Monroe, one of Steele's conquests and short-lived secretaries. Trudie and Steele were caught with their drawers down when vandals broke into the law firm.

"Joan, doesn't it seem strange that Steele didn't call either one of us, especially with Silhouette heating up?"

Steele was a corporate attorney, but often he got involved with high-profile litigation matters involving business issues. The current brouhaha was between Silhouette Candies, our client, and Sweet Kiss Confections, another candy company started up by a former owner of Silhouette. The issue involved trade secrets, proprietary information, and unfair competition—all right up Mike Steele's alley. The litigation attorneys on the case were Carl Yates, a name partner, and Fran Evans. That jarred another rock loose.

"Both Carl and Fran asked if I'd heard from Steele today," I told Joan. "And Jolene said she'd tried to call him, but he didn't answer."

"That's definitely not like Michael Steele," she agreed.

I got up and walked the few steps down the hall to Steele's office. Joan followed on my heels. Switching on the light, I went straight to Steele's chrome-and-black-lacquered desk and checked out his phone. The message light was blinking. I pointed at it.

Joan looked at the light, then at me. "But he could have picked up his messages and then received some more."

I hesitated. "Of course, you're right. It doesn't prove anything."

We went back to my office, and I closed up shop while Joan waited. Together, we left for the night.

As SOON AS I got home, I kicked off my heels, grabbed my address book from my tote, and headed straight for the phone in the kitchen. The thing with Steele was bothering me. I had to make sure about the messages.

Mike Steele and I might butt heads more times than not, but there was one thing we did have in common—mutual trust. He may be an ass, but he's an ass I can take to the bank on his word and his actions. And he felt the same about me. Since Steele lived alone and didn't have any family in the area that I knew of, I had an emergency key to his home and kept track of all of his passwords and codes, including the one for his office voice mail. He had entrusted this vital information to me after he'd been assaulted in the office just over a year ago, during the time of the Trudie Monroe debacle. I kept the passwords in two places: in my address book, carefully scattered throughout, and taped under a desk drawer at the office. The key to his Laguna Beach condo was upstairs in a desk drawer. I could have retrieved the voice mail password at work, but I didn't want Joan to know about it. It's not that I don't trust Joan; I do. But Steele also trusts me to keep quiet about it.

I called the office voice mail number and punched in Steele's extension. When prompted, I poked out his code on my dial pad. In short order, I was in his voice mail. He had twenty-three new messages and seven saved messages. Fortunately, the voice mail system automatically gave me the earliest-dated message first. Steele's first unheard message was from Saturday, two days earlier, the day he left town. He had not picked up messages since. In the past, even when Steele had gone out of the country, he had picked up messages at least once a day. He was extremely conscientious about his job and giving his clients quality attention, if not quality personality.

I sat down at the kitchen table and stared at the phone, wondering what to do next. I wanted to check his home phone, but that was one password I didn't have. Except for the spare key to his apartment, I had no access to Steele's personal life. Seamus, upset that I hadn't said hello to him yet, jumped onto the table and sprawled in front of me. I rubbed his belly with my free hand and listened to him purr while I pondered what this could mean. Another thing that nagged at me was that Jolene had tried to reach him on his BlackBerry and failed, nor had he responded to the message she had left. Anyone who even remotely knows Steele knows that the ubiquitous electronic device is nearly fused to his hand like an extra digit. He goes nowhere without it, and he almost always answers it. And he always returns calls.

Something was wrong, I just knew it.

My thoughts were interrupted by my own ringing phone. My heart did a leap, then dashed to the floor when I saw on the display Dev's name and not Greg's. Not that I wasn't happy to hear from Dev, but Greg was the one person I'd give anything to hear from.

"Hello," I said, after punching the answer button.

"Hi, it's Dev. Just checking to see if you're okay."

"Yeah, I'm fine. Not dandy, but fine." I paused. "And thanks for checking up on me. Any news about Donny?"

"Not a thing yet. I gave the information you gave me to the guys in charge, but you still might have to answer their questions."

"Whatever I need to do, I'll do." My voice was like cardboard, flat and dull. Too many things had happened in a short time. I was exhausted, emotionally and physically. Dinner, a hot bath, and an early bedtime were clearly in my future.

"Good girl," Dev said with forced cheer.

"Woof," I responded and panted into the phone. It got a half-hearted laugh, followed by a pause.

"I assume you haven't heard from Greg."

"Not a peep." I didn't want to talk about Greg. I didn't want to think about him either. Today was the first day in a very long time that I hadn't heard Greg's voice, and it was killing me, squishing my heart like it was in a garlic press. I decided to switch to another worry.

"Dev, when someone goes missing, how long before you can report it to the police?"

"Someone missing, Odelia?"

"I'm not sure, but I think Mike Steele is." I told him about the day and Steele's uncharacteristic lack of contact with the office.

"Steele said he was going to be gone, Odelia. And you know it was for personal business, so maybe he needs to focus on whatever called him out of town. I'll bet he'll be back by Wednesday. If he's not, then give me a call and we'll see what we can do."

What Dev said made sense, but only if we weren't talking about Michael R. Steele, Esquire. Whether I liked it or not, Steele had me as fused to him as the BlackBerry. Even when Greg and I took vacations, I had to set down ground rules with Steele about how often I would check in. It didn't stop him from leaving messages on my cell phone, but at least I controlled when I returned the calls. And two years ago, when Steele's mother passed away, he left quietly for a week to attend the funeral and take care of family matters. No one knew where his family lived, but one thing was for sure, he had called me every day, sometimes two or three times, to make sure things were still running smoothly in his absence.

The two men who called me the most were now not calling me at all. One left me sad, angry, and confused. The other left me curious. Both worried me.

I said goodbye to Dev, saying he was probably right about Steele, even though in my heart I didn't believe it.

A few minutes later, while I was scrounging in the refrigerator for some dinner, my phone rang. I jumped for it, only to be disappointed yet again. This time the display showed *no data*, meaning an unknown caller. I answered and got a huge shock.

"Odelia," the caller said after hearing my hello. "This is Sally Kipman."

"Sally?"

"Yes, quite a surprise, huh?"

I grimaced at the phone. "Yes, but a pleasant one."

She laughed lightly. "You never were a good liar, Odelia."

She was right, so I cut to the chase. Between Greg and Steele, I wasn't in the mood to play polite parlor games. "What's up, Sally?"

"It's about Donny Oliver. I was wondering if we could get together to discuss what happened."

"Whatever for? Did you kill him?"

"No, of course not, but the police are questioning me and have me in their sights."

"You?" I couldn't hide my surprise.

I tried to remember where Sally was when Donny came staggering into the reunion, shot and dying, but couldn't. But at that exact time I was dancing with Dev with visions of white gowns and flowers parading through my head. A pang shot through me like an electrical shock at the memory. Suddenly, dinner didn't seem important, but a box of Thin Mints definitely was in order.

"Why would the police suspect you?" I asked her while rummaging through the freezer for my private stash of the minty chocolate cookies.

She hesitated, no doubt weighing her answer with care. "Because Donny and I were … well, we were involved in a legal action many years ago."

"You?" I said again. After retrieving a box of cookies, I shut the freezer door and concentrated on the call.

"Yes, me. And the police are nosing around to see if it might be some sort of revenge killing."

"I take it Donny won the legal battle."

"Yes, Odelia, he did." Her voice was curt.

"May I know what it was about?"

Another pause. It made me wonder if she was going to tell me the truth, the whole truth, and nothing but the truth, or a watered-down version.

"Donny is the father of my son, Lucas."

My eyes popped open at the news. There was nothing watered down about an answer like that.

"When Lucas was eleven," she continued, "Donny found out he was the father and fought for custody. He won."

"He won? Who'd give that jackass a kid?"

"The court, Odelia. Donny made a strong case that I wasn't fit to raise a child, especially a boy. It was a morals issue."

I was speechless.

On the other end, Sally sighed. "It's rather ironic, actually."

She paused. I waited.

"You see, Odelia, you were right all those years ago. I am a lesbian."

EIGHT

TRYING TO LISTEN TO Dev's advice and not panic, I made it to Wednesday. There was still no call from Greg, still no call from Mike Steele. Two boxes of Thin Mints and three fingernails had been sacrificed to the cause, along with a bit of my sanity. Tonight, I was meeting Sally Kipman to discuss Donny Oliver's murder. Something told me that by tomorrow I wouldn't have a box of cookies or a single nail left.

I know I promised Dev I wouldn't get involved with Donny's murder. And Sunday I told Greg I had no interest in it. But this morning, while walking with Reality Check around the Back Bay, Zee had taken me aside and insisted on knowing if I was sticking my nose where it didn't belong. I couldn't or wouldn't give her a straight answer, which in itself was an answer. She had stared hard at me, hands on hips, for a long time. Then she shook her head, gave me a hug, and started walking after the others down the trail. Zee understood that when something bothered me, I couldn't let it go until I had answers, and that I would be relentless in my search.

I did this with both big and small issues alike. She also understood something about me that the men didn't, or didn't want to   that when I was in such an obsessive mindset, I would make up my own mind and do what I felt I should do, contrary to all good and sound advice.

Maybe Greg was right. Maybe I hadn't been part of an "us" relationship. Maybe I never could be, after being alone most of my life.

As I waited for my computer to boot up, I mentally reviewed the situation. I had spent part of Tuesday digging through Steele's desk, hoping to find a clue to his destination. I also searched the secretary's desk, hoping he had given even a scant piece of information to Rachel and that she had jotted it down somewhere on a sticky note or scrap of paper. Both times I came up empty-handed. The only trace of his trip was a note on the calendar that he would be out of the office Monday, Tuesday, and possibly Wednesday. Behind closed doors, I even listened to all of his messages, including the saved ones, hoping to find a tidbit of information to grasp, but all related to issues he was handling for the firm. Even his e-mails hadn't been picked up. All of them, from Saturday on, were marked unread—something else that was uncharacteristic, even when he traveled.

"Odelia," someone said to me.

I turned away from my computer screen and toward my office door to find Carl Yates looking at me. Carl was a man on the brink of sixty, very tall and angular, with thick hair the color of fading flax. He had an easy smile and manner, which belied the tough, take-no-prisoners litigator beneath. His jacket was off, his

73

tie askew, and his shirt sleeves rolled up. His reading glasses were perched on top of his head.

"Has Mike returned from his trip yet?"

"I haven't seen him." I turned in my chair and gave him my full attention. "In fact, Carl, I'm quite worried. No one has heard from him since he left. That's not like him. Has he called you?"

"No, he hasn't, and I've left a half-dozen voice mails for him, both here and at home. The Silhouette matter is heating up, and I need his input." He started to leave, then stopped. "And you're right; it's not like him at all. Hope nothing's happened to him."

"I don't want to seem panicky, but maybe we should call his emergency contact. He was due back today."

"Good idea, Odelia. Take care of that, and keep me posted."

Tina Swanson provided me with the emergency contact information from Steele's personnel sheet. It was for a Karen Meek in Santa Barbara. Tina didn't write down what Ms. Meek's relationship was to Steele, just her home and office number.

Looking at my watch, I noted that it was just about two thirty, so I tried the office number. A woman answered, "Karen Meek's office." She sounded young.

"Is Ms. Meek in?"

She asked my name and what it was regarding. I gave her my name, the firm's, and Steele's, and was put on hold. Shortly, another woman came on the line and identified herself as Karen Meek. Her voice was educated and efficient. I identified myself as Michael Steele's paralegal and told her we were concerned because he had not returned from a trip. I further explained that she was his contact information.

"But I saw Mike this weekend," she told me.

I sighed in relief. Maybe she was a girlfriend, although she didn't sound like one of his usual bimbos. Then it occurred to me that perhaps Karen Meek was his sister or some other family member. "Do you know where he is now?"

"He told me he was going to spend a couple of days at the Inn. Said he needed to think some things through, something about work, a trial or something, and wanted to do it away from the office. He said he needed some downtime."

"Downtime? Steele?"

The voice on the other end laughed, making me realize I probably shouldn't have been so candid.

"Yes, even Mike needs downtime every now and then. Hard to believe, isn't it?"

I laughed lightly. Whoever this Karen Meek was, she sounded cool.

"Ms. Meek, we haven't heard from Mr. Steele since he left Friday evening. That's highly unusual for him, even when he travels."

She laughed lightly again. "Sorry, but that was partly my fault. Saturday and Sunday he was at my house, and I wouldn't allow him to use his cell. He seemed preoccupied, and I wanted him to focus on family issues. I don't know why he didn't call after he left. Maybe he enjoyed being untethered from the office and decided to continue it. Like I said, he seemed preoccupied with something. Maybe he decided he could think about it better without any disturbance."

"You're family, then? Are you his sister?" I stopped and rethought my question. "I'm sorry, I'm being too nosy."

Again, I heard a light laugh from the other end of the line. "I'm like a sister to him, though not by blood. In reality, I'm his ex-wife."

Well, that knocked me over. I knew Steele had been married before. It was a tidbit of personal information he had let slip once. I remembered him saying it was during law school and short-lived. I had assumed that he and the ex had parted permanently, not remained close friends. But that was my assumption, not a fact, obviously. I also remembered him saying they had no children, and I wondered what family issues he had in common with his ex-wife. But I had reached my nosy quota with Karen Meek, at least for now.

"Well, Ms. Meek, maybe you're right about Mr. Steele deciding to remain incommunicado, but he hasn't returned yet and was due back in the office no later than today. So I'm sure you understand why we are so concerned."

"Of course," she replied. "And I'm getting worried now myself. Mike is always where he is supposed to be when he's supposed to be there. It's as much of a flaw as it is a good trait. True?"

I smiled at the comment. Yes, this woman did know Steele. "What was the name of the place he was going to? The Inn?"

"Yes, the Ojai Valley Inn & Spa. Do you want me to call them for you?"

"No, thank you, Ms. Meek, you've already been quite helpful. I'll give them a call. Maybe he's on his way back and is stuck in traffic."

"It's quite possible. But please keep me posted, won't you? Or have him call me when he returns so I won't worry."

"Of course, Ms. Meek, thank you." The list of people who wanted to be kept posted was growing by leaps and bounds

I looked up the number for the Ojai Valley Inn & Spa and dialed it. I asked for Michael Steele and was told there was no guest registered under that name. When I pressed for more information, I was transferred to the manager's office. I spoke to a Mr. Fernandez, who explained that he could only tell me that they had no guests registered under that name at that time.

My next call was to Dev Frye. I received his voice mail and left a message, which he returned within twenty minutes. I told him about Karen Meek and the inn, and how Steele had not shown up yet and not called anyone here at the office. I carefully left out the fact that I was meeting Sally Kipman tonight for dinner. After all, my call to Dev was about Steele and Steele alone. I also wasn't in the mood to be lectured. Dev told me to sit tight and he'd get back to me shortly.

Sitting tight is not in my genetic makeup. I was meeting Sally for dinner at seven at Houston's in Irvine, just off the 405 Freeway, and I was dying to know what she was going to tell me. I was still shaken by her admissions that she was gay and her child had been fathered by Donny Oliver. I was actually more surprised about her connection with Donny. If she was a lesbian, why and how did Donny manage to impregnate her? For all his faults, he hadn't seemed the type to force a woman. Maybe she wasn't gay then. Maybe her experience with Donny had turned her gay? Then I dismissed my last thought as pure poppycock. I knew better, and after all, I had survived Donny. Seven o'clock just couldn't come fast enough. I reached into my tote bag and grabbed some emergency Tylenol. All this sitting tight was giving me a headache.

Dev's call came on my cell phone just as I was leaving the office for Houston's. He had some information, although it wasn't really anything regarding Steele's whereabouts, just his non-whereabouts. It's never a surprise to me that cops know other cops. Dev knew some of the detectives involved with Donny's murder case, and it turns out he knows someone who knows someone in the Ojai Police Department. That person made a quick courtesy call to the Ojai Valley Inn & Spa.

According to Dev's source, Michael Steele was well known at the inn and had a reservation for two nights, Monday and Tuesday, but had been a no-show. Generally, he brought a female companion with him, but this time the reservation had been for one guest only and included a Tuesday morning tee time. After telling me all he could, Dev suggested that either I or the firm file a missing person report and he would be happy to facilitate it.

A formal missing person report—yikes. That really elevated Steele's absence to a new level, like the Homeland Security Advisory System upgrading its terrorist risk from yellow to orange and putting everyone on alert. I told Dev that I needed to discuss this with someone at the office and would get back to him.

Dev ended the call by asking me to dinner, but I demurred, saying I had a lot on my mind and needed some time to digest it. I still wasn't of the mind to tell him that I was about to add Donny's murder to my already full plate.

I made a quick call to Sally Kipman, telling her something had come up at the office and that I would be about thirty minutes late. I offered to reschedule, but she said she'd wait. That taken care of, I went in search of Carl Yates. I wasn't surprised to find him still hard at work. He was ensconced in a war room, a small conference room near his office that had been set aside to house the voluminous documents and work in progress for the Silhouette matter. With Carl were Joan Nuñez and Fran Evans. Joan looked up from the pile of documents in front of her and smiled at me. Fran frowned.

"I hope," Fran said to me in her usual frozen demeanor, "that you're here to tell us Mike Steele's back. We really need his help."

I ignored her and directed my words to Carl. "I have some information on that project you asked about."

For a second his look was blank, then understanding filled his tired eyes and made them spark. He turned to Joan and Fran. "There's nothing more we can do tonight, why don't you both go home." Joan nodded, but Fran started to say something. Carl stopped her. "Joan, can you be back here tomorrow morning around seven thirty or eight to go through those new documents that arrived today?"

Joan had already stood up and was rolling her neck and shoulders, loosening them. No doubt she'd been bent over documents close to ten hours today, with more facing her tomorrow. "Yes, of course, Carl. I'll be here by seven thirty."

"Good." He turned to Fran. "I need to give Odelia some time, and then I'm heading home myself. Get some rest, Fran; you've been hitting it pretty hard."

"But what about Mike?" she asked, looking from Carl to me. "Any news?"

"He still hasn't called me," I told her.

Before Fran could ask anything more, Carl directed me a few doors down the hall to his office. After closing the door, he took a seat behind his large, imposing desk and indicated for me to sit in a chair across from him. Carl's office was as cluttered as the war room, with expanding files, boxes of documents, and file folders stacked on most flat surfaces. Interspersed between the documents and files on his desk and bookcase were numerous family photos.

"What do you have to tell me, Odelia?"

"It's not good, Carl," I started. "Not terrible, but not good."

He leaned back in his chair, ready to hear more. Exhaustion was as noticeable on his face as his late-afternoon stubble.

"First of all, I called Steele's contact person, Karen Meek, his ex-wife. She saw him Saturday and Sunday in Santa Barbara, but not since. She said he was heading to the Ojai Valley Inn. My friend, Detective Devin Frye of the Newport Beach police, had someone in the Ojai PD do some checking. Mike Steele had reservations at the inn for both Monday and Tuesday nights, but never arrived and never called to cancel." I hesitated, swallowed, and continued. "The Ojai police also did a quick patrol of the roads, just in case Steele had an accident and went off the road somewhere, but they turned up nothing." I paused again. "Detective Frye suggested we file a missing person report." I started to say more, but stopped to get my thoughts in order.

"Anything else, Odelia?"

"Yes, Carl, something Karen Meek said." He nodded for me to continue. "She said Steele was going to the inn to think in peace for a few days—said he was preoccupied about something having to do with the upcoming trial." I paused, again trying to dig through my brain for anything I may have noticed before Steele left town. "I don't recall anything unusual about the Silhouette matter, but then I'm not working closely with it, just here and there as Steele needs me. Do you recall anything unusual about it?"

"Interesting," Carl said as he played with a pen, tapping it against the edge of his desk. "There have been some oddities here and there, but that's with every trial."

Carl leaned his head back and closed his eyes. Every now and then, he'd purse his lips. I knew he was mulling over the information, trying to decide how to proceed. Carl Yates had a methodical, orderly mind, not unlike a computer. He could quickly categorize information and yield a best course of action, all on the fly and with excellent results. I sat quietly and waited. After a few minutes, Carl opened his eyes, leaned forward, and looked me straight in the eye.

"So, Odelia, here's what we're going to do."

NINE

I arrived at Houston's exactly at seven thirty to find Sally Kipman at the bar toying with the stem of a nearly empty martini glass. She announced our table would be ready soon.

Waving her empty glass at the bartender, she said, "Grey Goose, extra olives." He nodded and looked my way.

Oh hell, why not? After what Carl Yates just told me, I could do with three or four martinis. "The same," I told him.

Sally looked good. She was dressed in neatly pressed light gray wool slacks and a pale blue silk blouse that accentuated her eyes and blond hair. On the back of her bar stool hung a matching gray blazer. She held her frame erect and her head high in self-confidence. The overall effect was quite striking.

We sat in silence until our drinks came. After giving her three olives a swirl in the alcohol, she lifted the glass in my direction. "Here's to new old friends."

I smiled slightly and clinked the edge of my glass against hers. She took a healthy swallow of her drink, and I followed suit. The strong alcohol caused me to sputter and cough.

"Something tells me," Sally said after I recovered, "that you're more used to drinking cosmopolitans and appletinis."

"This ... is fine." I coughed again.

"Would you like something else?" Her voice was laced with amusement.

"No, I'm fine. Thanks."

Truth is, I'm a lightweight when it comes to drinking. But I do have an occasional fondness for cosmopolitans, thanks to watching reruns of *Sex and the City*, and I can't remember the last time I had a regular martini, if at all. But I'll be damned if I'm going to let Sally Kipman know that. I was gingerly taking my second sip when the hostess announced our table was ready.

We sat opposite each other in a booth and picked up our menus. We were doing everything but getting to the reason we were there. The waitress came and took our order: grilled salmon with asparagus, and caesar salad to start, for both of us.

"I owe you a big apology, Sally," I told her after another sip of my drink, which I was really beginning to enjoy.

"For what?"

"For high school—you know, the lesbian thing."

She let her chin fall a bit forward and laughed almost into her drink. "You don't owe me anything, Odella. You were right, I was a lesbian—am a lesbian. I knew it even then. You, on the other hand, were never pregnant, yet I told everyone you were." She looked up, holding my eyes with hers. "It's I who owe you an apology."

"Why were we so hateful to each other, Sally? Do you even remember?"

She shrugged. "I'm not sure, but it probably had to do with us both being miserable and wanting to take it out on someone. I was angry about my parents' divorce and moving to California. I also knew I was different from the other girls and was trying to cope with that. There wasn't the support for gay youngsters there is now."

Sally paused, took a sip of her drink, and continued as if stepping on glass. "As I recall, Odelia, your mother disappeared about the same time. Am I correct?"

Although I remembered her personal history, I was shocked that she had remembered mine. Maybe, because I had spent thirty years trying so hard to forget, I had hoped everyone else would. Looking back, there were lots of things about my junior and senior years in high school I would have liked to have erased from my memory completely, not just the prom. Is it possible to invoke selective amnesia and not be considered delusional?

"Yes," I answered. "After she left, I was forced to go live with my father and stepmother. That alone would have made Mother Teresa malicious and spiteful." I shuddered, took another quick drink, and went eyeball to eyeball with one of the large olives in my glass. "To this day, I still don't know what happened to my mother."

We were silent for a moment, then Sally picked up her glass in an exaggerated toast. "Well, we may have been screwed up, Odelia, but at least we had good skin."

I snorted in laughter and raised my own glass in a toast of the truth. While other kids in school had battled acne, oily skin, and trips to the dermatologist, both Sally and I had enjoyed clear and beautiful complexions. And from the looks of it, we still did. Even as fifty loomed ahead, we both had creamy skin with few wrinkles.

Our salads came. Sally started eating. I picked up my fork, then put it back down and extended my right hand across the table. "Let's call it a draw, shall we? Let's just call it two teenage bitches that survived their parents and finally grew up."

She put down her fork, took my offered hand in hers, and shook. "You're on."

We picked up our drinks, clinked our glasses once again, and drained them. Sally ordered two more.

Over our entrees, I learned that Sally had gone to college at UCLA, the same college Donny had attended. She had graduated with an engineering degree, he with a business degree. They knew some of the same people and occasionally ran into each other. She became pregnant with Lucas their senior year, but never told Donny.

"Okay," I said, holding up a hand. "If you knew you were a lesbian in high school, what were you doing screwing around with Donny Oliver in college? Did you get drunk at some frat party and lose your mind? Did he seduce you on some bet?"

"No, actually I planned the whole thing."

"You planned it?" Suddenly, I was hit with a sense of déjà vu. "You *planned* to sleep with Donny?"

I shook my head in disbelief and immediately felt the effect of the two martinis. My skull felt like a huge and heavy pimento-stuffed olive lolling around in a tub of booze. I should've had a few of these the night Greg dumped me.

I steadied my head and tried to focus again on Sally. "You bedded Donny Oliver? Not the other way around?" Unable to control myself, I started laughing.

"Does that seem so far-fetched?" Sally tightened her lips and narrowed her eyes. "Do you think I'm that unattractive?"

"No, I didn't mean it that way." I waved my right hand in the air and continued to giggle. In my hand was my fork, and on the fork was precariously perched a bit of salmon. I pointed the fork at her. "Just one thing I gotta know." As I spoke, I bobbed the fork. The tidbit of salmon flicked across the table and landed in her martini glass.

Her look from across the table was stern. She put down her own fork and crossed her arms in front of her. When she spoke, her jaw was so tight her lips hardly moved. "And that is?"

I stopped giggling long enough to speak. "We may have a lot more in common than you realize." Decency told me to stop, so I told decency to sit somewhere else. There were things I wanted to know, even if just for entertainment value. "Was Donny Oliver your first?"

For a minute, I thought Sally was going to throw down her napkin and leave. But instead, she dabbed at her mouth with the napkin and replaced it in her lap. She no longer seemed cross, just annoyed around the edges, like a frayed piece of fine linen.

"Donny Oliver was my first and my last … man."

I started to speak but was hit with a case of hiccups. Picking up my glass, I drained it with one big, exaggerated swallow before continuing. "You're … *hic* … lucky."

I waved my empty martini glass in the direction of a passing waiter, but Sally reached out and took it from me before he could notice. "I think we've *both* had enough, don't you?"

"Truthfully, Sally, I haven't had nearly enough, considering the past week or so."

I looked across the table at Sally Kipman, my one-time high-school nemesis. It was my turn to narrow my eyes.

"Since Donny's murder on Saturday night, I have been dumped by my boyfriend, a man I wanted very much to marry, and my boss has gone missing. And before all this, I was smacked in the face with a leg of lamb in a fight at the market."

Sally interrupted with a short chuckle. "Yes, I thought I saw your photo in the paper."

I was not amused. Sally collected herself under my evil eye, and I continued. "Seems that just because I lucked out and solved a couple of problems in the past, one of my other bosses now thinks I'm just the person to find Mike Steele. That's my missing boss, who, quite frankly, is doing us all a favor by remaining gone. Which is why I was late tonight: I was getting my marching orders to put aside my other work in order to find the missing asshole. And now you've called to discuss Donny's murder. I should hang out a shingle: *Odelia Grey, P.I.* But in my case, the P.I. would stand for *plump* and *irritable*."

Finished with my rant, I leaned against the back of the booth, exhausted. A busboy cleared our plates, and our waitress stood ready for further orders.

"Do you still have that incredible brownie sundae with the caramel sauce?" Sally asked the waitress. She confirmed that they did. Sally turned to me. "Want to split one, Odelia?"

I took a deep breath. "No," I snapped. "I don't want to split one. I want one of my own, with extra ice cream."

The waitress looked embarrassed. She turned slightly toward Sally, awaiting instructions, her body language clearly stating that she thought me demented and Sally the sane one.

Sally didn't miss a beat. "Make that two brownie sundaes, both with extra ice cream." She glanced over at me, then back to the waitress. "And please bring two cups of strong, black coffee."

TEN

I got into the office early on Thursday, even foregoing my usual exercise. My night had been a restless one because of the information floating around in my brain. Nothing fit together. Bits and pieces of Steele's disappearance and Donny's murder swirled around in my semiconscious mind like cat hair adrift on an air current. It drove me nuts. On top of that, I woke up with another headache and a stuffy nose. The headache I could explain with the martinis, but the nasal congestion made me worry that I had caught Greg's cold. Oh well, at least I'd have something to remember him by.

Over a couple cups of coffee and the brownie sundaes, which also didn't help my sleep last night, Sally and I finally got around to discussing her history with Donny Oliver.

Like me, Sally Kipman had seduced Donny Oliver, but she had done it for a very different reason. In college, she had been involved in a serious relationship with an older woman. The two had even set up house together and talked about children. Near the end of her senior year at college, Sally and her partner decided it was time to start a family. They considered many men they knew as donors, and even a sperm bank, but for one reason or another, each one fell short. It was then Sally brought up the idea of Donny Oliver.

He was attractive, athletic, and intelligent. Sally knew something about his family and the type of people from which he had come, so there was little mystery to what they were getting. With the majority of his characteristics so favorable, the women figured the jerk gene could be overcome, so they fired up their plan.

Donny had been both an easy and potent mark, thinking he had won an easy lay, never suspecting he was the victim of a sperm holdup. In her sixth month, Sally and her lover broke up, leaving Sally devastated, alone, and very pregnant. The story was an old one—evidence that the same things happened to women over and over, both straight and gay.

Sally moved back in with her mother and awaited the birth. A few months after Lucas was born, Sally, armed with her recently acquired engineering degree, landed a job. Shortly after, she started work on her master's degree. A job, grad work, and a new baby—just the idea of all that stress made my head throb.

According to Sally, everything was going well. She got her master's degree, landed a great new job with the company she is still with today, and raised Lucas, who turned out to be a bright, charming boy with no signs of the jerk gene. She even found love again, this time with a woman named Jill Bernelli, whom she met through a lesbian mixer. They met shortly after Sally's mother passed away from a heart attack and just before Lucas's eighth birthday, and have been together since.

"I should have known," Sally had said to me as she cut off a piece of brownie with the edge of her fork, "that things were going too good to last." She took the bite and chewed it thoughtfully. "When things are going well, we tend to become complacent about happiness. That's always when some monster comes out from under the bed and scares the shit out of you. You know what I mean?"

I nodded, my own mouth full of chocolate pastry and creamy ice cream. I chewed and swallowed the concoction. "One minute you're dancing, thinking of white gowns and orange blossoms, and the next minute you're being called a corpse magnet."

"Huh?" Sally looked at me like I had a screw loose as she dabbed whipped cream from her lips with her napkin.

"Nothing." I took a sip of coffee. "So was Donny the monster under the bed?"

She shook her head. "No, he wasn't, but he was the monster the initial monster summoned, like a ghost summoning the devil." She pushed her dessert plate away and moved her coffee in front of her. "I'm stuffed."

I was full, too, but took a few more bites before giving up and pushing my plate away.

Sally drank some coffee. "When he was almost ten, Lucas became ill. It turned out to be some odd allergy, but for a long time we had no idea what it was. The doctors wanted to know his family's medical history. Of course, I knew mine, but Donny's was a complete unknown. As time went on and Lucas didn't get any better, I finally decided to go to Donny and ask about his family."

"He had no idea he had a son?"

"None at all, and he had no clue that I was gay. If I had my way, he never would have found out about either."

"Did you come right out and tell Donny you were a lesbian when you contacted him?"

Sally slowly shook her head and smiled. "He had no idea. Unfortunately, it was Lucas who spilled the beans about having two mommies." She took another sip of coffee. "I contacted Donny through the alumni association. He thought I was trying to shake him down for support money, but once he realized I wasn't, he wanted to know more about Lucas."

"And he wanted custody once he knew?"

"Again, it was like a monster hiding under the bed. At first, Donny was happy to help with the medical history. He met Lucas, and they got along great. Donny even got along well with Jill and me after he found out we were a couple. Donny had three daughters with his wife, Cindy, and often they took Lucas with them on day trips. Lucas always returned to us excited to have spent time with his father, and he grew quite close to Cindy and the girls. I began to be sorry that I hadn't let him know Donny sooner."

Our dessert plates were cleared and fresh coffee poured.

"So what spurred the custody battle?"

Sally sighed and suddenly seemed to shrink a bit. "Several months after Donny came into our lives, the doctors finally pinpointed Lucas's health problem. Like I said, it turned out to be an allergy, and once discovered was easily cleared up. During that time, Donny made no mention of custody issues. But as soon as Lucas was a healthy, vibrant boy again, Donny moved in for the kill.

"Out of the blue, one day we were served custody papers. Donny accused me of being a morally unfit mother, flaunting my perverted lifestyle in front of *our* impressionable preteen son."

She stopped, looked down at the coffee in her cup, and traced the cup with her right index finger.

"The court agreed with Donny. After all, he had a good job as an executive of a sports equipment company and was in a traditional marriage, complete with three children and a dog. It was the happy American family."

"But you had a good job and a stable home life."

"Yes, I did, and my lawyer trotted out many character witnesses, including my boss, coworkers, and even Lucas's doctor. But," she said, holding up her index finger, "in the eyes of the court, especially in the eyes of the male, ultra-conservative judge assigned to us, I was a woman living an unnatural and perverted lifestyle, a woman who spurned men and the natural order of the universe." She gave a short, rueful laugh. "That's almost exactly what the judge said in open court; that I was 'a woman who spurned the natural order of God and the universe.' And that such a woman should never be considered fit to raise a child, especially a male child, when the father had the desire and ability to do so in a more traditional manner."

"But that's downright ridiculous. Gay couples adopt and have children all the time."

"Now they do, Odelia. But that was fifteen years ago, and while some judges were starting to see the light, not all were."

"Didn't you appeal?"

"Yes, and we lost. Lucas went to live with Donny and his family, and I got limited visitation rights. I even had to pay Donny child support." Her voice was beginning to crack, like a hairline fissure in good china. "Even after all this time, it's difficult to talk about."

She looked up at me and gave me a weak half-smile. "And I haven't talked about it for a long time."

I reached across the table and patted her left hand where it rested on the table.

"I don't know what I would have done without Jill's support."

"Are you close now to Lucas? I remember you have a grand-son."

Sally squared her shoulders, and her face lit up with the mention of her grandchild. "Oh yes, Lucas and I never let this come between us. When he was fourteen, we petitioned the court, and Lucas was allowed to choose where he wanted to live. He returned to Jill and me. Even though I discouraged it, he never had many nice things to say about his father or Cindy, though he clearly favored Cindy over Donny. He said they fought all the time, mostly about Donny's drinking and carousing."

"Was Donny's wife at the reunion? I don't recall seeing him with anyone but Steve and a few of the other guys."

Sally shook her head. "I didn't see her there."

The waitress came to refresh our coffee. I declined, but Sally accepted more. After the waitress left, she leaned across the table and whispered, "I'm not sorry the bastard's gone, Odelia. Not sorry at all after what he put me, Jill, and Lucas through." She paused. "And after what he did to you at the prom, I doubt you've cried over his demise."

"Truthfully, I haven't. But, Sally, do you really think someone like Donny deserves to die?" I leaned forward, looking her straight in the eye. "Honestly, do you?"

She leaned back in the booth and turned her face away. After a moment, she turned back and looked directly at me. "As harsh as it sounds, yes, I do."

ELEVEN

I was still pondering what Sally had said last night, that sometimes people like Donny do deserve to die, when I received a call from Carl Yates asking me to come to the small, private conference room on the next floor. Woobie was growing rapidly and had recently expanded, taking over half of the floor just above our main floor. Grabbing a yellow pad and pen, I told John I was going into a meeting and headed for the elevators.

The evening before, Carl had decided two things: one, that the firm would file a missing person report; and two, that I would focus my time on finding Michael Steele, attorney-at-large. Carl had ended our conversation by saying he would run things past a couple of the other partners and give me the final word this morning.

Arriving at the conference room, I found the door shut. After a soft knock, I was admitted by Carl. He motioned me in and closed the door after me. Seated at the small conference table were Marc Boer and Katherine Brown. There are four name partners at Woobie: Wendell Wallace, my old boss who is now retired, Carl Yates, Katherine Brown, and Marc Boer. There are a few other partners, as well, such as Steele; but make no mistake, these top remaining three rule the roost and are quietly referred to amongst the employees as the Holy Trinity.

The Trinity greeted me with solemn faces as Carl asked me to take a seat.

"So, what's going on?"

The question came from Kelsey over a lunch of pastrami on rye, fries, coleslaw, and iced tea at Jerry's Famous Deli. The sandwiches are so large at Jerry's that we were splitting one. Joan, our other usual lunch buddy, was grabbing lunch back at the office while reviewing documents.

"Nothing," I replied while heaping coleslaw on my half of the sandwich. "I still haven't heard from Greg."

"I'm sorry, Odelia. Truly I am." She looked over both her shoulders and leaned forward in my direction. "But I was asking about the office. I came by your office this morning to see how you were, and that temp, John something or other, told me you were in a meeting upstairs."

"I'm in meetings all the time—part of the job."

"Yes, I'm aware of that. But Ani told me you were meeting with the Trinity."

Ani Markarian was Carl's secretary. "Ani should know better."

"It's about Steele, isn't it? Is he dead? Have a breakdown? In rehab?" She prattled on while holding a fry in her hand like a pointer. "I always thought he was on something—too nasty not to be."

I rolled my eyes. "Steele is not on drugs. He's too much of a health nut."

"Hmm, you're right." She bit the end off the fry like it was the head of an enemy. "Then my vote's for a nervous breakdown."

I took a bite of sandwich and studied Kelsey while I chewed. She was my friend, but I also knew the Steele matter was not to be discussed throughout the office. The party line would be that he was taking some unexpected but unavoidable personal time to handle family matters. But I knew Kelsey would never buy that. Like me, she'd been around Woobie too long to swallow fish stories whole.

"Truth is, we still don't know what's happened to him, but that's not what you'll be hearing."

She chuckled. "Typical."

I put down my sandwich and wiped my messy hands on a napkin. "Please, Kelsey, go along with whatever stories are fed to the staff. It's important."

She looked into my face a long time—studying me, probing my brain without permission. "They have you looking into it, don't they?"

With a sigh, I surrendered and confessed. "Yes, they do. The firm is filing a missing person report with the police. Then I'm to contact all his friends and family and see if I can turn up any information." I took a long drink of iced tea. "The firm has a valid reason to keep this quiet. Please don't say anything to anyone."

"Don't worry, pal, I won't, but only for your sake, not Steele's." She picked up her sandwich. Just before taking a bite, she said, "You're not going to end up in any danger, are you?"

"Danger? Sheesh, you're as bad as Greg about this stuff." But looking at Kelsey, I could see she was worried. "Trust me, Kelsey, all I'm doing is making a few calls to his gym rat buddies and talking to a few long-lost relatives. How dangerous can that be?"

Kelsey chewed and swallowed. "For a normal person, a day at the beach; for you, life-threatening."

TWELVE

INSTEAD OF GOING BACK to the office after lunch, I retrieved my car from the parking garage and headed for Laguna Beach. At this morning's meeting, I disclosed to the partners that I had a key to Steele's home, as well as his office passwords. They asked me to take a run by his condo if no one had heard from Steele by noon. They had read my mind. Before leaving for work this morning, I had fished Steele's key out of its hiding place with the idea of doing just that.

Steele lives in a condominium on Blue Lagoon Lane in Laguna Beach. I had never been there, but I knew the area and guessed that Steele must live almost on top of the beach.

Laguna Beach is about thirty to forty-five minutes from our office, depending on traffic; more if the freeway is tied up. Being that it was the middle of the day and not rush hour, I made it down the 73 Freeway and onto Laguna Canyon Road in good time. Laguna Canyon Road winds through a lovely rural park area, an area given to raging fires in some dry seasons, and comes out into the densely populated business district of the upscale beach town and artist enclave. Just before it reaches the web of small streets and boutiques, it passes two art areas. On the left is the location of the Sawdust Festival, which boasts over two hundred local artists during its twice-yearly art shows. On the right is the location of the Laguna Beach Festival of the Arts and home of the legendary Pageant of the Masters. My chest tightened, remembering that just a few months ago, Greg and I had attended the pageant and marveled together at the masterpieces reenacted on-stage by living, breathing subjects.

Pushing my personal grief aside, I continued, turning left onto Pacific Coast Highway. A few miles later, I turned right onto Blue Lagoon. I was not wrong; Steele did live almost on top of the beach.

I have to hand it to Steele, the man has wall-to-wall impeccable taste. Unlike his office, which is cold and austere in shades of black, white, and silver, with black-lacquered furniture, his home was warm and inviting, yet still very masculine. The flooring was travertine tile with muted area rugs in the entry and living room, and the walls were covered in textured taupe paint. In the living room was a large L-shaped leather sofa the color of a seasoned saddle, dotted with throw pillows of various earth tones and textures. Across from the sofa were two armchairs upholstered in a matching subtle print, one with an ottoman. Against a side wall was a substantial dark armoire, which probably housed the TV and audio equipment. On the walls were a couple of nice-sized paintings, and in the corners sat several large ferns. The living room was spacious and airy, with one wall a bank of windows looking out to the ocean. Peering out the window to the right, I could see tennis courts and a pool positioned a level below in a common area. This was living in style. Greg would love it.

There I go again. I must stop referencing Greg in everything I see and do. *He's gone, deal with it*, I told myself.

"Steele," I called out as I stepped farther into the condo. "Steele, you here?" No answer.

I found the kitchen, with its granite counters and gleaming top-of-the-line appliances. It looked like a kitchen from a model home, not a place where people cooked, mashed, and sautéed. Opening the double-wide side-by-side freezer/refrigerator, I noted that it was well-stocked with fruits and vegetables, but none looked freshly purchased. The freezer, too, was nearly full, and I smiled as I noticed several containers of Cherry Garcia ice cream. It was nice to know that at least Steele's palate was human.

Like my place, Steele's condo was built on two levels. The master suite was huge, with a California king-size bed and a leather headboard in the middle of it. Like the living room, the bedroom was done in earth tones with a mix of solids and prints. The master bath didn't have a tub, just a shower, but the shower was the size of one of my clothes closets, with multiple jets and a small built-in bench, making me wonder how much entertaining Steele did in his bathroom. Opening the medicine cabinet, or what stylishly passed for a medicine cabinet, I found various hair gels, antiperspirants, shaving implements, over-the-counter drugs, and first-aid products.

Nothing seemed out of order or used in quite a while. There were no stray hairs in the sink or crumpled tissues in the trash. I ran my fingers around the two sinks—both were slick and shiny, like they recently had been cleaned. Even the plush towels hanging on the designer rack looked freshly laundered. I stepped into the shower-a-rama. Neatly positioned on a stainless-steel rack were tubes and bottles of shampoo, conditioner, shower gel, and a bar of soap. I checked them all and found them dry. As with the sink, I passed my fingertips along the tile and the floor of the shower—slick, not a trace of soap residue.

Back out in the bedroom, I checked the linens on the bed. They were fresh and unused. I thought about the immaculate kitchen. This home had been cleaned and cleaned well since the last time Steele had been here. I made a mental note to find out who his cleaning lady or service was and make a call.

I did a thorough check of the second bedroom and bath and found both spotless. Like me, Steele used his spare bedroom as a combination office and guest room. Like the rest of the house, it was beautifully decorated and clean.

Pulling out my cell phone, I called Dev Frye. I filled him in on where I was and what I had found. I also told him that the firm wanted to file a missing person report. I told him I'd come to his office, but he said he'd rather come to Steele's place so he could look around.

After giving Dev Steele's address, I checked out the rest of the condo, opening closets and drawers, making sure someone still lived there. All looked in order. While there were few personal items downstairs, upstairs in both the master suite and office were framed photos. Some were of Steele in tennis togs with friends, others in ski apparel with other people. A couple of photos showed Steele with the same pleasant-looking woman. She looked about his age and had very long hair and a handsome face with strong features. In both photos they had their arms wrapped around each other. I wondered if this was Karen Meek.

While I waited for Dev, I sat at the desk in the guest room and went through some of the drawers. Everything was organized much as Steele kept things at the office. On the desk was a leather portfolio. Inside were recent billing statements from various utilities and credit cards. I sifted through them and found nothing unusual; they just appeared to be waiting to be paid. On the left side of the portfolio was a plastic sheet with windows for business cards. Inserted into the various windows were cards for a dentist, doctor, health club, and other services. In one sleeve was a card for a company called Melinda's Maid Service. I pulled out the card and put it in my pocket. Tucked behind it was a card for a company called Let Mother Do It. There was no address, just a simple card with a phone number under the name, maybe another cleaning company. I slipped the card out and put it in my pocket too.

I had just done a thorough search of the patio and garage when Dev Frye arrived. I let him into the condo and guided him to the dining table. From his inside coat pocket, Dev produced some forms. I sat down with him, and together we filled out the necessary information, which included a physical description of Steele, car make and model, present address, last known location, and other personal information. Dev told me that the Newport Beach police would put a description out over the wire to law enforcement agencies throughout California, such as the Highway Patrol, and would fax a copy of the report to the Laguna Beach, Ojai, and Santa Barbara police. They would be on the lookout for a car fitting the description of Steele's Porsche, but because there was no proof of foul play, beyond that there would not be any ongoing investigation.

I was torn about whether or not I should tell Dev that the firm wanted me to investigate on my own. The task had, after all, become part of my job description. In many ways, it was grandfathered in by my usual duties to look after Steele. The investigation had even been given its own internal billing number, and I was to post all the time I spent on finding Steele to that matter. The client was the firm, and the matter name was entitled Missing Link. The project title had been Katherine Brown's idea. I always did like that woman.

As usual, I took the middle road and told Dev that the firm wanted me to contact Steele's friends and see if any of them knew anything. He just stared at me, his face unreadable. When he did speak, I was surprised.

"That might not be a bad idea."

"Really?" I said, leaning forward. "I was sure you wouldn't be in favor of it at all."

Dev smiled slightly. "Calling a few of Mike Steele's friends seems harmless enough and might get us some leads. You never know. Besides, maybe this Steele thing is just what I need to keep your nose out of the Oliver matter."

My mind flashed back to the night before. Over the last couple of brownie sundae bites, Sally and I had made a pact—she would help me find Steele, and I would help her find Donny's murderer. Unbeknownst to Dev, my nose was already stuck into the middle of the Oliver matter. After all, promises made over chocolate and ice cream are nearly sacred.

"What makes you think I have any intention of sticking my nose into Donny's murder?" I tried my best to sound surprised and innocent.

Dev stared at me again, making me think I still had a bit of tell-tale hot fudge on my lip. "Like I said, Mike Steele's disappearance should keep you out of trouble, especially if your law firm is insisting you work on it. But you have to promise me one thing."

I looked at him, waiting for him to present the deal and wondering if it would be something I could honestly accept.

"You have to promise me, Odelia, that if you learn anything useful from his friends, that you will tell me immediately and not go off on a wild goose chase by yourself."

I leaned back in my chair. "Piece 'o cake."

"That's not what I asked you." He stared at me again, and I stared back, my nose twitching with mild irritation.

"Okay, okay, I will share anything I learn from his friends with you."

"Fine."

"Fine," I parroted.

The gravity of the matter hit home even harder when Dev asked for a current photo of Steele. In anticipation of such a request, I had printed out a copy of Steele's firm biography. At the top of the bio was a formal head shot of Steele, taken last year when the firm updated its website and all attorney bios.

Before handing it to Dev, I looked down at the handsome, intelligent face, and my stomach turned at the thought of Mike Steele being on a milk carton—of sorts. It is one thing to joke and tease about such things, but when it becomes a real possibility, the laughter is cut short like a soundtrack that is abruptly unplugged.

It's like telling Donny Oliver to eat shit and die, and then he does.

THIRTEEN

AFTER DEV LEFT, I returned to my office and made a list of Steele's friends, or at least the ones I knew about. The list wasn't that long. One was another lawyer named Timothy Weber. Tim worked for Goldberg-Rawlings, one of those international super-sized law firms. His office was in Los Angeles, but they also had an Orange County office that was housed just a couple of floors above our firm. When Tim's in town, he and Steele usually get together. They had met fresh out of law school at the first law firm they had both worked for. Other names on the list included Marvin Dodd, a financial analyst Steele plays tennis with frequently, and Walter Yamada, his CPA and golf companion.

Steele, of course, knew lots of other people, but these were his three key friends—his *amigos*—that I knew about. With Steele's computer password, I was able to find their private phone numbers on Steele's contacts list.

My plan was to call each of these people and see what they knew about Steele's plans. I also planned to drive to Santa Barbara and meet with Karen Meek, not only to question her, but to satisfy my raging curiosity.

My first call was to Karen Meek. She immediately asked if we had heard anything from Steele and seemed quite concerned when I reported we had not. She said she'd be happy to speak with me tomorrow at her office. We set the appointment for eleven thirty. Next, I called Marvin and Walter, but both were out of their respective offices. It was almost five o'clock, so I wasn't that surprised. I left voice mails for each, explaining who I was and why I was calling.

From going through Steele's voice mails, I remembered a couple of messages from Tim Weber telling Steele he was going to be in Orange County this week. I was pleased to find out when I called his cell that he was still in the area. As soon as he heard why I was calling, he asked me to come up to his office. I told him I'd be there in a jiffy.

Once you get past the designer lobbies, most law firms look the same, especially the larger ones housed in high-rise office buildings. Generally, the only distinction between them is what their reception area, or public area, looks like. Past that point, they become almost identical, with the attorneys on the outside with the window views and the staff in cubicles along the inside of the hallways. Out of view of the hallways, at the core of the floor plan, are the copy centers, kitchens, and file rooms. Most clients are seen in conference rooms just off the reception area and seldom see the inner workings of the firm they employ.

I felt right at home in the hallways of Tim Weber's firm. Except for the artwork, color of paint on the walls, and light fixtures, it could have been Woobie. Many of the staff were packing up for the day, but the same sense of purpose, the same clicking of fingers flying across keyboards, the same ringing of phones greeted me as I was escorted to his office by a pleasant-looking young man I recalled seeing from time to time in the elevators. Even the office Tim was using looked like the visiting attorney offices at Woobie— a simple desk, credenza, empty bookcase, computer, one swivel desk chair, and one visitor's chair. Since this wasn't his home office, there wasn't a single personal item in sight, except for his briefcase and suit jacket.

Tim thanked the young man who brought me to him and directed me to the visitor's chair. "I'm sorry about the office, but all the conference rooms are in use right now." Tim grinned. "Hey, caught that photo of you in the paper. Nice to see your black eye's gone."

I gave him a tight smile and murmured thanks. Sheesh! Did everyone on the planet see that photo?

Tim Weber was almost as tall and well-built as Steele, and almost as handsome, except that he was very fair and his light hair was starting to recede. So much so, I bet he'd be bald by the time he was fifty. He also seemed less rigid than Steele and far less self-focused. We had met on several occasions during the past couple of years, and I always found him pleasant. Tim was married to an heiress, old money from the East, and their names and photos often popped up in society columns reporting on charity events. He greeted me with proper politeness before cutting to the chase.

"So, Odelia, what's going on with Mike? Does anyone know where he is?"

"*No one* seems to know where he is. I was hoping you could shed some light on it."

Tim shook his head. "Wish I could. I knew something was up when he didn't answer my calls to his cell or his office. I called to let him know I was going to be in Orange County a few days, try to set up at least a dinner, maybe some tennis, while I was in town. It's been awhile since we've seen each other."

I gave Tim Weber a rundown of what we knew so far—the trip to Santa Barbara, the no-show at the inn, the preoccupation with a trial, the no response to calls and e-mails.

"It's simply like he's vanished," I said with a shrug of my shoulders.

"Very odd." Tim looked thoughtful. "Maybe I should go by his place."

"I already have, just today." When Tim gave me an odd look, I explained. "Steele gave me an emergency key to hold. The firm also filed a missing person report this afternoon, and I've left voice mails for both Walter Yamada and Marvin Dodd."

Tim hesitated and rubbed his chin with a hand. "Hmm, I was going to offer to do that for you, but it sounds like you already have all the bases covered."

"Tell me something, Tim." He looked at me with interest. "When I spoke to Karen Meek, she said something about wanting Steele's mind on family business while he was up there. I knew he'd been married before, but I didn't think he had any children."

"He doesn't, at least none that he knows of." He gave a slight smirk before continuing. "Karen wasn't referring to family as in children, she was referring to Family with a capital *F*. Karen Meek is a family law attorney and does a lot of pro bono work for children and their parents. She's the head of a nonprofit company called Family Bond, and Mike is on the board."

"So Steele and his ex-wife are friendly?"

He nodded. "Very. They were finalizing their divorce when I met Mike. Karen's a very neat woman, probably better than he deserved, considering how he treats the ladies. I believe they met early in law school but after graduation had very different ideas about the practice of law. She's a granola do-gooder type, and he's a hardcore capitalist."

Tim leaned back in his chair and thought a minute, then looked at me. "Funny thing: I don't think Mike's been in love since. Once in a while he brings Karen along on long weekends with my wife and me. Last winter we all went skiing in Vail." I remembered the photo in Steele's condo. "Roxanne and I—Roxanne's my wife—we always thought they might get back together if they could find some common ground, but it's plain now that's not going to happen."

Tim walked me to the front door of his firm and told me to please keep him in the loop on anything regarding Steele. By now, almost all the staff had gone for the night, and just a few attorneys lingered, still hard at work—just like at Woobie.

I was almost to my car when my cell phone rang. It was Walter Yamada returning my call.

"I hope I'm not disturbing you, Odelia, but you said it was about Mike Steele and an emergency."

"No problem, Mr. Yamada, I'm glad you called." I quickly gave him a sketch of what was going on.

"I'm sorry, but I'm afraid I won't be much help. I just returned from Chicago—was gone about ten days on a combination business and family trip. I haven't spoken to Mike in almost two weeks."

I remembered something I should have asked Tim Weber. "Mr. Yamada, you've known Mike Steele a long time, haven't you?"

"Yes, at least ten or twelve years."

"I know his mother has passed away, and he has an ex-wife, but what about other family members—father, brothers, sisters—where can I reach them?"

"I'm afraid when Mike's mother died, that was the last of the family. His father died in a car accident just before I met him, and his brother died tragically from a drug overdose a year later. I don't believe he had any other siblings."

"Thanks, anyway, Mr. Yamada. But if you hear from Steele, please let me or the firm know immediately."

"You bet I will, and vice versa, okay? This isn't like him at all."

Everyone was in agreement—this disappearing act wasn't something Steele would do under normal circumstances. I suddenly had an image of him sprawled dead in a ditch on the side of the road between Santa Barbara and Ojai, maybe thrown from his car when it spun out of control on a turn he took too fast. Driving fast and recklessly would be like Steele. I know, I've ridden with him in that land rocket he calls a car. But I also reminded myself that the Ojai police, as a favor to Dev, had search the main road to the inn and the area around it. Still, he could be anywhere, and maybe not dead. People have been known to survive crashes and crawl with broken limbs back to the road for help. Why not Steele?

I searched my recent calls on my cell phone. When I found what I was looking for, I hit dial. Soon Sally Kipman was on the other line.

"I'm heading to Santa Barbara tomorrow morning to meet with Mike Steele's ex-wife, want to come?" Before she could answer,

I added, "I'm also going to comb the highway between Santa Barbara and Ojai for his body."

"His body?"

"Well, for signs of a possible car accident. You know, broken shrubs and tire tracks, stuff like that."

"What about Donny's murder?"

"Bring what you have so far, and we'll discuss that, too. Remember, we agreed to team up on both, and I'm on the move beginning *now*."

FOURTEEN

As soon as Sally saw my ancient Toyota Camry, she insisted we take her Jeep Grand Cherokee. Sure, why not? I love my car—it runs well, looks fine, and is paid off—but any chance I get not to drive, I take it.

It's about a two-hour drive to Santa Barbara from where I live, so we had agreed to leave my place no later than eight thirty to allow for unexpected traffic problems. If we arrived early, we could grab a cup of coffee somewhere.

We were on the 405 Freeway heading north, approaching the section of road where the Getty Center perches on a bluff overlooking the freeway, when my cell phone rang. It was Marvin Dodd.

"Thanks for calling back, Mr. Dodd."

"What's this about Mike Steele missing?"

"Seems that way. No one has seen him in several days. He went out of town for a few days, was due back in the office on Wednesday, but never showed."

"Hmm, not like him at all."

As with Tim Weber and Walter Yamada, I gave Marvin Dodd a quick rundown of events.

"Well, we played tennis last Thursday night at his place, and he grilled up some salmon after. I haven't seen him since."

Thursday was just two days before his trip and four days before he disappeared. "Did he say anything to you about his trip to Santa Barbara or Ojai?"

"Nothing you don't already know. He was going to see Karen about some business, then spend a couple of days at the inn." He chuckled.

"Something funny, Mr. Dodd?"

"It's just … well, over dinner he showed us that picture of you in the *Register*—too funny."

I stuck my tongue out at the phone, sorry he couldn't see me do it. But Sally did see it.

"What was that about?" she asked once I ended the call. "Wasn't he cooperative?"

I rolled my eyes and told her, making her laugh.

"Seems your boss was proud of you."

I stuck my tongue out at her, but even as I did, something nagged at me, something that Marvin Dodd said about the incident in the grocery store. I mean, the whole idea that Steele was parading that photo around was annoying enough, but something that Mr. Dodd said gnawed at me like a hungry termite.

After smiling at my childish behavior, Sally reached up and retrieved something tucked under the visor, which she handed to me. It was several sheets of folded white paper—maps printed from the Internet, more specifically, Mapquest.

"There are two ways to get to Ojai from Santa Barbara," she explained, nodding in the direction of the paper in my hands. "I printed out both of them." I unfolded the sheets in my hand and looked at them while she explained. "One route retraces back down 101, then swings north again on 33. It's not the most direct route, but it's the fastest."

The colorful map in my hand showed a path that looked like a big *V*. As she said, the road went south, back toward Los Angeles, before connecting with 33 in a sharp northward path to Ojai.

"The second way is shorter in mileage but longer in time. That route is along 150 by Lake Casitas. I've taken 150 before. It's a beautiful drive but curves a lot." She looked over at me. "Which do you think your boss, this Steele guy, would have taken?"

"Good question." I studied the maps in my hands. Steele loves to drive, and I could picture him relishing the twisty scenic route, especially in his sports car. "Depends on how much of a rush he was in at the time."

I refolded the maps and tucked them into my trusty tote bag. Maybe Karen Meek could shed some light on Steele's mood and timetable when he left her.

Changing the subject, I asked Sally, "Have you had time to find out anything about Donny?"

She smiled and looked at me, her eyes hidden by stylish Ray-Bans. "You're not the only one who's been busy since Wednesday night."

I smiled back, put on my own sunglasses, and settled in for her report. We had about another hour on the road, might as well get some work done.

"I called Cindy, Donny's wife," Sally began. "I told her in spite of everything, I was very sorry for her loss; after all, Donny was Lucas's father. I asked about funeral arrangements—which, by the way, are on Tuesday."

"That's Halloween, isn't it?"

Sally nodded. "Seems fitting, doesn't it?"

"No time like Halloween to be in a cemetery." I paused. "You going?"

She nodded again. "Yes, we all are—me, Jill, and Lucas and his wife and baby. Whether I like it or not, Donny was family." She focused on her driving, deftly maneuvering around a slow-moving car in the fast lane. "When I asked Cindy why she wasn't at the reunion, she said Donny didn't want her there. Claims he told her she'd cramp his style."

"His style? Being an ass and getting killed is a style these days?"

"That's what she said." Sally looked at me. "Honestly, she didn't seem too upset that Donny was gone. In fact, she actually came out and told me she was glad he was gone."

"You're kidding."

"Nope. Apparently Cindy felt comfortable enough with me to spill her guts. Guess she considers us sisters in some sort of I Hate Donny club now."

"Hmm." An association for women Donny Oliver had screwed and screwed over—could be fun.

"According to Cindy, she was planning on leaving Donny right after Christmas. Said she'd had enough, that there was no reason to stick around when he obviously didn't want her."

"Very interesting."

"Yes, but here's the kicker. She said whoever killed Donny did her a favor, because Donny told her recently that if she ever left him, he'd destroy her."

"Maybe she did herself a favor."

"It's a distinct possibility."

Turning straight ahead, I looked out the window and watched the traffic, thinking about what Sally just told me. We both were quiet for several miles until I turned back to her.

"Sally, what do you say to paying Mrs. Oliver a little visit sometime this weekend?"

She turned, and a slow grin formed on her face. "I'm sure Jill would love to bake a bundt cake for the widow."

FIFTEEN

THE LAW OFFICE OF Karen Meek was located in a Spanish-style single-story duplex on the corner of De la Guerra and Anacapa, just a block from State Street, the main shopping and dining area of Santa Barbara.

I love Santa Barbara. It's one of the most charming places in all of California and a close weekend getaway for those of us who live south of it. Thoughts of Greg and the many weekends we'd spent here tried to crowd themselves into my mind, but I forced them back with a mental whip and chair as if they were wild animals.

Walking into Karen Meek's office felt nothing like walking into Woobie or Tim Weber's office. Instead of expensive floral arrangements, impressive artwork, and staid furniture, we were greeted by sweet and subdued Laura Ashley wallpaper, sheer curtains, and wood floors. A French country coffee table was positioned on an area rug in the middle of the large waiting room, and on it were various periodicals, including many children's magazines, all stacked neatly. The chairs were a collection of wooden kitchen chairs, all painted in either white or rose lacquer, with some child-size chairs in a corner around a small pint-size table. Green plants were scattered about in various pots. It was absolutely charming and very suitable for Santa Barbara.

In one corner of the large room, near a door in the far wall, was a large desk on which sat a computer, phone, and various files. Like the chairs, the desk looked refinished to match the décor. We weren't in the office long when a young woman came out of the far door carrying more files. She was in her twenties, tall and willowy, dressed in a lilac cardigan sweater and well-worn jeans. Her face was naturally pretty, and she wore her blond hair in two braids, with long bangs.

"Oh, hi," she said to us. "Sorry I didn't hear you come in. May I help you?"

"I'm Odelia Grey," I told her. "I have an appointment with Ms. Meek at eleven thirty, and this is my friend, Sally Kipman." She put the files down on a small credenza and looked at the appointment book open on the desk.

"We're a little early," I added.

The young woman smiled warmly. She could have been a model pushing fresh milk, good dental hygiene, and wholesome living. "Karen's with a client right now, but she should be done shortly. Would you ladies like some coffee?"

"I'd *love* some coffee," piped Sally. "Thank you."

I nodded in agreement. As soon as the young woman left back through the far door, Sally and I each took chairs near the large coffee table.

"Cute place," Sally said, looking around. "You sure she's a lawyer?"

"That's what I'm told; family law, works a lot with children."

"Smart woman to leave the intimidating surroundings to the other guys."

Sally was right. If Karen Meek worked with children and families, she was wise to give them a place where they at least had the illusion of warmth and safety, rather than a cold, impersonal waiting room. I had looked up Family Bond on the Internet. Its primary purpose was to heal children living in the midst of chaotic and troubled family situations, with issues ranging from child abuse to poverty, including helping families deal with raising a child with a mental or physical handicap. The organization also helped fund shelters for abused women and children.

The young woman returned with colorful mugs of hot, aromatic coffee. She told us her name was Tanya. We thanked her for the coffee. With a smile, she returned to her desk and began sorting through the files on the credenza.

We were halfway through our coffee when the door near Tanya's desk opened, and out came two women, one holding a small boy by the hand. The woman without the child was the same woman in the photo with Steele—Karen Meek. As they walked to the front door, Karen spoke in low tones to the other woman, who was crying softly. The child walked alongside them, head down. He must have been only about five years old. He was neat and tidy, and dressed in jeans, red high-top sneakers, and a blue hooded Dodgers sweatshirt and Dodgers cap. When the three of them reached the door, he turned, and I could see that his other arm was in a sling and tucked under the sweatshirt, the empty sleeve hanging down like a windsock in dead air.

I was about to look away when the child lifted his head and glanced at Sally and me. I almost gasped. Even with the cap pulled down low on his head, I could see that one side of his young face, the same side as the injured arm, was bandaged. Sally must have noticed, too, because I felt her nudge me in my side.

Careful, I told myself, *don't jump to conclusions just because Karen works with dysfunctional families and traumatized children. The boy could have taken a nasty spill.*

The woman thanked Karen, and Karen said she'd be in touch the next day. Before they left, Karen knelt down to the boy's level, looked him in the face, and whispered something to him. She was smiling when she did. The boy, once again looking down at the floor, nodded.

Once the woman and boy left, Karen turned to us. "One of you must be Odelia Grey."

"I am," I said, holding out my hand. "And this is my friend, Sally Kipman." Karen smiled, officially gave me her name, and shook my hand. She did the same with Sally. I was dying to know the story on the boy, but I knew better than to ask.

"Why don't we go into my office?"

We followed Karen past Tanya and through the door, into a hallway with various rooms branching off from it. At one end of the hallway was a small kitchen. She directed us toward the other end. Along the way, we passed the bathroom, a room that served as a file and copy room, a small office, and finally into a large office at the end of the hall. Like the waiting room, Karen's office was decorated in soothing prints and refinished antiques. In spite of the numerous files stacked on tables and the floor, the place seemed tidy and organized—much like Karen herself.

Karen Meek was dressed in tailored tweed wool trousers and a dove gray silk blouse. Her long hair was pulled back and held with a becoming clip. Around her neck was a strand of pearls, with matching pearl studs in her ears. She was trim and held herself very erect, almost in a pose, like classically trained dancers often do. Her face was attractive but not beautiful, and her brown, wide-set eyes snapped with kindness and energy. I quickly noted that on her left hand was a large diamond ring. My heart ached for a fleeting second, and just as quickly I pulled myself together.

There was a small sitting area in one corner of the office, and she directed us to sit there. Sally and I perched side by side on a delicate settee; Karen sat stiffly in a matching chair.

"If you're here, Odelia, I guess Mike hasn't surfaced."

"No, I'm afraid he hasn't." I put my tote bag down on the floor by my feet and folded my hands in my lap. "Our firm has filed a missing person report."

"Good. I was beginning to wonder if I should do one myself."

"No need. A friend of mine is with the Newport Beach police. He filed it and had a copy sent to the Santa Barbara, Ojai, and Laguna Beach police departments." I swallowed. "The Ojai police even did a quick drive along the roads between here and the Ojai Valley Inn, but they turned up nothing."

"That's just not like Mike. Not at all." Karen toyed with her necklace. "I'm starting to get very worried."

I leaned slightly toward her. "Karen, what sort of mood was Steele in when he left—and exactly when did he leave here?"

She smiled at me. "I see you call him Steele, not Mike, and I'll bet he calls you Grey. Am I right?"

I nodded. "He calls everyone by their last name at the office."

"He called me Meek most of our marriage."

Sally scoffed. "How romantic."

Karen looked at each of us in turn before leaning back in her chair in a more relaxed position. "Actually, he could be, but most of the time he's pretty intense." She looked at me. "That's why I made him shut off his cell while he was with me. We had business to discuss, true, but mostly I wanted him to relax."

"He was here to discuss matters regarding Family Bond?"

"Yes." Karen sat up straighter. "I asked him to come up so we could have a face-to-face meeting on some issues. He and I are the directors—the only directors since my uncle passed away about three months ago. Usually we handle all business by phone or e-mail, but I felt it was time to meet, go over year-end matters, and consider a new board member to replace Uncle Vince."

"I read up on Family Bond on the web. You do a lot of good work for children."

"We try, but it's like trying to hold back the tide armed with a shovel and sand pail." Karen smiled, but it was a sad smile. "Like that mother and child you saw earlier. We're relocating them to a safe house. But for every situation like that we help, three more crop up."

"Has Steele always been involved with Family Bond?"

"Why, yes; in fact, it was his idea to set it up, get nonprofit status, apply for aid, grants, donations. I was killing myself trying to do it on my own, and he stepped in, found some angels who helped fund it initially, and did all the corporate work."

"Was this after you were divorced?" Sally asked.

"It was. Mike and I remained very close after we broke up, more like brother and sister or cousins." She adjusted herself in the chair and crossed her legs, then started fiddling with her ring.

"Did you remarry?" I asked, indicating the ring.

"No, at least not yet, but I am engaged. That was another reason why I wanted to see Mike. I wanted to tell him in person that I was getting remarried."

"How did he take it?"

"Fine, or at least I thought so. He was more upset about my other news." As if on cue, both Sally and I leaned forward. "I told him I wanted to put my fiancé on the board with us."

"Why was he against that?" I asked.

She hesitated, again playing with the pearls around her neck. "Mike often felt that I led too much with my heart and not enough with my head."

"Meaning he thought this man wasn't right for you?"

"No," she answered quickly. "Meaning he thought Tom and I would not make good business decisions for Family Bond and would force them through with a two-against-one vote."

"But," I said, putting my thoughts in order, "wasn't it two against one when your uncle was on the board?"

"Yes, it was two against one, but I was the one. Uncle Vince was a lot like Mike, very focused and intense. He practically raised me. Maybe that's why I gravitated to Mike in the first place." She looked at me, then Sally. "Though I must admit, that's probably why Family Bond did so well after Mike formally set it up. The two of them ran it as if it were Microsoft. I had to go to them and plead my case for anything beyond day-to-day expenditures."

"And this Tom is more like you?" Sally asked.

Karen smiled. "Yes, even though he's a big business tycoon himself, he's much more interested in helping the children than the bottom line, and he has some very creative ideas. But I'm sure it would have worked out. Mike could still hold the business reins while Tom and I did the good deeds."

Yeah, I thought, *I could see that now. Steele happily doling out cash for decisions he felt were wrong and on which he'd been out-voted.*

"If your fiancé, Tom ... ," I hesitated.

"Bledsoe," Karen added. "Thomas Bledsoe. He has his own company."

Sally and I gawked at each other with open surprise before I turned back to Karen, my mouth still hanging open. "Amazing Games Software—*that* Thomas Bledsoe?"

"Why, yes. We met at a charity event for children, and he became one of our angels, a major contributor. Mike met him that night, as well."

Sally shook herself out of her shock. "Odelia and I went to high school with Tommy ... I mean, Thomas Bledsoe." Sally glanced at me. "In fact, he was Odelia's prom date."

"Really?" Karen looked at me with interest. "What a coincidence."

"Yes, isn't it," I said, still stunned. "Tommy and I were lab partners, never dated except for prom."

Karen smiled. "What a small world. I'll have to make sure I tell him when he calls. He's in Japan right now, something about launching a new game there next year."

"Our high-school reunion was last weekend," Sally said. "Too bad you and Tommy … Tom … didn't come." She looked quickly in my direction. "Although maybe it's best you didn't."

"Ah, yes, the reunion where the man was killed."

Sally and I nodded in unison, like a couple of bobbleheads.

Karen started to say something more but hesitated, as if choosing her words with care. Then she simply added, "I saw the story on the news."

After studying Karen for a quick moment, I cleared my throat and tried go back to the task at hand. As much as I'd like to comment on it being a small world, the facts were that Steele was missing and Donny was dead. With Steele's existence still up in the air, I wanted to concentrate on the possible living.

"Back to Steele," I announced. "Karen, before Steele left to go to Ojai, did you iron out things about the board?"

Karen shrugged. "Not really. According to the bylaws, we'd both have to agree to it, and Mike told me he would not agree to Tom being on the board until after we'd been married awhile. He said he wanted to get to know him before making up his mind."

Sally softly cleared her throat. "How long have *you* known Tom?"

Karen blushed. Quickly, she got up and walked to her desk, where she busied herself with some papers. Sally and I both got up and joined her. Her body language was telling me the discussion was over, but Sally was persistent.

"I don't mean to pry, Ms. Meek, but it sounds as if Mr. Steele was trying to protect you. He must have had some concerns about Tom."

Karen looked up, her eyes narrowed. The hand sporting the diamond went to rest on one hip. While Karen and Sally faced off, I dropped my eyes down and did a quick scan of her desk. Something caught my eye on the edge, but I didn't want to draw attention to the fact that I was snooping, so I looked back up at Karen.

"Look," she told us, "Tom is *my* business, not Mike's, and certainly not yours, even though you all knew each other way back when. He has nothing to do with Mike disappearing." She sat down at her desk and opened a file. "Now, if you'll excuse me, I have to prepare for a meeting in a few minutes."

That was our not-so-subtle signal to leave. Sally started for the door. I went back to the settee and retrieved my tote. Karen ignored us both. Just as I was about to pass Karen's desk, I turned.

"Karen, would you answer one last question … please?"

She looked up at me with impatience but waited for me to speak. We had definitely hit a nerve by prying about the length of time she'd known Tommy. I put my heavy tote bag down on the edge of the desk.

"What kind of mood was Steele in when he left your house Monday morning?"

"As I recall," she said in a very professional voice, "Mike was quite cheerful. He was looking forward to his time at the inn and some golf." She hesitated briefly. "But like I told you on the phone, he was preoccupied with something at the office." She shrugged. "I asked about it, but all he would tell me was that something was fishy, and he couldn't put his finger on it."

There was something *fishy* about the Silhouette trial? My mind wanted to pore over every tidbit of information I knew about the case right then and there, but I didn't have the time.

"When Steele left here Monday morning, would he have gone to Ojai via 150 or head south to meet up with 33, then north?"

"That's a different question, Grey."

I flinched inwardly at the use of my last name. Karen Meek might be a granola do-gooder, as Tim Weber said, but something suddenly told me not to cross her if at all possible. But then, she'd have to be tough to be an advocate for abused children. I had lost sight of that, disarmed by the pearls and Laura Ashley.

Pushing ahead anyway, I rephrased my question. "Which route would he have taken to Ojai?"

Karen Meek released an exaggerated sigh. "Mike would have definitely taken 150. He knew it like the back of his hand."

SIXTEEN

DURING A BRIEF LUNCH at a place called Ruby's on State Street, I showed Sally the small piece of paper that just happened to get stuck to the bottom of my tote bag when I placed it on Karen's desk. It was a telephone message, the white top of a carbon copy set. It noted a call to Karen from Tim Weber and was marked urgent. The call had been made yesterday just after I had seen him at his office.

"This looks pretty suspicious," Sally commented.

"Absolutely." I drank some iced tea. "I got the feeling he wasn't in contact with Karen much, except through Steele. But maybe I got the wrong vibe. Thinking back, he did say something about his hopes for Steele and Karen reconciling not happening now."

"Do you think he knew about the engagement? Even before she told Steele?"

"Could be. She might have been asking for input on how to tell Steele, but I doubt it. The fact that he made the call to Karen just minutes after I left him makes me think he might have been giving her a heads-up about something."

Sally mulled it over before speaking. "Or he could have been asking her his own questions about the last time she saw Steele."

"Could be," I said again. "There's no law against Tim Weber calling Karen Meek. After all, they've known each other a long time. But the timing of the call and the fact that it's marked urgent is not sitting well with me. And she seemed awfully fidgety, didn't she?"

Sally nodded. "Like a cat in a room full of rockers."

After lunch, we gassed up the Jeep and followed the Mapquest directions through Santa Barbara, Montecito, Summerland, and Carpinteria, until we finally hooked up with 150, heading for Ojai. The road led us past numerous nurseries, farms, and ranches, and wound through groves of various trees—avocados, oranges, lemons, even persimmons hanging like heavy orange orbs in the October sunlight. But it was quite awhile before I spotted any area where a car might have gone off the road and not been noticed.

"How about here?" I asked Sally. She slowed the Jeep down. Fortunately, there was no one behind us.

"I don't think so, Odelia." She reached in front of me and pointed out the window. "Look along the road—there's a fence a few feet back, hidden by the shrubs. If he went off here, he wouldn't have been able to go far and would have been spotted quickly."

She was right. We kept moving slowly along Route 150, occasionally pulling into turnouts so that faster-moving vehicles could pass us. Here and there, I made her slow down so we could scan the road and embankment for any sign of skid marks and broken vegetation—but there was nothing. On one stretch of the road, the right side disappeared down into a deep ravine. I had Sally pull the car over so I could get out and check it out more closely.

I walked along the side of the road for a few hundred yards, often walking a few steps into the heavy growth to see if there were any signs of a crash—again, nothing. I was both disappointed and relieved. I also had the beginnings of a sore throat and runny nose. Sally pulled the Jeep up alongside me.

"Even though it's farmland," she said through the open window, "it's still pretty populated and the road too well-traveled for no one to have spotted an accident, especially in the daytime." Reluctantly, I agreed and climbed back into the vehicle.

"You feeling okay? You're a little flushed."

I shrugged. "I might be getting a cold, that's all."

I wasn't in the Jeep long when my cell phone rang, but when I answered all I got was static. Looking at the display, I saw that the call was from Woobie. I tried calling back, but the call kept dropping.

"Wait until we clear this hilly area," Sally advised. "We're almost to Ojai."

The 150 intersected 33 here, and we turned left in the direction of the town of Ojai and, according to the map, the location of the Ojai Valley Inn & Spa.

There was a voice mail on my cell. I quickly connected to it and listened. It was Carl Yates, asking me to call him as soon as possible. His voice didn't sound excited or upset, just tired. I dialed Carl's direct line. He picked up on the second ring.

"Hi," I said into the phone. "It's me, Odelia. What's up?"

"It's Mike Steele," Carl said, his tone as tired as on the voice mail.

"Did he finally come in?"

"No, Odelia, he didn't." He paused, and I stopped breathing, waiting for the worst-case scenario. "But they found his car." I started breathing again.

"But no Steele?" I grabbed a tissue from my tote bag and wiped my drippy nose.

"No, not a trace of him. The car was found in a parking lot at LAX. His BlackBerry was in the glove compartment."

"LAX? They found his Porsche at LA International?"

"Yes, in the long-term parking lot for the international terminal. Looks like Mike took a trip."

After I finished talking to Carl, I turned to Sally and told her about the conversation.

"Do you think maybe he was upset by his ex-wife's news?" Sally asked. She had pulled into the parking lot of Starr Market while I was on the phone and parked, leaving the car to idle.

I shrugged. "I know a lot about Steele, but I have no clue about his long-term relationships. In fact, I just found out about Karen Meek. All I knew before was that he'd been married once. Steele is hardly the type who wears his heart on his sleeve." Leaning my elbow on the edge of the car window, I looked out across the parking lot and watched the people walking to and from the store. I thought about what Karen told us: about her upcoming marriage and her desire to put her fiancé on the board of Family Bond. Without turning back to Sally, I said, "Karen said Steele seemed okay with the marriage. She said it was the board appointment of Tommy that got him riled up."

"It's definitely puzzling." Sally paused to take a drink from her bottle of water. "Tommy has built himself a corporate empire. You'd think that would be exactly the type of board member you'd want for a nonprofit—someone who brings experience and good business sense to the table. There must be something else that set your boss off. I got the feeling Karen hasn't known Tommy long. Maybe that's it."

I turned around and faced Sally. "Especially the way she became cold and snippy when you asked her how long she'd known him." I shook my head in wonder. "Tommy Bledsoe and Steele's ex-wife, can you believe it?"

Suddenly, remembering something, I reached for my cell phone, punched redial, and once again found myself connected to the office. Ani answered Carl's extension this time, but Carl came right on the line when she told him it was me on the other end.

"Sorry to bother you, Carl. But when I met with Steele's ex-wife today, she said Steele told her there was something fishy going on at the office regarding a case. She didn't say, but I'm assuming it's the Silhouette matter." I listened a minute. "Yes, fishy; that was her exact word, not sure if it was Steele's or not. She said he was preoccupied with it but couldn't put his finger on the problem. Anything you can think of about Silhouette that you would call *fishy*?" Again, I listened while Carl hemmed and hawed and processed my question.

"Hold on, Odelia, let me shut my door." I waited. In a few seconds, Carl Yates was back on the phone with me. "There *was* something odd going on, a lot of discrepancies in the information we had initially and the information we have now; almost as if documents had been removed from key files and replaced with documents that are similar but not quite the same."

"But aren't those Bates stamped?"

Bates stamping is a form of sequential numbering done to documents produced in litigation cases. It keeps the documents in order and assures the parties that nothing has been omitted or added, and it provides a number for referencing certain documents or pages of documents in other documents.

"Of course, but the strangest thing is, the believed discrepancies stopped as soon as Mike went missing."

I froze. "Carl, are you telling me you suspect Michael Steele of tampering with trial documents?"

"I don't know what I'm telling you, Odelia. I just know that Mike is missing, and the documents ready for production seem to be different from when they were initially prepared. Even Joan and Fran are perplexed about it."

"And now Steele's car has been found at the airport." It was a thought I said out loud.

"Exactly. I don't know yet what's been going on, but many of the documents we were counting on to prove our case are no longer helpful, and a lot of the originals have gone missing. These were corporate originals, Odelia, sent to Mike by the client, who didn't have the sense to make copies first or the sense not to send the originals in the first place. With Mike's sudden disappearance, it isn't looking very good right now."

"First of all, Carl, I may not be Steele's biggest fan, but one thing I know: he's not crooked, not in the least."

"I'm not saying he is, Odelia, just that I wish he were here to discuss this with me." He hesitated. "Odelia, there's something else; some of the missing documents were found in Mike's car."

The information floored me for a second, but I quickly recovered. "Maybe he took them with him to review. Maybe he was making sure no one tampered with them further."

Carl said nothing, but I could hear him breathing on the other end.

"And secondly," I said, not waiting for a response, "I don't buy for a minute that the fastidious Michael Steele parked his beloved Porsche in the general long-term parking lot at LAX. When Steele travels from Los Angeles, he uses a very pricey special garage for his car, and they chauffeur him to the airport and pick him up when he returns."

"But, Odelia, would Mike care about his car if he wasn't coming back?"

He had a point.

On the way back to Orange County, I sat silently on my side of the vehicle and mulled over everything Carl had said. The case documents had been tampered with; some of them had been found in Steele's car at the Los Angeles airport—in the international terminal parking, no less; Steele was missing, now thought to have hopped a plane out of the country. I didn't buy Steele's involvement in the fishy business for a heartbeat. If he had those documents in his car, he had a good reason. And, just in case Steele has me fooled and his ethics are as sketchy as the rest of his personality, I don't think he would have said something to Karen about his concerns about the pending trial. And what about motive? If Steele did tamper with the documents, what would be his purpose? What would he gain to help the other side win and his firm, the firm he held an equity interest in, lose?

"This is just not adding up," I said to Sally, finally breaking the silence.

Sally nodded in agreement. "It is really odd; much odder than Donny being killed. At least we know the killer's motive—anyone who knew Donny wanted to kill him."

Donny—in all the mystery surrounding Steele, I had forgotten about Donny. The scratchiness in my throat had grown. Remembering I had a couple of breath mints in my bag, I pulled them out and popped them in my mouth, hoping they would soothe the dryness.

"Not a good thing, Odelia, especially considering both you and I are still being scrutinized by the police."

Sally was right, we were still under suspicion; not primary suspects maybe, but not totally out of the woods yet either. I was just about to say something to her when, as if by magic, my phone rang—it was Dev Frye.

"Where are you?" he asked as soon as I answered. "I went by your place, saw your car, but got no answer when I knocked."

"We're on 405 south, just passing Long Beach. We went to Santa Barbara today to meet Steele's ex-wife."

"We?"

Uh-oh. Dev knew that I was going to investigate Steele's disappearance, but he had no idea I had teamed up with Sally Kipman to do it.

"Yes, Sally Kipman and I went to Santa Barbara together."

Silence. I waited it out.

"I didn't know you and Sally Kipman were pals," Dev finally said. "I got the definite idea from you that the two of you couldn't stand each other."

"We've patched things up."

"I see. So why is she helping you find Steele? I know your firm asked you to check things out, but doesn't she have a family and a job? Did she know Mike Steele?"

Why did the men in my life ask questions I didn't want to answer? It was annoying.

"Odelia, are you and Sally Kipman teaming up in the Oliver matter?"

"I told you we went to Santa Barbara to see Steele's ex-wife."

"And I believe you. But I also know you have a habit of only telling half the truth, especially when cornered with a question you'd rather not answer."

Who, me?

"You do know that Sally is being questioned in connection with Donny Oliver's death, don't you?"

"Yes, I do. Like me, she had an ugly past experience with Donny."

He started to say something but stopped. I could almost see him weighing his words, like apples at the grocers. "Odelia, I want you to call me once Sally drops you off. You are going straight home, aren't you?"

"Actually, I wanted to stop by my office first. Sally and I are going to check something out, and then she'll bring me home."

"No, Odelia, come straight home. That's an order."

Excuse me! was what I was thinking, but instead I asked, "What's up, Dev?"

What Dev told me made me want to jump from Sally's moving Jeep. The only thing that stopped me was the fear of being either run over or dragged down the 405 Freeway at seventy miles per hour. Instead, I told her to pull off at the next exit because I had to pee.

SEVENTEEN

"So what did Detective Frye tell you?"

Sally had pulled off the freeway and traveled a short distance until she spotted a Starbucks. As soon as she parked, she turned to question me.

"Nothing, just wanted to know when I'd be home."

"Bullshit, Odelia. You turned white and almost leapt from the car."

I said nothing, just stared at her.

"It's not what you think, Odelia."

"So, tell me, what *am* I supposed to think?"

"I'll bet the good detective told you that I tried to kill Donny just a few months ago."

I swallowed and nodded. "He said you were charged with attempted homicide—that you almost killed Donny with a butcher knife."

"And he's right."

My hand tightened on the door handle. Sally noticed.

"I was only charged, Odelia, not convicted. The charges were dropped."

"That's great for you, but it doesn't negate the fact that you tried to kill him."

"Like I said, it's not what you think." She looked over at the coffee shop. "Let's get some coffee. We always do well over coffee." She gave me a small smile. "You like pumpkin pie?" I nodded, still in shock, still thinking I should run, and now I *really* had to pee.

When I came out of the ladies' room, Sally was seated at a table with two very tall cups. I sniffed mine and was rewarded with a lovely spicy aroma, just like pumpkin pie. I took a small sip of the hot brew. It was absolutely delicious.

"It's their pumpkin spice latte," she explained. "They only have it in the fall." She was unwrapping cellophane from a sandwich. "Want half? It's chicken tarragon salad." When I hesitated, she held out half of the sandwich to me. "Come on, Odelia, it's been hours since lunch, and you only had a salad. Besides, you don't look so hot."

I accepted the half sandwich and took a small bite. It was a bit on the dry side but very tasty. After I swallowed, wincing as it passed down my sore throat, I focused on Sally. "Why didn't you tell me you tried to kill Donny?"

"Because I knew you'd freak out, which you did, and I needed your help. I knew eventually you would find out or be told, but I thought we could make some headway before that happened." She sipped her coffee. "I know I'm a prime suspect, considering what's happened between Donny and me, but I didn't kill him, Odelia."

"But you tried to?"

"Yes, and truthfully, I'm sorry I failed." She looked me in the eye. "You want to hear my side, or do you still want to run?"

I glanced over my shoulder first, to make sure of my options. "I'm all ears."

"It was this past June. We were all supposed to go to this award dinner for Lucas. He's a teacher, and he and several other teachers were receiving special awards from the school district. At the last minute, Davy's babysitter—Davy's my grandson—cancelled, so Jill said for us to go and she'd stay with the baby. We didn't want to leave her behind, but we couldn't find another sitter on such short notice."

She took a bite of sandwich, chewed, and washed it down with her coffee. "Lucas had invited Donny and Cindy to the award dinner also, and they came. Donny showed up half drunk and was sipping from a flask most of the evening. He asked about the baby, and we told him Davy was home with Jill. When it was time to leave, Donny was nowhere to be found. We ending up taking Cindy home." Sally blew out a deep breath. "Boy, was she angry."

She started playing with the cardboard holder on the outside of her coffee cup, nervously peeling it away in small strips. "After we dropped Cindy off, we headed to Lucas's house. When we got there, we found Jill and Donny fighting."

"Donny had gone to Lucas's home?"

"Yes. Jill was blocking the door to Davy's room, and Donny was calling her every obscene name in the book, saying he was taking Davy. Lucas made a dash for Donny but not in time to stop him from punching Jill in the side of her head." Sally's eyes started to tear as she talked. "Jill fell to the floor like a ton of bricks. I thought she'd been killed."

"In the movies, this is where you would run into the kitchen, grab a knife, and go after him."

"And that's exactly what happened. I got him pretty good, too. Stuck him like the pig he is . . . was." Sally swallowed hard. "When I saw Jill lifeless on the floor and Donny yelling that Davy belonged with him, I went insane. I couldn't let him hurt another person I loved."

"What happened to Jill? She's okay now, isn't she?"

Sally nodded. "She had a concussion from the blow and spent the night in the hospital. Donny was in the hospital for a few days. I was charged with attempted murder, and Donny was charged with assault and attempted kidnapping. In the end, all the charges were dropped, and the police wrote it off as just another family squabble."

Sally dabbed her eyes and wiped her nose with a napkin. "Like I told you before, Odelia, I'm not sorry he's gone. I didn't kill him, but I want to shake the hand of who did."

EIGHTEEN

IT'S A FUNNY THING, trust. Everyone wants to trust and be trusted. Yet, as adults, we know better than to trust everyone we meet. And very early on we teach children not to trust strangers. Somewhere along the road of life, hopefully we learn who to trust and who not to trust, for the truth of it is, sometimes we can trust strangers more than we can trust those closest to us.

Because of my non-date with Dev, Greg now had a trust issue with me. Dev rightfully accused me of editing my responses to questions, so his trust in me regarding my word was shaky. On the other hand, Carl Yates trusted me to find Michael Steele and to keep confidential the problem with the Silhouette lawsuit. Sally trusted me to help her prove she didn't kill Donny Oliver, but at the same time she was asking me to trust her even though she didn't tell me earlier about her attempt to murder Donny.

It was Saturday morning, and I was barely able to trust myself to scramble an egg without a major accident. I had gone to bed the night before feeling like crap and woke up feeling crappier. I definitely had a cold.

By the time we'd finished our pumpkin spice lattes, I had agreed to continue to help Sally investigate Donny Oliver's murder. She called Cindy from her cell before we left Starbucks and asked if we could drop by either Saturday or Sunday. Cindy said Saturday would be best, so today at two o'clock Sally was going to pick me up once again, and we would head for Donny's house, a bundt cake baked by Jill in hand.

Sally said she was still available to help me with Steele's disappearance, but I wasn't sure about that situation any longer. With his car found, the firm may decide to see if he eventually turns up. But no matter what the firm decided, I still wanted to check out the situation with the documents, and I still wanted to know what happened to Steele. As I scrambled eggs in my misery, I prayed he was somewhere, anywhere but skipped out of the country. Because, if Steele, for whatever reason, did tamper with legal documents and then vamoosed for greener pastures, I vow on my last Thin Mint to hunt his miserable ass down.

You can trust me on this.

Originally the plan after Santa Barbara was to go directly to my office. It would be near the end of the day and most of the staff would have been gone by the time we got there, especially on a Friday night. But because of Sally's duplicity and Dev's warning, I decided to make the trip to Woobie alone. Sally said she understood.

As soon as I got home, I called Dev back and let him know I was safe and sound. I also told him what Sally had told me, and got the response I expected. Although Dev seemed sympathetic toward

Sally about what had happened earlier this year, he reminded me that the bottom line was that she had, indeed, tried to kill Donny Oliver, and that she was one of the people in attendance at the reunion when he was murdered. I wanted to remind him that I was also in attendance at the reunion when Donny was murdered, and that I had killed someone. Seems I was one up on Sally Kipman after all.

But in spite of Dev's cautionary remarks, somehow I knew that if the police had hard evidence against Sally, she wouldn't be wandering the streets right now; she would be in jail or at least would have been brought in. According to her, she'd only been questioned so far.

Originally, Dev had called to tell me about Steele's car being found. I told him that the firm had already told me the news. Dev didn't seem to know much more than that, or at least he didn't mention anything else. I wondered if the firm had swept the document thing under the rug and why.

Halfway though my discussion with Dev, my sore throat got the best of me, and I decided to skip the office and go in on Saturday morning. Fewer people were there then anyway, so fewer questions. My call to Dev ended with him telling me to stay away from Sally. I never mentioned that we were meeting again, this time to visit Donny's wife. Hey, he didn't ask; I didn't tell.

After breakfast, I decided to throw a quick load of laundry in the washer. As I bent down to pick up the dirty clothes, my head about imploded. It felt almost like it did the night I was swilling martinis with Sally, but without the accompanying nice buzz. Steadying myself by holding on to the washer, I stared at the containers of detergent, bleach, and softener on the shelf above the machines to regain my focus. Stuck to the bottle of laundry detergent was a hot pink sticky note from Cruz Valenz, my cleaning lady. *Need more* was all the note said.

Cruz has been cleaning my home every other Wednesday for several years, and during that entire time I have begged, cajoled, requested, and even ordered her to write down the items I needed to replenish on a note pad in the kitchen, where I would easily see it. But no, instead, she continues to stick notes on near-empty bottles, cartons, and containers. Since Cruz does such a wonderful job and is such a nice lady, I finally caved, and now after each time she comes to clean, I scour the house looking for the notes as if they were clues to hidden treasure at the grocery store. I must have missed the one on the laundry soap the last time she was here.

As I studied the note, I knew it should mean more to me than to just buy more detergent, but what? Laundry forgotten, I sniffled and studied it until it finally came to me. Locating my tote bag, I rooted around inside for the two business cards I had taken from Steele's home, but came up empty-handed. I know I took them. Scrounging around in my soggy memory bank, I replayed my activities the day I checked out Steele's condo in Laguna Beach.

Let's see, I remember taking the cards out of the plastic sleeve and putting them ... putting them ...

I dashed upstairs and rummaged in my closet to find the suit jacket I had worn to work that day. Sure enough, the two business cards were tucked inside one of the pockets.

First, I called Melinda's Maid Service but only reached a recording. I left my name and cell phone number at the tone. Then I made a call to Let Mother Do It. On the third ring, a woman answered, sounding slightly out of breath.

"Hi," I said, hoping my sniffling didn't make me sound like a pervert. "I found your business card and was wondering if you are a maid service."

The woman hesitated long enough for me to wonder if we were still connected, then said, "We can do most anything you need to be done—*anything*." The woman, who I guessed by her voice to be older, really stressed the word *anything*. If she'd been writing it, it would have been underlined and circled, followed by an exclamation point.

"Anything? That's pretty broad."

The woman laughed. "Let's just say we're open to special requests. Doesn't mean we'll accommodate them, but we certainly try." The woman's voice was warm and cuddly, like a favorite plush toy—just the sort of voice you'd expect manning the telephone of a business with the word *mother* in its name.

"Really, how interesting." I paused. "But you do provide housekeeping services, correct?"

The woman hesitated once again. "Primarily, yes."

"Cute name, by the way."

"Thank you. Did you call with a special request, dear? Or are you just looking for someone to clean your home?"

"Neither, really. I just need to ask you a quick question, if you don't mind."

"Of course, go right ahead."

"Do you do housecleaning for a man named Michael Steele? He lives in Laguna Beach."

The hesitation this time was the longest. "We really can't divulge our client list, dear. Most of our clients strive for privacy."

"I understand," I said, though I really didn't. I thought house-keepers were thrilled to provide reference names, unless, of course, Let Mother Do It had a lot of celebrity clientele. Celebrities don't just strive for privacy, they often hunger for it, especially in Southern California.

"Is that how you found out about us, from this Mr. Steele?"

"Sort of. I found the card at his home."

"What is your name, dear?"

"Odelia, Odelia Grey. I work for Mr. Steele."

Another hesitation. "Then why don't you ask him personally if he uses our services. If you work for him, then that should not be a problem."

"Unfortunately, Mr. Steele is missing. That's why I'm calling. I wanted to know if you clean his house regularly or had cleaned it recently. I was hoping I might find out something to help me find him."

"Missing? Heavens! Sounds like you need one of those private detectives, not Let Mother Do It."

"You're probably right." I wiped my runny nose with a nearby tissue. "I'm sorry I bothered you. Thank you for your time."

"You know, dear, considering the unusual circumstances, I don't think it would be too terrible to give you a little information." She paused. "I mean, what harm would it do to tell you that Let Mother Do It has never worked for a Mr. Steele in Laguna Beach, or anywhere else for that matter. Maybe he was given our card by a friend of his. All our new business comes from referrals."

"Are you sure you've never done work for Mr. Steele? No errands, laundry, cooking, anything?"

"I'm positive, dear. After all, I'm Mother, and Mother knows everything."

I laughed, but it came out like a snort. "Father knows best, but Mother knows everything?"

"Father knows best only after Mother tells him what he knows."

I laughed again, and this time it came out with a cough. "Excuse me, but I'm nursing a cold."

"Don't forget to take some tea with honey, dear. You'll feel a lot better."

Tea with honey? If I wasn't meeting Sally in four hours, it would be tea, all right ... tea followed by a NyQuil shooter or two.

NINETEEN

AFTER DECIDING THAT THE laundry could wait, I grabbed a quick shower and headed to the office. As I expected, it was mostly deserted except for a couple of attorneys using Saturday to catch up or to get a jump on the week ahead. I went straight to my office and closed the door.

Seated at my desk, I pulled out the upper right-hand drawer and felt underneath. Taped to the bottom of the drawer was a small envelope in which I kept Steele's passwords. Also inside was a small key that fit a special compartment in Steele's custom-made desk. Only two of these keys existed—Steele had one and I kept one. And as far as I knew, only the two of us knew about the compartment and where my key was hidden.

I peeked out my door and saw that no one was around, then quickly covered the several yards between my office and Steele's. As usual, his office door was closed. I opened it and slipped inside, gently closing it behind me. It wasn't unusual for me to go in and out of Steele's office, but I didn't want someone to see me and stop to make small talk. I had just a few hours to check out a couple of things and then head back home to meet Sally.

After settling into Steele's chair, I opened his right-hand bottom drawer. It was a very deep drawer. Inside, color-coded folders hung suspended from slim metal rails. Inside each hanging folder were well-labeled manila file folders containing information Steele needed at his fingertips. Some of the folders contained personal information, such as the legal associations he belonged to, and others contained information on various Woobie internal committees. I pushed the files back and out of the way. Underneath them was a false bottom with a small keyhole. The key in my hand fit the tiny lock perfectly. After a quick turn, I was able to pull up the lid. It was only open halfway when I saw what I was after—Steele's passport. It was resting on top of a neat stack of papers.

Steele used this false-bottom drawer mostly as a personal safe deposit box. Inside, he generally kept things like his passport, will, birth certificate, and important papers on other aspects of his life that he liked having immediate access to but didn't want to keep at home. The first time I found out about the drawer was when a client brought in some old bearer bonds. Steele stashed them in this drawer for temporary safekeeping and gave me the spare key. I've had it since. Once he had me bring his passport to him after he arrived at the Orange County Airport and realized he'd forgotten it.

I looked down at the passport in my hand. If Steele hopped a plane out of the country, he would need this. If he forgot it, as he did before, he either would have called me or returned on his own to retrieve it. Steele was methodical and seldom made mistakes. If he was up to something shady that involved skipping the country, he would not have forgotten this. But then, just because Steele's car was in the parking lot for the international terminal didn't mean he took an international flight. Still, sifting through what little I did know about real-life white-collar criminals, it would seem that if he *did* do something illegal and tank his impeccable legal career, he'd want to leave the country. And knowing Steele, it would be somewhere that boasted warm weather, sandy beaches, and a bikini-clad Welcome Wagon.

My head hurt like hell. I closed my eyes, rubbed my temples, and tried to think. As I started swinging gently in Steele's chair, I heard the familiar *squeak... squeak*. Damn if I didn't miss the *squeak... squeak*. I sat like that for a short while—thinking, concentrating, and squeaking—when an idea struck me like a thunderbolt. At the same time, Steele's office door was suddenly flung open by a shocked Fran Evans.

"Oh," she said, quickly recovering her usual frosty demeanor, "I thought maybe Mike was back." She tugged at the hem of the cream tunic sweater she was wearing and smoothed it down over her jeans.

"Nope, just me." Before Fran could get any closer, I pulled some of the hanging file folders over the hidden box and rummaged through a few of them, hoping I looked like I knew what I was doing. I slipped the passport into one of them while I rifled. "Some things came up on Steele's calendar, and I thought maybe I should attend to them instead of waiting for him to return."

"Such loyalty is so commendable, Odelia."

I glanced up at her. The words sounded sincere, but I immediately saw from her eyes that they were said to mock me.

"My loyalty, Fran, is to the firm. Steele may have vanished, but his work did not. If Steele misses a deadline, it reflects badly on the firm, which can affect all of us."

"You're such a good little paralegal, Odelia. Always looking out for the firm and that arrogant ass Steele."

My first impulse was to throw my bulk at the bitch, but instead I sniffed and rolled my eyes, not caring if she saw me or not.

"Funny, isn't it?" she said, eyeing me warily. "Steele is missing and so are the documents we need to prove our case for Silhouette."

"Nothing *funny* about that at all."

"I didn't mean funny as in *ha ha* funny, Odelia. I meant funny as in strange or suspicious."

"If you're accusing Mike Steele of doing something unethical, Fran, don't beat around the bush, just come out and say it."

"I'm not saying Steele did anything wrong, just that everything seems, shall we say, too coincidental."

Hmm, let's see, I calculated to myself, *if I climbed up onto Steele's desk, I could launch myself at Fran with much more velocity than if I tried it from ground level.* As if reading my mind, Fran took a step backward, closer to the open door.

My headache increased. I scrunched my eyes at her as I spoke, hoping it made me look mean and not just in pain. "I don't know what you mean, Fran. Steele is missing, but that doesn't mean he had anything to do with those documents." I paused and sniffled. "Besides, you were handling them as well. Maybe it was *you* who tampered with them?"

Her mouth fell open in indignation. "What? Are you accusing *me* of doing something with those documents?" She was outraged. "How dare you!"

In equal outrage, I snapped back. "And how dare *you* accuse Michael Steele of the very same thing, and he's not even here to defend himself."

"No, he's not, and that's the point, isn't it?" She took a deep breath and started to leave. Just before walking out the door, she turned to me. "Maybe we should be checking *your* car for those documents, Odelia. Maybe you had something to do with this. I've often wondered about the two of you. Maybe you planned this together, and he left you behind to take the heat. It's something he'd do and something you'd fall for."

Had Fran delayed her departure by another minute, I know I would have assaulted her and probably been fired for it. Hmm, might have been worth it, especially since I know it would have felt great, and I could use a little instant gratification right now.

As soon as Fran left, I tried to get my thoughts back on track. I had an idea, but it was one that was rather outrageous. But first I had to close up Steele's desk. It wouldn't do to leave it open for anyone to find and rummage through. Locating the file where I dropped his passport, I pulled it out and dropped it back into the secret box, but when I tried to close and lock the lid, something got in the way. I opened the lid wider and felt around inside. Something was definitely stuck, papers of some sort.

Dropping the lid, I went to work removing the hanging folders until the entire box beneath them was exposed. This allowed me to pull up the lid all the way. It was a good-sized box, taking up the entire lower portion of the file drawer. Inside, in addition to the personal documents I expected to see, was a file folder. It was squished into the box down at the far end and was interfering with the hinge. After wiggling it a bit, I was able to free the folder and pull it out. Inside were documents, original documents, all pertaining to Silhouette and the other parties to the lawsuit.

What did this mean? Was Steele behind the document tampering after all? And what about the documents found in Steele's car? Where those more originals or just good copies of these?

I stopped speculating and tried to put myself in Steele's head. Once I did, I saw a different picture. Maybe Steele hid these documents to protect them. Karen had said he was preoccupied with the case, with something fishy. Maybe he had discovered the tampering himself and hid the originals to make sure nothing more happened until he could figure out what was going on. Now that sounds more like the Michael Steele I know.

I checked my watch. It was almost noon. Quickly, I put the file back into the hidden box and locked it. After the hanging files were replaced, I looked over my handiwork to make sure the false bottom was not noticeable to anyone snooping around the drawer. Satisfied, I returned to my office, grabbed my bag, and headed for Laguna Beach and Steele's condo once again. If I hurried, I could make it there and back home before Sally arrived.

With no weekday traffic, the trip to Laguna Beach took less time than it did before. However, when I arrived in the seaside town itself, it was alive with people out and about enjoying the warmer-than-usual late October. This time, I didn't dawdle to take in Steele's décor and to wonder if anyone was home. Instead, I went straight up the stairs to the extra room and to Steele's desk. On the desk, right where I'd last seen it, was the portfolio containing bills waiting to be paid. I sorted through them until I located a couple of credit card statements. I also dug around the drawers to see if I could find a checkbook of some kind. I don't recall Steele ever having a checkbook on him. I knew he paid almost everything by either credit card or debit card and paid his bills online. But even so, I was sure he would be the type who would keep meticulous entries. I located the checkbook and its register in the middle drawer and was pleased to see I was right. Items were entered and immediately subtracted from the balance. Except for a check he'd written a day before his trip and a cash withdrawal on the same day, there hadn't been any deductions for his mortgage, utilities, car payment, or credit cards since late September. It looked like Steele paid his bills all at once at the end of the month. I checked the entries for several months and located only two credit card names. These matched the two statements I had taken from the portfolio.

I tossed the checkbook and the statements into my bag and grabbed my address book and cell phone. Flipping open the phone, I came face to face with a photo of Greg I had saved to the screen. I looked at it, screwed up my face to chase back the tears, and was pleased that this time I won the battle of the blubbering. The pain was getting easier to take, maybe because a week had gone by or I had thrown myself so deep into finding Steele that I didn't allow the break up with Greg to take center stage. Whatever the reason, I vowed to get past it and keep moving. A moving target is more difficult to hit; it's true for dodging both bullets and emotions.

Taking a deep breath, I punched in some numbers from a cryptic entry in the address book. Immediately, I heard a mechanical voice telling me to leave my name and number, nothing more.

"It's me, Odelia," I said into the phone, almost in a whisper. "Call me on my cell if you can." I didn't leave my number. There would be no need.

When my cell phone rang just a few minutes later, I jumped. But when I answered, I didn't find the person I expected, but Melinda of Melinda's Maid Service.

Once I was over my surprise, I asked her the same questions I had asked Let Mother Do It. This time I received a positive response in a negative tone.

"Yeah, I used to clean that selfish bastard's place."

I nodded to myself. *Yep, this sounded like the right person.* "Used to? I take it you don't anymore?"

"Not for about three weeks," Melinda scoffed. "He called me about three weeks ago and demanded that I make an unscheduled cleaning visit. Said some plants had been delivered, and the delivery company had made a mess. Wanted me to drop everything I was doing and come right over and clean it up."

"And you didn't?"

"Hell, no. I was in the middle of my daughter's baby shower. I told the fool where he could find his vacuum cleaner and broom, and said I'd be by on my regular day, which was in just two days. I always cleaned his place on Friday."

"Knowing Mr. Steele as I do, I'm sure that didn't go over very well."

"Like the proverbial freaking lead balloon. He said he wanted me there that night. Now, mind you, it was already eight o'clock in the evening. I wasn't going anywhere except to bed after the baby shower. I had a full day of cleaning scheduled the next day—always do every day."

"And Mr. Steele fired you on the spot?"

"No, not then and there, but the next night he called me and said he'd found someone else to do his cleaning—someone, he said, who was more flexible."

I shook my head. It sounded as if Steele was just as charming outside of the office as he was in the office. "Melinda, do you know who he hired to replace you?"

"It was a company I'd never heard of before—had a cute name too. He said someone at the office gave him the referral."

"Let Mother Do It," I suggested.

"Yeah, that's it. Let Mother Do It. He told me they provided lots of extra services besides cleaning. He was really rubbing my nose in it."

Hmm, and Mother claimed they had never done any work for Steele.

"I'm very sorry, Melinda. I've worked for Mr. Steele for a while now, and I feel your pain. But are you sure Let Mother Do It took over the cleaning?"

"Positive." She paused and I could feel her get ready to blow. "You know, I cleaned once a week for that bastard for over four years, and he tossed me out just because I wouldn't leave my daughter's shower to sweep up some dirt. He and that Mother company can just kiss my saggy old ass."

TWENTY

THE CALL I WAS waiting for came just as I was pulling into my garage. When the phone rang, I checked out the display. It was a blocked call. It always was.

"Hello, little mama, nice to hear from you."

"Hi, Willie, thanks for calling back. I need to ask you something."

Willie Porter was once known as William Proctor, the CEO of a high-flying Internet investment company known as Investanet. The company turned out to be a scam, and Willie hit the trail with hundreds of millions of dollars, leaving behind just as many broken dreams and broken lives. Willie and I crossed paths when I was looking into the sudden death of Sterling Price, one of Woobie's clients. Somewhere during the investigation, Willie and I became friends, and while I'm not in the habit of having fugitives on my Christmas card list, from time to time it does come in handy—like now.

Every few months, Willie calls me, and we chat about life, books, movies, whatever comes to mind. I think in some way I provide a sense of connection to his past "normal" life, which he misses. He also gave me a number to reach him if I ever had the need. The area code is for somewhere in Idaho, but I'm sure it's just a simple land phone line connected to an answering machine in an empty room or closet. Every now and then, the number changes, and he gives me a new one. I have no idea where Willie is, and I never know when he's going to call; knowing how sophisticated he is in staying hidden, I'm sure I'd never be able to trace him. This was only the second time I had called him, the first being on the anniversary of the day I killed someone.

"What's on your mind, little mama?"

I gave him a quick rundown of recent events, including Donny's murder and the fact that I didn't believe for a second that Steele had skipped the country.

"So what do you think?" I asked when I was done.

He laughed. "For someone so intent on living the straight and narrow, you sure do get tangled up in some pretty wild messes."

"That's hardly the issue here, Willie."

He laughed again. "No, but it is fun to think about." He paused. I waited. "If your boss was following my lead and skipping the country, that passport you found wouldn't mean a thing. Criminals don't travel under their own names and with authentic ID. If he did mess with those documents for his own personal gain and is as methodical as you say, he would have planned it in advance, giving himself enough time to obtain a fake ID and passport."

"Is it that easy to get a fake passport?"

"You're so damn cute when you're naïve." Willie laughed again. I frowned. "Fake passports are very easy to come by but very expensive, especially those that are virtually undetectable."

"So finding his real passport means nothing?"

"'Fraid not, little mama, but I will tell you what I do find interesting, and that's his car. No self-respecting high-level crook would leave his car pointing in the direction he traveled. That's the big red flag to me. If your boss is as smart as you say, he would have left the car there and taken a cab away from the airport, maybe to a boat, or train, or another waiting car. Or—" He stopped.

"Or what?"

"Or someone planted the car at the airport to make it look like he skipped town." He paused. "Did your boss have any enemies?"

"Almost as many as you have, but for different reasons."

He chuckled, then cleared his throat. "Little mama, I don't want to be the bearer of bad news, but it could be your boss stepped on the wrong toes—lawyers do it all the time, especially upstanding ones."

I nearly fainted as I pictured what Willie was trying to tell me. "You mean he might be dead?"

"It's a distinct possibility. A carjacker would have taken his fancy car and left him by the side of the road. But someone with a score to settle might make sure he's never found."

A single involuntary sob escaped my lips.

"You okay, little mama?"

"Yeah, I'm fine. Just have a bad cold."

There was a moment of silence before Willie continued. "Are the police involved yet?"

"Yes, but not really. There has been a missing person report filed, but when his car was found, I think most people just assumed he left California. They say there's been no evidence of foul play."

"And that stuff with the legal documents just backs it all up?"

"Exactly." I remembered the statements in my bag. "I have Steele's checking account number and his credit card numbers. I was going to ask my friend Detective Frye if the police could run them and see if they've been used lately and where. Wouldn't that show something? I mean, Steele did withdraw three hundred dollars from his checking account just before he left town, but that wouldn't get him very far unless he was also using his credit cards or bank card."

"It's something to look at, but again, if he's on the run, he would have gotten new cards with his new identity. If his cards are being used, chances are it's by someone who stole them, but that might net you some answers."

I looked at my watch. Sally was due here in just under thirty minutes. "Willie, I have to run. Someone's meeting me in a few minutes about Donny Oliver. You've been a big help, thanks."

"One last thing, little mama. Let me run those cards for you. I have resources and contacts the police can only dream about. If these cards are being used, I'll find out faster and maybe even find the person who is using them."

"Are you sure?"

"It would be my pleasure."

Another thought crossed my mind. "While you're at it, Willie, could you also look into two companies for me—Silhouette Candies and Sweet Kiss Confections? These are the two companies involved in the lawsuit. To be honest, I can't figure out for the life of me what motive Steele would have to tank his own client and turn on the firm."

"Money, what else?"

"Maybe in your case, but it doesn't make sense for Steele—not unless he was in some sort of a jam, but even then it's hard to imagine."

"Give me this guy's full name; I'll look into him as well. And what's the name of that cleaning company that lied to you? Might as well throw them in for good measure."

"Let Mother Do It? Don't waste your time. It's just a cleaning and errand company run by an old lady. She probably had a senior moment and forgot they'd done work for Steele."

"You never know. What kind of a snoop would you be if you didn't look at every lead?"

He had a good point. "I'll take care of that, then," I told him. "I can easily check it out online to see if it's registered with the Secretary of State or filed as a fictitious business name. It would have to be one or the other to be legally doing business in the state under a name like that."

I gave Willie what details I could off the top of my head about the two companies in the lawsuit, along with Steele's full name, birth date, and the numbers of his credit cards and checking account from the information I'd taken from his home. When I was done, I thanked Willie from the bottom of my heart.

He laughed. "Now run along, little mama, and stick your nose into that murder. Leave the missing person stuff to me for now."

TWENTY-ONE

I WASN'T QUITE READY when my doorbell rang just before two o'clock. After speaking with Willie, I gave Zee a quick call to touch base. She'd been very worried about me since the break up with Greg, but I'd been so busy with the Steele matter we hadn't had time to get together. I promised to call her tomorrow and to take care of my cold, and assured her I was doing fine under the circumstances. I never mentioned Sally or the upcoming visit to Donny's widow, and I certainly never mentioned my call to Willie Porter.

"Be right there," I called in the direction of the door as I slipped into a new nubby-textured cream and black knit cardigan sweater. I had worn jeans to the office, but once home I had done a quick change into a pair of nice black trousers and a black knit short-sleeved jersey. My sneakers were replaced by black suede flats and long, black trouser socks. I felt like crap, but I didn't look half-bad.

After grabbing my tote bag, I opened the door, ready to climb into Sally's Jeep and hit the road. Instead, I almost hit the floor.

The person at my door wasn't Sally. In fact, it wasn't even a person. On the other side of the door sat Wainwright in all his golden furry glory. Hanging from his mouth by a black strap was a plastic pumpkin bucket, the kind kids would carry trick-or-treating three days from now.

"Trick or treat," a voice said from out of my range of vision. "If you've got the treats," it continued, "I can do some tricks." Then, on cue, Wainwright sat up and whimpered.

I was close to whimpering myself.

When the big dog sat back down, I threw my arms around his neck and gave him a squeeze. I had missed his soft fur and doggy smell. Still hugging the dog, I turned my head to see Greg sitting just to the side of the door. I wanted to squeeze and smell him, too, but held back.

"So, do you do tricks for treats, too?" I asked Greg.

"Depends on the treats."

I smiled, remembering both our tricks and treats in happier times.

He smiled and studied me. "You look very nice. You on your way out?"

"Yes, I am. A girlfriend is picking me up any minute. I thought that's who was at the door."

An awkward silence settled over us. I didn't know if I should invite him in, at least just until Sally arrived, or if I should rush him off before she arrived. My decision was made for me when Seamus, standing behind me a few feet inside the door, meowed a greeting. Without further ado, Wainwright dropped his bucket, pushed past me, and trotted inside, where he immediately began slobbering over the cat.

I turned to Greg. "Would you like to come in, too? At least just until Sally arrives."

He answered by rolling toward the door. I stepped aside so he could maneuver the doorway better. Once he was inside, I closed the door, but he didn't move deeper into the house. Instead, he reached up, tugged on the front of my sweater, and gently pulled my face down toward his own. Once in range, he kissed my cheek, letting his lips linger against my face. I had to struggle not to cry.

"Be careful," I warned him. "I have a cold."

"A cold I gave you." He looked deep into my eyes. "Seems only fair for you to give it back." With that, he planted a hungry kiss directly on my mouth. When it was done, we rested forehead to forehead. "I've missed you so much, sweetheart," he told me in a whisper.

Part of me wanted to crawl into his lap and never leave, both of us wheelchair bound for the rest of our lives. Instead, I stood straight and backed away a few steps.

"I've missed you, too, Greg. I've missed you a lot."

I hesitated, wondering if I should say what was on my mind or leave it for when we had more time. But me being me, I plowed ahead, caution be damned. "Is our break over, Greg?"

When he didn't answer, I continued. "Was today the big day, the day scheduled for you to forgive me? Did I neglect to write it on my calendar?"

He hung his head in a gesture I knew well. It was a gesture of frustration—not with himself, but with other people. This time, I'm sure he was frustrated with me.

"Don't be like that, Odelia," he said, finally raising his head to look at me. "I miss you, and I wanted to see you. I had hoped you would want to see me."

"I do, Greg, more than anything. But under the circumstances, I would have appreciated a call first to discuss how you feel instead of a surprise visit. Did you expect me to be overwhelmed with gratitude for this sudden change of heart?"

"Odelia, please."

"No, Greg, you *please.*" I struggled to control my emotions while I spoke. "Please understand that I have been through hell for the past week, and you showing up like this throws me off what little emotional balance I have left. And since you haven't bothered to call, you have no idea what else is going on around here. This entire week has been an absolute nightmare, and it isn't all about *you.*"

That got his attention.

"What else is going on, Odelia? Is it Horten?"

"My father is fine, Greg. Thank you for your concern." I glanced at my watch and wondered about Sally. I really wasn't sure I wanted to get into it with Greg right now, but I decided to forge ahead — no time like the present. "Mike Steele is missing."

For a moment, Greg's mouth hung open like an airplane hangar.

"Steele is missing," I continued. "His car was found abandoned at LAX. Important documents have been tampered with, and people think he did it and skipped the country."

"And what do you think?"

"I think something bad has happened to him, and he's being set up to look like he tampered with the documents."

"Something bad?"

"Yes, Greg, something bad—as in maybe he's even dead."

I tried to stop myself from cascading into the depths of snotty bitchhood, I really did, but in the end I failed. "Remember, I'm a corpse magnet."

We stared at each other—me, indignant and sniffling, and Greg, in shock. Just then, my doorbell rang, making us both jump a little. It was Sally. I introduced them, then told Sally I'd be out in a minute. After she returned to her Jeep, I studied Greg before speaking. He studied me in return; both of us, I'm sure, sizing up the terrain, wondering if we had the stuff to continue traveling our previous path. I was the one who broke the short silence.

"Sally is one of my high-school friends. We are on our way to pay our respects to Donny Oliver's wife." Again, I wondered if I should leave it at that, knowing that Greg would find visiting a grieving widow acceptable. But again, I couldn't stop my big fat mouth. "Both Sally and I, especially Sally, are on the suspect list for the murder, so we're also hoping to uncover some information to help us prove we had nothing to do with it."

Greg started to say something, but I stopped him.

"Yes, Greg, I'm back in the murder business, this time doing double duty between Donny and Steele, and I'll make no apologies for it."

I gathered up my bag and opened the door. As I started over the threshold, I turned half around. "I really am glad to see you, Greg. I love you, and I hope when we have more time we can hammer all this out. But I can't do that right this minute. Now please excuse me, and make sure you lock up when you leave."

"Everything okay back there?" Sally asked once we were on the freeway.

"Who knows?"

And that was the truth—who knew? Greg had made an overture of making up, and I had put him on hold. I felt great and devastated at the same time. I also resented that he seemed to think things could be patched up so easily, especially when nothing had changed. He was still going to hate the fact that from time to time I got sucked into a vortex of murder and mayhem, much as I tried to avoid it, and I was still going to stick my nose wherever people needed help.

I mean, not that I really saw myself as some sort of middle-aged avenger for the dead, wrongfully accused, and missing, but given the opportunity, would Wonder Woman turn her red, white, and blue bustier-clad back on Sally and Steele?

TWENTY-TWO

THE OLIVER HOME WAS located on a hillside in La Habra Heights. It took us just shy of an hour to reach it. It was a very large multi-level yellow house surrounded by lots of mature vegetation, and a winding brick path lead from the street, up the incline, to the front door. Hanging on the door was a fall wreath with a calico bow that gave the property a welcoming feel.

We had to wait a few minutes after Sally rang the bell for the door to open. From the other side, we heard the barking of a dog and someone asking someone else to take it somewhere. When the door finally opened, we were face to face with a woman a bit younger than us, probably just past forty. She was trim and wore gray sweatpants and a pink tee shirt. Her blond hair was gathered up on her head haphazardly with a clip. In spite of the dark circles under her eyes, she was very attractive. Sally introduced her to me as Cindy Oliver and handed her the bundt cake.

The inside of the house was inviting and cozy, with hardwood floors, and walls and furnishings in various earth tones, accented here and there with a splash of bright color. It had an upscale yet lived-in feel to it. From every window was a spectacular view.

"It's a nice day," Cindy said. "Would you like to sit outside?"

She showed us outside to a pleasant and well-tended deck overlooking a lower-level yard. The back yard was large but sloped with more mature vegetation, including tall eucalyptus trees bordering the property. At Cindy's bidding, we sat at a round teak table while she disappeared inside with the cake. A moment later, she returned and settled in at the table. Soon after, an older version of Cindy appeared with a tray holding cups and saucers and a carafe. Several slices of the fresh cake were arranged on a small dish next to a stack of napkins.

"I made some coffee for you ladies," the woman said. "But if you prefer tea, just let me know."

"Coffee will be fine, thank you," Sally said for the both of us.

The woman gave us a small smile tinged with stress and sadness. "And thank you so much for the cake. Once the girls see it, it will be gone in a jiffy."

After the woman put down the tray, Cindy put a hand on the woman's arm. "This is my mother, Carolyn Poppin. She and my father flew in right after … after it happened." Cindy smiled up at the woman. "She's been a godsend, especially with the girls."

Carolyn Poppin smiled down at her daughter and squeezed the hand on her arm. "I'll let you ladies talk. Just don't tire yourself too much, Cindy."

"How are you doing, Cindy?" Sally asked after Mrs. Poppin returned to the house.

"Okay, I guess, but it has been much more difficult for the girls."

"They around?"

"No, my dad took them to the movies to keep their minds off things."

Sally hesitated but continued. I could tell she wasn't used to pressing people when it came to personal matters—unlike me, who was fast turning it into a second career. "Cindy, you know there was no love lost between Donny and me, but please know I hold no hard feelings against you and the girls."

"I know that, Sally. The girls and I have always liked you and Jill, and we've always considered Lucas part of our family." She paused and looked off in the direction of the lower yard, then back at Sally. "I always felt he was wrong taking Lucas from you like that, but he wouldn't listen to anyone. By the way, how is Lucas taking this?"

"He's doing well, thank you. In spite of everything, Donny was his father, so, of course, it's natural for him to be having mixed feelings of both grief and relief."

Cindy nodded in understanding.

After taking a couple of sips of the excellent coffee, I got down to business. "Cindy, why didn't you go to the reunion with Donny that night?"

She focused her tired blue eyes on me. "Are you also going to ask if I have an alibi?"

"Excuse me?"

"That's what the police did. First, they wanted to know why I didn't go with Donny to that stupid reunion. Next, they wanted to know where I was that night, who I was with, and if anyone could prove it."

"And you said?" Just as I asked the question, Sally deftly kicked me under the table. I shot her a semi-dirty look. After all, we didn't come here for coffee and cake, we came here for answers. My attention settled back on Cindy, waiting for her answer to my question.

Sally stepped in. "Cindy, you told me you didn't go to the reunion because Donny said you'd cramp his style. What do you think he meant by that?"

Cindy took a piece of cake and placed it on a napkin in front of her. She picked at the edges. "That reunion was important to Donny. It was his return to his glory days. He talked about it for weeks. I knew I'd end up sitting in a corner, bored into oblivion. It was better for both of us that I stayed home. Besides, it had been a long time since we'd gone anywhere as a couple, why pretend for that night?"

"So you were home that night?" I asked.

"Yes, Odelia, I was home that night. My two oldest daughters were with me. We ordered pizza, made popcorn, and watched movies. My youngest was at a sleepover. The pizza guy can confirm I was here, as can a neighbor who stopped by to say hello."

Despite Sally's sturdy shoes and good aim, I persisted in my line of questioning. "Were you and Donny separated?"

Cindy looked at Sally. "Nosy thing, isn't she?"

Before Sally could say anything, I jumped in. "Yes, I am, especially when I've been under suspicion myself, and so has Sally. I know *I* didn't kill Donny. And I'm pretty sure Sally didn't kill him, but you I don't know."

Cindy Oliver leaned forward and locked eyes with me. "I didn't kill my husband, Odelia, but I'm not sorry he's dead. It saved me the trouble of a divorce."

"Is that a yes on the separation question?"

Sally kicked me again. This time I turned on her, spitting ten-penny nails in spite of my cold.

"You kick me one more time," I warned her, "and I swear I'll throw you over the edge of this deck. You asked for my help in clearing your name, and I'm doing just that. After all, I'm not the one who tried to kill Donny a few months ago, and I was dancing with a cop at the time of the murder, so it's not like I'm here to save my fat ass."

Sally held up both hands, palms out, in surrender. "Since you put it that way, go right ahead."

Turning to Cindy, I gave her a look that I hoped would loosen her tongue. It did.

"Donny and I were not separated," she began. "At least not yet. But we were going our separate ways more and more. I was going to file for divorce right after Christmas. I would have sooner, but I didn't want the girls to have to deal with that over the holidays."

I looked from Cindy to Sally, and back at Cindy. "Now that wasn't so hard, was it?"

The two of them looked at me like I was crazy, which I was beginning to think myself. The incident with Greg and my increasing discomfort from my head cold had definitely put an edge on my already cranky demeanor.

Returning to my questioning, I asked Cindy, "Why were you going to divorce him? I mean, I know he was an ass, but what specifically caused you to want to do it now instead of a year or two ago?"

Cindy looked away. I took the opportunity to sip more coffee and nibble on a bit of cake. "Jill's cake is fantastic," I whispered to Sally. She gave me a look that was as good as a kick under the table.

"I fell in love." The words came from Cindy and were almost lost in the slight afternoon breeze. She cleared her throat. "I wanted to leave Donny a long time ago, but he was always threatening to take the girls from me if I did. I remember how horrible he was to Sally over Lucas, so I stayed to make sure my girls always had me with them."

"But Cindy," Sally said, "that probably wouldn't have happened to you. Donny won because I'm a lesbian and the judge was a narrow-minded, bigoted fool."

Cindy turned back and gave us a fake rubbery grin. "And I'm a drug addict."

I dropped the tidbit of cake I was holding, and Sally openly gasped.

"You mean you once were a drug addict?" Sally asked.

"Once a druggie, always a druggie." Cindy recited the words calmly, as if she were telling us the world was round. She sighed. "I've been clean almost four years. I became addicted to painkillers after I had a hysterectomy. Donny said he would file for custody based on my being a drug addict and an unfit mother. I couldn't let him do to me and my girls what he did to you and Lucas."

The three of us sat quietly as the breeze flowed through the trees like an autumn lullaby, as if its only job were to soothe bad memories and kiss emotional boo-boos. If it were only that simple. Donny had scarred the three of us, but me the least. I don't know what I would have done in Sally or Cindy's shoes.

Finally, I broke the reflective silence. "You said you fell in love."

Cindy looked at me, and I noted small tears running down her smooth cheeks. "Yes, just over a year ago."

A slight sound and movement caught my attention. I turned quickly and caught Mrs. Poppin watching from the kitchen window; no doubt she was listening, too. As soon as she realized she'd been caught eavesdropping, she moved out of sight.

"Is that why you were finally leaving Donny?"

"Yes, but not in the way you think." Cindy wiped away her tears with the back of her hand and pulled a nearby chair closer so she could prop her feet up. She gave a short laugh. "Maybe if I get comfortable enough, I can pretend this is a visit to my shrink and spill my guts."

I found myself liking Cindy Oliver.

With her feet elevated, she leaned back in her chair and looked up at the deck covering, then to us. Exhaustion covered her face like a film, dulling what I was sure was celebrated beauty in better times.

"Like I said, I fell in love, but I wasn't leaving Donny for him. I met him quite by accident at the car dealership, of all places." She smiled when she spoke. "We were both getting our cars serviced and had to wait quite awhile. Eventually we struck up a conversation. He was so nice, so mellow and kind. So unlike Donny. I was sorry when they told him that his car was ready. When he went to pay for the repair, he discovered he had forgotten his wallet, so I offered to put his repair work on my credit card."

I was incredulous. "You did that for a stranger?"

She shrugged. "By then, I didn't feel he was a stranger. Also, it turned out he knew Donny. Later that day, like the gentleman I knew he was, he called and asked if he could take me to lunch to thank me and to give me the cash. I almost told him just to mail me a check, but at the last minute I said yes to the lunch. We met for lunch the day after and once a week since then, until just a couple of months ago."

Sally leaned forward with interest. "You don't see him anymore?"

Cindy shook her head. "No, though we have remained very close friends. He's married, but unlike me he was merely going through a rough patch, not a rough marriage. From the beginning, we both knew we wouldn't end up together. It was just too complicated, and he did really love his wife—still does. We were there for each other when we needed to be. I have no regrets."

"So you *weren't* going to leave Donny for this man?" Sally was still leaning forward, soaking up every word.

"I was leaving Donny for myself and for my girls. I didn't just fall in love with Victor, I fell back in love with myself, and it was time to take care of myself and face whatever Donny threw at me in court. It was because of Victor that I saw myself as being capable of—"

I cut her off by holding up a hand. Even with my cold-medicine-dulled mind, the name Victor caught my attention. "Victor? The guy's name is Victor, and he knew Donny?"

Sally shot me a wide-eyed look. I glanced her way, then refocused on Cindy. A cold, hard possibility had just struck me broadside across my brain. After thinking about what I wanted to say, I forged ahead.

"You didn't come to the reunion because you thought you'd be bored. You didn't come because you didn't want to meet Victor's wife or see Victor and Donny together."

Sally leaned back in her chair and ran her fingers through her short, blond hair. "Christ on a cracker."

Cindy said nothing. She looked down at her hands, which twitched and moved with nervous tension. A new river of tears started down her cheeks. When she did speak, she never raised her head to look at us.

"Victor and I were over, but he was still supporting me as a friend." She sniffed and so did I, but for different reasons. "Two months ago, Donny and I had a particularly nasty fight, and he struck me several times—blackened my eye and almost sent me through a window. It was the first time he'd ever hit me, but I remembered what he did to Jill that time—almost killed her. The next day, I called Victor and he came by. We've met several times since. He's been helping me make plans for leaving Donny—things like hiding money, gathering evidence to help me fight Donny in court, even setting up a safe place for me to go and start over with the girls, if need be."

A safe place. I thought about the woman and child I'd seen at Karen Meek's office. But no place would be completely safe until the tormenter was gone. Prisons were filled with women who had killed their abusers.

"Do the police know about Victor Morales?"

Cindy looked at me and shook her head.

"They didn't ask you about any lovers, past or present, nothing like that?"

"They did, but I didn't tell them about Victor. As for others, until then, there had never been anyone except Donny." She swallowed. "I knew Donny had been cheating on me for years, but I didn't know any specific names to give the police."

Sally and I looked at each other, our eyes communicating the same thought.

Cindy gasped. "You can't believe Victor and I had anything to do with this!"

TWENTY-THREE

"You knew about Victor and Cindy?"

"Yes and no," I said to Sally as I rummaged through my tote bag.

After saying goodbye to Cindy and Mrs. Poppin, we climbed back into Sally's Jeep and headed for the highway. We were almost back on the 5 Freeway when I asked Sally to pull over. She made a turn into a parking lot for a Burger King and pulled into a spot near the back.

"Johnette told me at the reunion that she thought Victor was having an affair. She followed him once and saw him with a pretty young woman."

"Cindy's very pretty, but she's not that young."

"Younger than us," I observed. "And from a distance, with that nice figure and long, blond hair, she could look a lot younger."

"True." Sally watched me root around in my bag. "What are you looking for?"

"My address book. Johnette wrote down her address and phone number for me at the reunion. I didn't have time to transfer it into my address book, but I remember sticking the paper in there."

I finally located the small, red, leather-bound address book and flipped through it. About two-thirds into it was stuck a folded piece of paper with the information I wanted. I held it up to Sally in triumph.

"How do you feel about paying the Moraleses a little visit?"

"Right now?"

"Why not? Unless you've got a hot date."

She hesitated. "Actually, I do. It's our anniversary, Jill's and mine."

Suddenly, a hot, searing pain of envy shot through me. Sally had a life—a life with Jill—and I had left my chance at a similar life back at my townhouse with instructions to lock up. Still, I don't know how I could have handled that differently at that given point in time. I choked down the urge to cry and plastered a mostly sincere smile on my face.

"Congratulations."

"Thank you." Sally beamed at me before her glow diminished. She turned in her seat and reached out to gently stroke my shoulder. "Don't worry, Odelia, it's going to be okay between you and Greg."

I sniffed, took a tissue from my bag, and blew my nose. "I wish I had your confidence."

"You'll see. And if for some reason you cannot patch things up, there will be someone else even better for you. You are too wonderful not to have someone special." She paused. "That detective you brought to the reunion seemed rather stuck on you."

I sniffed again. "That's part of the problem, though not all of it." After one more blow into the tissue, I said, "Thanks, Sally, you've been rather wonderful yourself." I looked at her. "Too bad we didn't become friends sooner."

She gave me a warm smile before glancing at the dashboard clock. "It's only about four thirty now. Jill's and my dinner reservations are for eight. We could squeeze in a visit to Johnette and Victor if they live close by."

"You don't have to go, Sally."

"No, I want to, especially after what Cindy told us. Seems like Victor should be on the suspect list, if he's not already."

"I agree." I looked at the address. "They live in La Mirada. That's pretty close."

"Figures, especially since Victor and Cindy were at the same car dealership."

Sally reached behind my seat and pulled out a Thomas Guide for Los Angeles County. "This is rather old, but it should still get us there."

I looked up the address from the slip of paper on the street guide and followed it back to where we were currently located.

"Doesn't look like it's more than four or five miles away."

Before we took off, I called the number on the slip. On the second ring, I got Victor.

"Hi, Victor, it's me, Odelia." I paused. "Guess what? Sally Kipman and I are just a couple of miles away and thought how much fun it would be to stop by and say hello … if you folks have time, that is." I listened again. "Great, we'll be there shortly." Another pause. "Uh-huh, no, don't worry, we have the address. See you soon."

After closing the cell phone, I turned to Sally. "Victor said Johnette went grocery shopping but should be home very soon. He thought our visit would be a nice surprise for her."

"With any luck, we might get some time alone with him while we're at it."

"You're reading my mind."

As we pulled out of the parking lot, I noted a motorcycle parked between two cars near the entrance of the restaurant. The motorcycle was bright green and sporty, like a racing bike. The rider was perched on it, helmet on. I could have sworn I'd seen that bike a few minutes earlier as we left the Oliver house.

"Sally, do you recall seeing that motorcycle before?"

She looked over at it and shrugged. As she did, the rider turned away from us and looked in the direction of the front door of Burger King, lowering the visor.

"No, looks to me like he's just waiting for someone."

"Probably."

Giving Sally directions from the map, we were in front of Johnette's home in less than fifteen minutes. It was a pleasant-looking ranch-style home in peach stucco, located on a quiet cul-de-sac. Most of the front area was taken up by a wide driveway that could easily accommodate several cars on one side and that branched off toward the garage on the other side. I remembered that Johnette and Victor had two grown sons. The driveway must have come in handy when all of them were coming and going in separate cars. The lawn and landscaping on the sides of the driveway and garage and in front of the house were beautifully maintained.

We pulled into the drive. Before we rang the doorbell, the door opened and Victor stood in front of us, wearing jeans and a loose

Hawaiian shirt. He seemed genuinely happy to see us, which made me feel guilty, considering the real root of the visit was hardly social.

"What a nice surprise. Come on in—Johnette will be so happy to see you girls."

He steered us inside and through a spacious living room that held an impressive grand piano. On the far wall were sliding glass doors that looked out onto a tidy lawn, patio, and large pool. Unlike the Oliver home, which had oodles of natural vegetation surrounding its hilltop perch, the plants in and around the Moraleses' yard were planned and cultivated and as manicured as my nails. The patio doors were open to the fall breeze.

"I see Johnette still plays the piano," I said as we followed him into the kitchen and to a large dining nook surrounded by large windows on two sides. He invited us to sit at a large oak table with fake antique high-back chairs. Each chair held a ruffled cushion that matched the window curtains, wallpaper, and even the kitchen towels and appliance covers. The place was cute but too matchy-matchy for my taste.

"Yes, in fact, after she quit teaching two years ago, she started giving private lessons."

"Why did she quit teaching?" asked Sally.

"When budgets started getting slashed, she found it too stressful, and the kids were so disrespectful, not at all like when she started out."

"My son is a teacher," Sally commented. "It's scary what some kids are into these days."

Victor smiled sadly. "She still does some substitute work but prefers to just have a few private piano students. Once our boys grew up and left home, we didn't need the second income as much."

"You're a school principal now, as I recall from the reunion."

While Sally chitchatted, I surveyed the room, noting all of the family photos scattered about. Tacked to the refrigerator were a couple of masterpieces by small children.

"Yes, I am, at a high school. I started out as a coach and math teacher." He rose from the table. "Would you like some coffee?"

We'd just been plied with coffee at Cindy's, but I didn't want to seem impolite. "Do you have something cold to drink?"

"How about some lemonade? Johnette makes it fresh, like her mother always did. No concentrated lemonade in this house."

"Sounds great," Sally said.

As soon as Victor turned to get our drinks, Sally widened her eyes and nodded at me as if to say *what are you waiting for?* Something told me this time she wouldn't be kicking me under the table.

The lemonade was delicious, a bit on the tart side, with an unusual bite to it. If I remembered, or if it wasn't too tacky after my nosing around, I'd have to get the recipe for Zee. Great lemonade is one of her favorite things.

I was trying to decide how to open a dialogue when Victor did it for me.

"What brings you out this way?" he asked us. "I know you live in Newport Beach, Odelia. What about you, Sally?"

"I live in Orange County, too—in Lake Forest."

"We were visiting Cindy Oliver, paying our respects." I watched his face for a reaction and wasn't disappointed. He almost paled. "They don't live very far from here," I added.

187

Quickly, he collected himself. "That's right, they don't."

"Did you stay in touch with Donny after high school?"

He shook his head and took a sip of lemonade. "Not really. We went to different colleges. I saw him at the five-year reunion, and we met occasionally after that for a couple of beers. But it'd been years since I'd seen him, until last Saturday. He was a big-shot VP at a national sporting goods company and I taught high school—not exactly the same circle."

"What about Cindy, how well do you know her?"

Victor got up abruptly from the table and strode over to the kitchen sink. He still held his glass of lemonade in his hand. When he turned around, I thought he was going to throw it at us. Instead, he put it down on the counter and covered his face with both hands for a moment. When he took them away, his eyes were wet.

"I know Cindy Oliver very well, but I suppose you already know that."

Sally and I both nodded.

"And I suppose you'll feel obliged to tell Johnette."

"She already thinks you're having an affair, Victor. She told me so at the reunion. She followed you at least once, but I don't think she knows who you were seeing."

"She followed me?"

"That's what she told me."

He turned back to the sink and hung his head while gripping the edge of the counter. "The thing with Cindy has been over quite awhile. It started up quite by accident. She was miserable with Donny. Johnette was going through some issues and we hadn't been intimate for a very long time, not physically or emotionally."

"Issues? Was she sick?"

"Johnette went into a very bad depression just after she retired from teaching." He turned back to face us. "In fact, the depression was one of the reasons she quit teaching, but it got worse after she left her job. She was in and out of a residential facility for a while, and when she was home she was almost a zombie from the meds. I was slipping into a depression myself over it."

"That's when you and Cindy hooked up?"

"Yes. We found each other and gave each other strength, but we both knew it was only temporary. We finally broke it off but remained close. We kept tabs on each other, supported each other through e-mails and phone calls, but the affair itself came to an end."

It was the same story Cindy had given us. "And Johnette is much better now?"

He nodded. "I finally took her to a new doctor, one Cindy recommended, and it has made all the difference in the world. She still has low periods, but they're manageable. Most days she's her old self." He smiled.

My throat was getting scratchy again. I took a drink of my lemonade before continuing. "Johnette saw you with Cindy recently, so you are still seeing her, at least in some capacity."

He moved back to the table, but instead of sitting down, he stood with his hands on the back of a chair. His face was growing haggard. "Didn't Cindy tell you why?"

"We'd like to hear it from you."

He told us about Cindy getting a beating from Donny and how she called him for help in making the break. Again, it was pretty much what she'd told us. Once he was done, he looked us over with open suspicion.

"Why are you two nosing around? Why can't you just mind your own business and let us solve our own problems?"

"Because we're both suspects in Donny's murder, and you're not," Sally said in an even tone. "Seems to me you should be on that list either with us or in our place."

"You two are suspects?"

"Yes, especially me." Sally sighed. "Did you know that Donny was the father of my son?"

Victor nodded. "Cindy told me what happened. I'm very sorry, Sally."

I chimed in. "With what Donny did to Sally and what he did to me at the prom, we both made the short list of suspects—lucky us. But the police don't know about you."

"But I didn't kill Donny!" He looked first at me, then at Sally. "You were there," he said to Sally. "When Donny came stumbling in, the two of us were talking about our kids, remember?"

"Yes, I do. And Odelia was dancing with her friend."

I took a deep breath though my mouth, my nose being almost useless. "And Cindy was home with two of her daughters, and the police have checked out her story."

I dug around in my bag and produced a pen and an old power bill in its envelope. On the back of the envelope, I wrote all three of our names and Cindy's. "Okay," I said, pen poised over the back of the envelope, "who else would have reason to kill Donny Oliver?"

"Try everyone," snorted Sally.

"No, seriously, who would have wanted him dead? He was very popular in school. Most people liked him even if they thought him a jerk from time to time. Maybe it was someone from his work or the husband of some woman he was seeing on the side."

"I don't know," Sally commented, "but I can't help but think that it wasn't an accident that Donny was killed at our reunion."

Victor sat back down at the table, and the three of us put our heads together to think. It was Victor who spoke first. "How about Tommy Bledsoe?"

"Tommy Bledsoe was in Japan at the time," Sally told him.

I nodded and sniffled. Reaching for a tissue, I found the little purse packet I keep in my bag empty. "Do you have some tissues, Victor?"

"Sure, Odelia." He got up and retrieved a box from a small counter near the refrigerator. In his other hand, he held a remote control he had picked up near the tissue box. "Damn remote," he said, indicating the item in his hand. "I was looking for this all last night. It goes to the TV in our bedroom."

As he handed me the box of tissues, an idea struck me. "Remote control."

"What?" asked Sally, turning to look at me.

"Remote control—that's the answer, or at least a possibility."

Victor held out the TV remote control to me. "You want the clicker?"

"No, I don't want the clicker," I said in frustration, with a nasally voice. I held up a finger indicating for them to hold on a minute. I turned away and blew my nose twice. Finished, I got up and deposited the dirty tissue in a nearby trashcan.

"Remote control," I stated again while I washed my hands. "A murder can be done by remote control. A murderer doesn't necessarily have to be the one who pulls the trigger." Looking at my two companions, I saw the light dawning on both of their faces.

I continued. "Someone not at the reunion could have hired someone to kill Donny."

"Someone like Tommy Bledsoe," Victor said. "He certainly has the money to do it."

Sally leaned forward, elbows on the table, and held her head in her hands. "But if someone was hired to kill Donny, then we're back to square one."

Victor looked at her. "Why's that?"

I returned to the table and took a drink of lemonade.

"Sally's right, because if someone was hired to kill Donny, then anyone could have done the hiring, including Cindy or any one of the three of us."

Just as Victor was about to say something more, the door leading to the garage opened and in walked Johnette carrying a few plastic bags of groceries. We had been so caught up in our talk of murder, we hadn't heard her drive in.

"Odelia, Sally ... what a wonderful surprise!"

TWENTY-FOUR

THE PHONE RANG ONCE, then twice, then a third time before I hung up.

"What are you doing?" I asked myself out loud as I paced from the kitchen to the living room and back again.

After Sally dropped me off at home and sped away to meet Jill for their anniversary celebration, I scoured the downstairs of my townhouse, looking and hoping for a note left behind by Greg, much as I searched for clues left behind by Cruz. I didn't need much, just some sign that he'd call soon, drop by again, was sorry, loved me, hated me—anything that evidenced he'd been here when I left and was leaving the lines of communication open. I would have settled for a broken dish in the sink. I found nothing. That's when I placed the call and hung up.

My cold was worse, and I felt a bit dizzy. That was when I realized I hadn't eaten since breakfast except for a bite of cake, cups of coffee, and some lemonade. I was drowning in caffeine and sugar but hadn't eaten anything substantial or healthy. I wasn't hungry, but I knew I should eat, so after changing into some warm jammies, I located some split pea soup in the pantry and heated it up. I had managed to get a few spoonfuls down and was in the midst of shoveling another into my mouth when my phone rang. The display said it was Greg, and the surprise caused me to slosh green soup down the front of my clean pajamas.

I grabbed the phone and tried to calm myself down before hitting the answer button. It rang a second time. I took a breath as deep as my congestion would allow. "Hello."

"You don't sound so hot."

"I'm afraid my cold is winning the fight."

"You mean our cold."

I smiled at his use of the word *our*. I took it as a good sign.

Before I could say anything, he asked, "You called?"

I hesitated, wondering how he knew, then remembered that his phone recorded missed calls. Putting the soup down, I tried to concentrate. "Yes, I did. I wanted to apologize for rushing off so rudely today. I really was very happy to see you and Wainwright."

"But you were right, Odelia, I should have at least called before coming over."

There was a period of silence. I wasn't about to say *no, that's okay,* because it wasn't, but I wasn't ready to ask him the details about his motive for the visit. I was worried that whatever reasons had prompted him to show up, he had changed his mind after hearing about my recent activities. But then I had made it clear what I was doing, so why should I hide it now? I had spelled it out, and Greg was far from illiterate. It was Greg who broke the ice on the topic.

"I'm sorry about Mike missing. That was quite a shock. Any leads?"

"Not really."

I wondered if I should say more, wondered if Greg was really interested or just being polite by asking. Then I decided Steele's disappearance was good neutral ground.

"Most people think he sabotaged a huge lawsuit and left the country, but that doesn't sound like something he'd do, and I can't think of a reason why he would do it in the first place." I brought Greg up to speed on what I had found out so far and how the firm had asked me to look into it. I carefully edited out my S O S to Willie Porter.

"It seems odd that that cleaning company doesn't remember him, especially when they supposedly were just there in the past couple of weeks. Mike Steele is hardly a forgettable guy."

I laughed and followed up with a cough. "You're right about that, but the woman I spoke to seemed a bit dotty. Maybe she just takes the calls and sends the cleaners out. I should call her again."

Talking about it reminded me that I had wanted to look up Let Mother Do It to see if it was a registered company or fictitious business name. I would make sure I did it after my call with Greg.

There was another long pause on his end. "And how did your visit with the widow go?"

Talking about Steele's disappearance was one thing, but Greg was actually asking me about Donny Oliver's murder. Was this acceptance on his part or just morbid curiosity?

"Interesting, to say the least. Turns out Donny smacked his wife around pretty good recently, and she was getting ready to leave him."

"Abuse could be a motive for murder."

I thought about my afternoon and all the information and ideas newly crammed into my muddled brain.

"Greg, do you know anything about hit men?"

"What?"

"Hit men, contract killers—what do you know about them?"

He laughed. "Sweetheart, you may be exasperating at times, but you are never dull."

Sweetheart, he called me sweetheart. My heart fluttered.

"Why do you ask? Do you think that high-school chum of yours was whacked by the mob or something?"

"Actually, I hadn't thought about the mob. I was thinking along the lines that an individual might have hired someone to bump off Donny. All of the usual suspects seem to have airtight alibis, including me. So if one of us did it, we would have had to do it through someone else. Killing by remote control, so to speak."

"À la Robert Blake?"

"Exactly."

"Interesting theory and plausible, but all I know about such things is what I've seen on TV. I wouldn't have a clue how to go about finding a gun for hire."

"And I'm thankful for that, Greg."

He laughed again, this time longer. I took it as another good sign, grabbing for it like a thirsty man for a drop of water. There was another long pause.

"Odelia, I know this is going to fall on deaf ears, but please be careful."

I took note that Greg had stopped laughing and his voice was now somber.

"If someone did hire a contract killer to take out Donny, that person could also hire someone to do the same to you."

Holy crap. I hadn't thought of that, but Greg was right.

"I know you want to help your friends, Odelia, but please stay out of it. Let Dev and his pals handle the murder. If you *must* stick your nose into something, look for Mike Steele. It seems the less dangerous of the two evils."

Then I had another thought, one that wasn't going to make Greg happy. "But what if Steele is the victim of a contract killer? What then?"

This time the pause was so long I almost thought he'd quietly hung up on me. When I heard him clear his throat, I silently said thanks.

"How's your dad, Odelia?"

It was a deft and effective change of subject, but at least we were talking again.

Following my chat with Greg, I went upstairs to my computer and fired it up. Using my office password for Lexis, it didn't take me long to check out the name Let Mother Do It. I billed the search to the Missing Link matter. I found nothing filed in California under that name: not a corporation, a limited liability corporation, a partnership, a fictitious business name, nada. I expanded the search to cover all of the United States—again, nothing. Whatever Mother was doing, it wasn't through proper channels. If it were, there would be a record of it somewhere in California. My guess was she didn't file taxes on the money she made either and took the fees under the table. This seemed odd, especially since she alluded to having important clients. Those folks write off everything, and to do that they would need receipts, and receipts would flag a small business, at least eventually.

Following my line of thought, I searched Lexis for Melinda's Maid Service. Bingo! There it was—a fictitious business name filed properly in the Orange County Clerk's Office evidencing that Melinda's Maid Service was an assumed business name for Melinda Thompson.

It was just before nine on a Saturday night, but still I made the call. The phone at Let Mother Do It rang at least a dozen times before I gave up. Not even an answering machine had picked up.

I gave up, too, on my investigation, at least for the night. Giving in to my growing discomfort, I changed into a clean nightshirt, took a big shot of NyQuil, and headed to bed. Seamus was already in his spot on the bed, snoozing as only a cat can.

I was dreaming about serving lemonade to Robert Blake—a Robert Blake with white hair, not black—when I was startled by the phone next to my bed. I don't know if it was on the second or third ring when I picked it up, but when I did, I was talking to Zee.

"How are you doing today?"

"Not bad." I checked the clock—it was close to nine thirty in the morning. "Except for a bathroom break early this morning, I slept twelve hours."

"Good. I hope you're going to stay in bed today. If not, at least stay put at home. You need your rest."

"Yes, mother." The sarcastic comment made me think of the elusive Let Mother Do It. Zee was a bubbling brook of minutia. In that remarkable skull of hers, she retained everything she ever read, saw, or heard, or at least it seemed like it to me. "Zee, have you ever heard of a company called Let Mother Do It? It would be a cleaning company or personal services company, something like that."

"Hmm, doesn't sound familiar. Where are they located?"

"Not sure, but their phone is an Orange County exchange."

"Problem is, with all the cell phones now and transferable numbers, that doesn't always give a correct location."

"True. I believe they did some cleaning work for Steele and he's in Laguna Beach, so I'm thinking they might actually be in Orange County."

"Knowing you, you've already searched on Lexis." Zee once worked in law. In fact, we had met at Woobie years ago.

"Yes, last night, and nothing showed up anywhere in California—or the rest of the country, for that matter."

"Sorry, but if I recall something, I'll give you a call. You *are* going to be home today, right?"

It wasn't a question as much as a direct order. "That's the plan, Stan."

"Good, stick to the plan." There was a pause, and then she got to the real reason she had called. "Did you hear from Greg?"

"Funny you should ask."

"Not funny at all. He and Seth and some other guys got together yesterday morning for some basketball. Seth said Greg looked so hang-dog he should've been put down."

"Did Seth tell him to come over?" I was getting my dander up over the fact that the visit might not have been Greg's idea.

"Not exactly. According to Seth, Greg was asking him every five minutes whether or not he should call you. Finally, my hubby told him what he told you a week ago—crap or get off the pot."

I laughed, which brought on a fit of coughing. Once I got my breath back, I filled in my best friend on both Greg's visit and the call last night.

After my talk with Zee, I settled back under the covers for a bit more snoozing. Seamus was at his usual post at the foot of the bed. I was just about out when the phone rang again. This time it was Dev.

"Just seeing how you're doing."

"My cold is worse, but I'm hanging in there. Thanks for asking." I adjusted the pillows and sat up. "Any more news on Steele?"

"No, but no one is really looking for him except for you and your firm."

Dev hesitated, and I knew he was going to tell me something I didn't want to hear.

"Odelia, the missing person report is still in effect, and if there is a sighting, it will be reported. But as long as there is no evidence of foul play or criminal activity, the police are not going to actively look for him. Adults disappear every day, mostly because they want to disappear."

"But Dev, what if *I* think there's been foul play?"

"You do?" I could tell from the tone of his voice that his interest was sparked. "Why's that, Odelia? Is there something you haven't told me?"

"I checked his personal papers at the office, and his passport is still there."

"But he could have flown domestic and still stashed the car in the international terminal lot."

"True, but honestly, Dev, something has happened to him. I just know it. Steele isn't the type to just walk away from his life—ask anyone." I thought about the papers in his car. The firm was either keeping that quiet or they didn't have proof of anything being illegal. "And he's not the type to get involved in dealings so shady he'd have to run."

On the other end of the phone, Dev let loose a big sigh. "Odelia, most of the people who walk away from their lives don't fit a specific type except for being under extreme stress, emotionally or financially. But if there was a specific type, I'd say Mike Steele fits it perfectly."

"How so?"

"Besides the stress factor, he's smart enough to plan it and execute it, and he has the resources to carry it out."

Again he paused. I was beginning to read his pauses and hesitations. A short pause meant nothing out of the ordinary, but a long one definitely called for concern. This pause was neither, so it threw me off.

"I also called with some pretty good news for you."

"Excuse me." I quickly blew my nose. "Okay, shoot. I could use some good news."

"You are officially off the suspect list in the Donny Oliver case."

"Officially? You mean they think I couldn't have done it or wouldn't have done it?"

This time, the pause came with a deep chuckle. "Don't press your luck, Odelia. They haven't found any evidence to link you with Oliver's death. Should that change, you'll be back in their sights." A longer pause. "But your pal Sally is still under consideration."

"Anyone else? Say ... his wife?"

"Let's just say there are a few others, which brings me to another issue." Another pause—a very long one. Uh-oh. "What the hell were you doing at Donny Oliver's house with Sally Kipman yesterday?"

Yikes. That threw me, but only for a moment.

"We went to pay our respects to Donny's widow. After all, Donny was our classmate and the father of Sally's son. We even brought her a bundt cake."

"Yeah, right."

"It's true, ask her. Better yet, ask her mother, Mrs. Poppin, Carolyn Poppin, she was there." Now it was my turn to pause. "Hey, how did you know about yesterday?"

"Let's just say I got a call from one of my cop buddies telling me to keep my girlfriend in line."

Girlfriend? But, of course, I was at the reunion with Dev. The police working Donny's murder knew that.

"Dev, I was thinking about the murder."

"I told you to stay out of it, Odelia, and I mean it." His tone had turned harsh and demanding.

"But—"

"No buts about it. I'll not have you getting mixed up in this type of thing again. How many times do you have to have a brush with death to understand how dangerous it is or how dangerous your involvement could be to other people? I can't do my job if I'm worried about you."

He'll not have me? The possessiveness of his tone bothered me. Seems without my permission I had been handed from one man to another, and neither was tolerant or accepting of what I wanted to do. In my heart, I knew they were both right to be concerned about me, and I did appreciate it, but I had ideas and opinions and felt frustrated that I wasn't able to tell Dev about them. Actually, the frustration came from him not being willing to listen.

After turning down an invitation from Dev for brunch and a movie, I rolled over and tried to get back to sleep, and it was almost mission accomplished when the phone rang again. It wasn't even ten o'clock yet, and I'd had three phone calls in less than twenty minutes. It must be National Call Odelia Day. I rolled over and answered it.

"Hi, stranger."

"Excuse me?"

"Don't you know who this is?"

"Look, I'm in bed, sick, and not in the mood for games. Tell me or buzz off."

The caller laughed. "Just as charming as ever, I see. It's Tom Bledsoe."

"Huh?"

From the other end, I heard him laugh again. "I knew you'd be surprised."

Surprised wasn't the word. I shot straight up in bed so fast Seamus scurried for cover. "Tommy?"

"Hope you don't mind, Odelia, but I got your phone number from Karen. She gave me three of them ... home, office, and cell; thought I'd start with your home number." He paused, probably waiting for me to say something, but I was still too stunned. He continued. "Wow, what a coincidence, huh? I'm engaged to your boss's ex-wife. What are the chances?"

Finally, I found my tongue. "Sorry, Tommy—I mean Tom—but I'm still in shock. Aren't you in Japan?"

"I came home yesterday, a few days early. Karen is quite upset about Mike being missing."

"Did she also tell you about our thirtieth reunion?"

"Yes, of course. Between the reunion and Mike, you've had quite a time. Too bad, though, that I missed the reunion. I wouldn't have minded seeing Donny with a bullet in him."

It seemed that Sally and Cindy weren't alone in their celebration of Donny Oliver's death. As much as I detested Donny, I still thought his death a tragedy. Was I being too naïve, too much of a goody two-shoes, or just in denial about my own deep and true feelings about his death? It made me wonder what it would take, what boundaries someone would have to cross, for me to wish a person dead. And how does one properly wish someone dead? Is it done while blowing out birthday candles or upon seeing the first star of the evening?

I wish I may,
I wish I might,
See [fill in the blank] *killed tonight.*

I didn't equate telling Donny to eat shit and die as being the same as wishing him dead in a serious way. But seeing that no cosmic wisdom was providing me with a solid answer, I turned my attention back to Tommy Bledsoe.

"The suspect list is impressive, even I made it, but I've since fallen off the hit parade."

Hit parade, strange choice of words, I thought to myself. Obviously, I was still thinking about the idea of a contract killer.

"Did you kill Donny, Tom?"

"Me? I was in Japan, you know that. And so do the police. They tracked me down and asked me questions."

"Then let me rephrase the question. Did you have Donny killed?"

He laughed, not a little chuckle or a smirk that could be heard in his voice but a full-out laugh. "Wish I had thought of that, Odelia. I would have considered it a good investment."

He paused. What's with men and their pauses? It's as if they're setting the stage for some sort of verbal brilliance that never materializes.

Okay, yes, I'm being cranky. I'm sick and people keep calling— I'm entitled.

"Odelia, may I ask you a question?"

"Of course."

"How many people do you come right out and ask if they've killed someone?"

The question made me wonder if Tommy knew of my experiences as a corpse magnet. "More than you would imagine."

"Uh-huh." He laughed again. "And how many of those people would you expect to answer you truthfully if they did kill some one?"

"Maybe I'm hoping I'll shame someone into telling the truth."

Tom Bledsoe laughed harder. "Halloween's in two days, Odelia. Make sure you go as Diogenes. You can wander Southern California in search of an honest man."

"Or woman."

TWENTY-FIVE

"The number you have dialed is no longer in service. If you feel you have reached this recording in error, please hang up and dial again."

True to my word to Zee, I had stayed home all day Sunday, doing laundry and taking care of my cold. I had to admit, I did feel much better. Sunday I made two calls to Let Mother Do It and received no response. Monday morning I tried the number again, then again shortly after ten o'clock. Now, for the third time, a canned voice was telling me that the number for Let Mother Do It had been disconnected. Three strikes, I was out. What the hell was going on?

I had hit a wall on both Donny's murder and Steele's disappearance. Instead of narrowing down the suspect list, with the idea of a contract killer I had expanded it to virtually anyone who currently had or ever had a grudge against Donny Oliver. Considering what a jerk he was, that could encompass most of Los Angeles and Orange Counties, with San Diego County thrown in for good measure. But to be realistic, I think whoever killed Donny had some very personal reasons. Not that humiliating me and Tommy wasn't personal, but that was thirty years ago. The embarrassment might still be alive and well in our minds, but both of us had pretty much moved on. Tommy wasn't totally in the clear, but I doubt if being pantsed and dumped in a fish tank when he was eighteen held much importance to him now that he was a gazillionaire, though I've been known to be wrong before about people. And even though I still cringe and want to crawl in a hole every time I think about my prom, it wouldn't be enough for me to seek revenge three decades later. Had I wanted revenge, I would have carried it out a long time ago when the wounds were fresh and bleeding, and certainly not by way of a bullet. Even though what he did to me is unforgivable in my eyes, I hadn't joined the Rah-Rah, Die, Donny, Die club. No, there were others with much more current and personal axes to grind.

As much as I was getting to know and like Sally, she still could be the killer. She certainly had motive. And Cindy Oliver certainly had motive. And what about Victor Morales? Did he do away with Donny to help Cindy in her quest to be free? And were Cindy and Victor being honest about their romantic relationship being in the past? Maybe Victor and Johnette weren't doing so hot as a couple, and Cindy and Victor joined forces to get Donny out of the picture and pave the way for their own relationship?

Or was I meowing up the wrong scratching post?

Maybe there was still someone else not yet unearthed who wanted Donny dead more than those already under the shadow of suspicion.

Questions, questions, questions—they gave me the urge to go home and settle under the covers with Seamus and a good book, preferably not a murder mystery.

Putting aside the Donny dilemma for a bit, I thought about Steele. Over the weekend, Carl Yates had sent me an e-mail telling me to continue working on Missing Link as time permitted, but to also make sure I spent time on my other work. In lawyer-speak, that meant it had been downgraded from a category 5 hurricane to a bad tropical storm and no longer merited sucking up all of my billable time. But it also meant that I wasn't to ignore it. Seems my special assignment was not so special anymore now that they had found Steele's car and all seemed in order, at least as far as foul play went.

Dev was right; people disappeared all the time, of their own accord, and there was no reason to believe any harm had come to Steele. On the surface, it appeared that he simply decided to vanish from his day-to-day life for a few days, maybe even forever, and that it was his decision. But in my gut, this theory curdled like sour milk.

Picking up my phone, I punched in three numbers to an internal extension. On the second ring, Carl Yates answered. "Yes, Odelia?"

"Carl, I have something you should see."

"Bring it on down. I'm leaving soon for lunch with a potential client, but I have a few minutes."

"Actually, Carl, if you don't mind, I need you to meet me in Mike Steele's office. It can wait until after lunch, but the sooner the better."

He mulled it over less than ten seconds before agreeing to meet me in Steele's office in five minutes. When he arrived, I was waiting inside with the door shut. Carl entered and closed the door behind him.

"Did you learn anything new, Odelia?"

"Not exactly new, but important." I held out the small key to Steele's private box. Carl took it.

"It looks like a safe deposit key."

"You're close." I walked to the edge of Steele's desk. "Open Steele's right-hand drawer."

Carl had a puzzled look on his face but he followed my directions. Opening the drawer, we both saw the same well-labeled hanging files I saw Saturday.

"Now push those files back—all the way back."

He did as he was told and immediately saw the special compartment. "It's a false-bottom drawer."

I nodded. "That key goes to that lock. Go ahead, open it."

Again, Carl did as I asked and soon had the box opened about halfway.

"Steele keeps a lot of his personal papers there. See his passport on the top? Unless he's traveling under a false name, he would never have left that behind."

"And if he is traveling under a false name," Carl said, looking directly at me, "it doesn't look very good for him."

"I agree." I indicated the box. "Go ahead and dig around. There's a surprise in there for you."

Carl looked at me with a half-grin. "I'm not going to get bit by anything, am I?"

"I hope not." I smiled at him. "Bonuses are in a few weeks. I wouldn't want mine to be fed to the shredder."

He chuckled, then returned his concentration to the box. Digging inside, he immediately found the file and wiggled it until he could pull it free. After looking inside, he dropped into Steele's chair.

"These are the missing original documents."

"All of them?"

Carl fingered through the small stack of signed originals. At the bottom of each was a Bates number. "They're here, every one of them." He looked up at me. "But how? And why are they here?"

"What about the ones found in Steele's car?"

"I never saw those. They were described to me over the phone."

"This is just speculation, Carl, but Steele had a habit of stashing stuff in here for safekeeping. Remember when Jake Wells brought in all those old bearer bonds?" Carl nodded. "Well, this is where Steele kept them until they could be processed. And Steele knows I have the only extra key to this box."

I moved closer to Carl and tapped the file folder with an index finger. "I think Steele discovered someone was monkeying around with the documents and put the originals in there to protect them while he figured things out. The documents in the car might have been very good copies of the originals, and they might have been there because Steele was going to review them while he was staying in Ojai. Even his ex-wife said he was preoccupied with a problem with the case."

"Are you sure you and Mike are the only ones who have a key to this drawer safe?"

"As far as I know, we are."

"And no one else knows about these papers being here?"

"I don't think so." I hesitated, remembering Saturday when Fran barged in on me, thinking Steele was back. "Fran saw me in here Saturday when I was checking the drawer, but I'm pretty sure she didn't see anything."

"Good."

He sat back in Steele's chair and raised his face to the ceiling. He swiveled and we heard the familiar squeak. After a moment or two, he focused on me.

"Odelia, if you don't mind, I'd like to rescind my e-mail and put you back on Missing Link in full force. I'm beginning to think Mike's in danger. For what reason, I don't know, but we need to find out what happened to him. Do you think it's possible for you to uncover anything new?"

Thinking about Willie, I said, "I have some special feelers out, but I don't know how long it will take for them to produce anything."

"I know Joan Nuñez is your friend, but do you trust her completely?"

I thought about that for a second, then answered truthfully. "Yes, Carl, I do. I don't think she'd do anything unethical any more than I think Steele would."

"Good, I feel the same way." He handed me the file folder. "Make copies of these and put the originals back in here for safekeeping. Then I want you to get together with Joan and have her show you the differences between these originals and what is now in our production documents. Maybe the two of you can think of how this happened. Meanwhile, I also want you to keep looking for Mike."

"The documents haven't been produced to the other side yet, have they?"

He shook his head. "No, we were about to produce them when Joan started noting discrepancies. I've been stalling on the production."

I walked to the window and stared down at the traffic moving many floors below. I was upset at the thought of Steele being in danger and me possibly being his only hope. Talk about feelings of inadequacy.

Looking back at Carl, I weighed my words carefully before speaking. "Who else had access to these original documents, Carl? Anyone else besides Fran, Joan, and Steele, and, of course, yourself?"

"Most anyone who works here, Odelia, you know that. Ani handled them regularly, as did our copy center and central filing. It's not like we needed to keep files under lock and key, at least until now." He stopped and thought a bit. "I'd really rather not think about an employee tampering with important documents, but I don't know what else to think. If it's true and it gets out, it'll be the last straw for our relationship with Silhouette. They are already talking about firing us and hiring another firm. This would send them right over the edge."

I was shocked. Silhouette had been a client almost as long as I'd worked for Woobie. "Why would they fire us?"

"They want this case resolved one way or the other as soon as possible. And they're not happy that Mike's out of the office right now, or that I've been putting off moving forward without him. They don't know the truth about Mike or the documents, so they just think we're dawdling. There's a new CEO at Silhouette, name's

Ben Walker, and he's trying to sell their board on the idea that they need fresh and more aggressive representation, especially since they're thinking about taking Silhouette public in the near future. He's been making noise about jumping to Goldberg-Rawlings; says he doesn't think we have enough muscle to carry the company into the future."

Goldberg-Rawlings—Tim Weber's firm. "Carl, have you ever heard of Tim Weber? He's an attorney with Goldberg."

He shook his head. "I know most of the partners in their office upstairs and some in their LA office, but that name doesn't ring a bell. Should I know him?"

I shrugged. "Just an attorney I know from that firm, that's all."

After making the copies, I replaced the originals in Steele's drawer and called Joan. Carl had already given her a heads-up. In a jiffy, she was seated with me behind closed doors at the small conference table in Steele's office with the documents in question, both her copies and mine spread before us.

It was true, the supposed copies of the documents in Joan's file did not match the originals. They looked alike and at first glance could easily be taken as true and correct copies, but upon close examination of the text, it was clear that they had been doctored. Key phrases in agreements and correspondence had been altered that totally changed the meaning of the document, and not in favor of our client. Had this not been caught in time it would have damaged our case horribly, perhaps irreparably. We would have produced documents claiming they proved our case when, in fact, they proved it for the other side.

"Whoever did this went to a great deal of trouble and knew what they were doing," I remarked to Joan. She nodded in agreement.

Upon examination, it was clear that whoever did the tampering knew the ins and outs of office equipment and word processing. They would have had to have scanned the originals into word processing documents, made the changes, and reprinted them, making sure the fonts, line positions, and margins all matched exactly. Somewhere along the line, the originals would have had to have been copied on a high-quality color copier to maintain the color of ink on the signatures and letterhead. The copies of the signatures, letterhead, and Bates numbers were probably then pasted on each new page in exactly the same position, then copied again. With a high-grade copier, the result would be copies that looked like they came straight from the original, until you took the time to read the text. It was genius, and it had been time-consuming.

Joan shook her head while she pored over the documents. "What upsets me, Odelia, is that it's definitely an inside job."

"Or at least someone in Woobie managed to get the originals to someone else just long enough for them to be copied. The copies weren't done here, Joan. We don't have a color copier. And to get this fine quality duplication on signatures and letterhead, you would have to first make a high-resolution color copy, otherwise the signatures would have looked like a copy of a copy instead of a copy of an original."

I thought about Greg and his company, Ocean Breeze Graphics. I had learned a lot from Greg and Boomer, his assistant.

"The thing is, it could have been even more high-tech than that. It's so easy now to replicate documents." Looking out the nearby window, I watched a lone fluffy cloud while I thought about how and why this might have happened. "This seems like a lot of trouble over two candy companies fighting about a non-compete issue, doesn't it?"

Joan knitted her brows. "You know what I think?"

Giving her my whole attention, I leaned forward.

"I don't think it's about the lawsuit, Odelia. I think this is about making Woobie look bad—about making the firm look incompetent and damaging its reputation."

Quiet, sweet Joan had hit the nail directly on its head. Considering what Carl had told me and the documents in front of me, I'd bet my Christmas bonus Joan was right. Well, okay, maybe not my whole bonus, but certainly the taxes on it.

TWENTY-SIX

I BEGGED OFF LUNCH with Kelsey and Joan and opted for a salad at my desk. In spite of Carl giving me the green light on Missing Link, I really didn't know where to go next. Steele had vanished into thin air. There were no witnesses or tracks, and certainly no bread crumbs dropped from the pockets of an Armani suit. I hadn't heard from Willie since Saturday, and without new information, I was at a dead end.

Goldberg-Rawlings—was there a connection between Steele's disappearance and the fact that one of his best friends worked for the firm our client was thinking about hiring in our place? I could be grasping for straws, but at this point I had nothing else to grab. Would Steele have said something to Tim while searching for advice? I could see Steele asking a trusted friend about the document situation without disclosing the client's name, but Steele is a cagey and cautious attorney. If he knew that Goldberg-Rawlings was our competition for Silhouette's legal business, he would never have mentioned the problem with the altered documents, not even hypothetically.

But did Steele even know about the possibility of Silhouette transferring its business to Goldberg-Rawlings?

I knew Carl had a lunch appointment, so I waited until close to two thirty before calling him. Ani picked up his line.

"Ani, it's Odelia. Is Carl around?"

"Not right now."

"It's very important that I speak to him for just a second. Could you call me as soon as he's back in the office?"

"If it's urgent, try him on his cell. He's on his way back to the office right now. I just spoke to him."

I immediately punched in the number Ani gave me. Carl picked up on the first ring. I could hear traffic noise in the background.

"Carl, it's Odelia. I have one quick question for you."

"Shoot."

"Did Steele know about Silhouette considering Goldberg-Rawlings?"

Carl paused. I could almost see him thinking the question over and prayed he didn't look to the ceiling or close his eyes as he did in the office when lost in thought.

"No, I'm pretty sure he didn't. I just found out myself on Friday."

After hanging up, I leaned my elbows on my desk and rested my chin on my clasped hands. I just couldn't seem to wrap my brain around all the facts and corral them into making sense. Going around in mental circles was tiring and confusing, like a dog chasing its own tail. I needed caffeine. No, what I needed was a pumpkin spice latte, but with a cold I knew I shouldn't be indulging in milk products. Oh, but what the hell.

Starbucks was a short walk from our office building. By cutting through our parking garage, I could make better time. I had skipped my usual morning walk because I felt lousy, but now it felt good to be on the move, even if only for a block and with a slightly runny nose.

I was on my way back when I spied Tim Weber walking quickly on the far side of the parking garage. Hmm, might be just the person I needed to see. I started to call his name when he stopped and looked about. He continued walking, constantly keeping watch over one shoulder or another. Instinctively, I ducked behind a parked car and watched. Someone in another parked car lightly tapped a horn. Tim gave a subtle wave in the direction of the horn and started toward it. Clutching my latte, I dashed between two SUVs parked a little closer.

I couldn't see who he was meeting, so I started tiptoeing between cars, moving from one hiding place to the next as quietly as I could to get a closer look, all the while hoping no one else would see me and report me as a suspicious character.

Poking my head over the hood of a red Ford Focus, I saw the top of Tim's head several cars over just before it disappeared. Then I heard a car door shut. Whoever he was meeting, he had gotten in the car with them. I listened but heard no engine running or one start up, making me think they must be having their meeting in the parked car. Abandoning the Focus in favor of a larger Oldsmobile sedan, I managed to move a bit closer, trying not to let the heels of my pumps make too much noise on the concrete.

Worried that they might drive off before I could get a look at who Tim was with, I put down the latte, squatted, and moved another two vehicles over, all the while praying they were too preoccupied with their discussion to notice a two-hundred-plus-pound woman duck walking—in a skirt, no less. To add to my difficulty, my nose started running in earnest. I dug into my suit jacket pocket but only produced the change and receipt from my latte, not a single scrap of tissue. Disgusted, but under pressing circumstances, I wiped my nose with the back of my hand and sniffled lightly. I was now hunkered down sideways between an SUV and a minivan just a couple of cars away from my prey, thankful to find two large vehicles in such close proximity. I could hear two voices—Tim's and a woman's. They sounded like they were arguing.

"You think I'm overreacting?" It was Tim's voice.

"Yes, overreacting." The woman's voice was angry. He shushed her. She lowered her voice and said something else I couldn't hear.

Tim responded, but he also had lowered his voice. I was straining to hear but didn't dare get any closer. Every now and then I heard Tim say a word or two, but that was all. But when I heard Tim say "Mike," I stopped breathing. The woman said something else and whatever it was, it agitated Tim Weber. He pushed the door open and got out of the car.

"No!" Tim said, raising his voice. "I told you he's not to be harmed. We'll just stick with the original plan, and that's final."

The woman said something else. I strained to hear, trying to recognize the voice, but I came up empty.

Just before Tim shut the door, I heard him say, "We'll talk about it Wednesday when I'm back in town. We'll meet here, same time, if that's okay with you. Until then, let's relax and not do anything stupid." Again, the woman said something I couldn't hear.

As the Honda drove off, I stayed hidden, giving Tim time to walk back to the building. I watched him through the windows of the SUV, gradually starting to stand as he walked away. I was partway erect when I turned my head and smacked the side of my face on the large side mirror. Immediately, I dropped down and clamped a hand over my mouth in case I let out a yelp. Just what I needed, another black eye, especially when the other was finally healed. Oh well, at least this time there wasn't a photographer standing by to memorialize my humiliation.

It was then that a bit of important information floated to the top of my swampy brain. Marvin Dodd had said that over dinner, Steele had shown him the photo of me in the scuffle at the grocery store. No—what Marvin Dodd had said was that Steele had shown it to *us*. Steele generally hung out with Marvin Dodd, Walter Yamada, and Tim Weber. Mr. Yamada told me he had been out of town. Tim Weber said he hadn't seen Steele in a while. But Marvin Dodd had definitely used the word *us* when talking about Thursday-night tennis and dinner at Steele's place.

When I got back to my office, I was shaking. To make matters worse, I had left my latte in the parking garage. I placed a call to Marvin Dodd. He came on the line almost immediately.

"Has Mike turned up yet, Odelia?"

"No, sorry, not a sign of him, though his car was located at LAX. Looks like he left town."

"Strange, very strange."

"Mr. Dodd, I'd like to ask you one very quick question."

"Of course, go right ahead."

I cleared my throat. "That Thursday night, the one right before Steele disappeared, you had dinner at his place, correct?"

"That's right. He and I played tennis, then he whipped up some dinner. Did you know that Mike's a great cook? Better than my wife any day of the week."

"No, I didn't." Another hidden talent I knew nothing about. "So it was just the two of you for tennis and dinner, right?"

"Yes and no. Mike and I played tennis, but Tim Weber came by for dinner."

"You're sure about that?"

"Sure am. Tim dropped by after a meeting at his office." He paused. "Why? Is there a problem?"

"No, just wanted to make sure I had my facts straight. We're going over every detail of Steele's last days before he disappeared."

"Good idea. Please keep me posted."

Dollars to donuts whatever happened to Steele, his good buddy Tim Weber knew all about it. I thought about calling Dev, but after my last attempt to tell him anything, I was hesitant to bring up the subjects of Donny Oliver and Mike Steele in any capacity. Besides, there was absolutely no evidence that Tim was talking about Mike Steele. I mean, I was pretty sure he was, but even if the police decided to listen to me and question Tim, I knew he would somehow explain the conversation away, like any good scumbag attorney would. Then all eyes would turn to me—the crazy woman who eavesdrops while squished between cars.

Besides, now I had an added worry. If I did go to the police, would whoever was in the car with Tim decide not to listen to his orders and hurt Steele in some way? I never did get a look at the woman in the car or the license plate. All I saw was a dark-colored, late-model Honda driving away.

I temporarily solved the issue by blowing my nose and going home.

TWENTY-SEVEN

HALLOWEEN—A NIGHT FOR pint-sized ghosts and goblins. Generally, I love Halloween. Greg and I would dress up and hand out candy to the little kids who came to his door. Most were from the neighborhood, and they all knew Greg and Wainwright. Even Wainwright would get into the act by allowing us to stick something on his head in a makeshift costume.

This Halloween, I was home alone. Greg did call and ask if I wanted to come over, but I declined. My cold had flared up overnight, and I had called in sick. Most of the day, I fretted over Steele and whether or not I should tell Dev. But when Dev called in the early afternoon to see how I was doing, I clammed up, even after he apologized for speaking so harshly to me before. He offered to come over and keep me company, but I turned that down, too.

I called my dad to see how he was doing, and he invited me over. I was already on pins and needles, and the last thing I needed was an evening with my nutso stepfamily, although Halloween did seem like an appropriate holiday to spend with them. Again, I used my cold as a good excuse, just as I used it as an excuse to not attend Donny's funeral earlier today.

The last call I made was to Sally. She'd called the day before while I was making my Starbucks run, and I didn't return the call until tonight. We chatted briefly about Tom Bledsoe's call to me, but both of us were empty-headed on where to go from here with Donny's murder.

Everything in my life seemed to be at a stalemate.

Starting at about six thirty, small batches of kids and their parents rang my doorbell. Each time, I would put on a smile and dispense sugar and chocolate to happy ghouls and fairy princesses. After eight, the trick-or-treaters were sparse. It was just before nine when I decided to turn off my front light. Just as I reached the switch, my doorbell rang. I grabbed the candy bowl and opened the door.

"Trick or treat," squeaked a miniature pirate. Next to him stood a grownup in his own snazzy pirate costume.

"Nice costumes, guys," I said, holding out the bowl to the child. "And you're my last trick-or-treaters of the night, so take a big handful."

The little boy stuck his small fist into the bowl and lifted out an amazing amount of candy. The adult followed, but as he leaned forward to grab the candy he whispered to me, "Hello, little mama, long time no see."

I started to drop the bowl, but Willie caught it.

"So, is this your new bodyguard?" I asked Willie once I recovered from my shock and ushered him and his little companion inside.

"Absolutely. I believe in training them young."

He turned to the boy, who was about five. "Henry, somewhere around here is a kitty cat. But if I were you, I'd use my hook hand to play with him. He's not too friendly."

"I need to go potty," Henry whined.

I looked at Willie, who was making himself comfortable on my sofa, then at Henry, who looked pained. With a sigh, I steered the little guy down the hall to the guest bathroom. I left Henry to do his thing and returned to the living room. I don't know much about little boys, but I do know that good aim in one is considered a virtue.

I sat on the sofa and turned toward Willie. "I'd say what a nice surprise, but that would be an understatement. Where's Enrique?"

"Enrique's busy, but he sends his love." Willie studied me. "Boy, you have a nasty cold."

I grabbed a tissue from a box on the coffee table and wiped my nose. "And you have an uncanny knack for showing up unexpectedly."

"I could have called, but the desire to see your smiling face was overwhelming."

"And what if I'd had company?"

"I would have improvised." He grinned. "I'm good at that."

"And what if it had not been Halloween?"

"Then I would have been the pizza delivery guy." He took off his hat to expose the familiar pale forehead and balding pate. "One way or another, we would have had this conversation in person."

"It's that important?"

Willie reached out and placed a hand on my arm. "Odelia, this is very important, and you need to listen to every word I have to say."

Now he had my full attention, at least until Henry wandered in and sat down with us. Willie stopped and chuckled. "Hmm, I didn't think about what I'd do with Henry once I got inside, but I'd rather he not hear this. His mother would skin me alive if he started babbling in an inappropriate manner."

I turned to the boy. "Henry, you like videos?" The boy nodded. "I have a small TV in the kitchen with a video player. Would you like to watch something, maybe *E. T.*? There's also cookies and milk in the deal for you." The child nodded again, this time with more enthusiasm.

After I settled Henry at the kitchen table with his snack and started the video, I returned to Willie. In each hand, I carried a cold bottle of Samuel Adams for us.

"Is this about Steele?" I asked, handing him the beer.

"Yes and no, little mama." He pushed aside the beard and took a big swig of his beer. "Good grog, wench. Arghhh!"

I stared at him with furrowed brows, but my attempt at a menacing look was diluted by the sniffles. Willie only laughed.

"Like I said, yes and no." He reached into his pocket and produced a flash drive, which he handed to me. "There are some interesting photos on here concerning both matters."

I turned the small, black rectangle over several times in my hand and stared at it, as if merely looking at it would produce the pictures.

"Starting with your old pal Donny Oliver, there's a photo of him and a woman who is not his wife coming out of a motel on a couple of occasions. The husband of the woman commissioned the photos."

"You mean he was having her tailed?"

He shook his head. "Nope. And here's where it gets interesting. For whatever reason, seems the guy's client paid to have Oliver followed and photographed. The guy who took the pics said when his client saw them he almost had a heart attack."

"Who's the woman?"

"Guy wouldn't say." Willie chuckled. "He had no ethics at all about selling me the photos of Oliver, but said he couldn't reveal his client's name because it would breach his client's confidentiality."

"That's asinine."

"Well, so is making your living snapping photos of cheating couples."

"But why didn't he turn these over to the police? This woman or her husband could be Donny's killer."

"Money, little mama, it's all about the money." He took another draw from his beer. "Confidentiality, or lack of it, aside, this guy was going to try to blackmail his client, but once I put the word out that I was looking for anything to do with Oliver or his murder, the guy shopped them to me. He figured I'd pay more money for them. He was right."

"How much did you pay for these? I'll pay you back, of course."

Willie threw back his head and laughed. "God, I love talking to you. It's like *Leave It to Beaver* but live and in color."

I twitched my nose in annoyance. "Well, I don't expect you to foot the bill since I asked for a favor."

"Trust me, little mama, you can't afford these photos. Besides, it's my pleasure. Call it an early Christmas gift."

Again, I fiddled with the flash drive as I spoke. "You said there were other photos."

"Yes. I had people tailing the key people of both candy companies since Saturday. They took photos, asked questions, and in general found out everything they could." He took another swallow of beer. "Sweet Kiss seems on the up-and-up, and so does your client, Silhouette. The only thing we found interesting is the company the CEO of Silhouette is keeping these days. On Sunday, Ben Walker, the CEO of Silhouette, had brunch in La Jolla with a couple of people, a man and a woman, both attorneys. My associate took photos and traced the plates on their cars. The woman is Frances Elizabeth Evans, an attorney at your law firm, I believe."

"Yes, Fran is working on the Silhouette case. Was the man Carl Yates?"

"The man was an attorney for another law firm—Goldberg something."

"Tim Weber of Goldberg-Rawlings?" My voice was getting nasally, so I took time out to blow my nose.

Willie nodded. "Yes, that's the guy."

I leaned back into the sofa cushions to think about what I'd just learned.

So Fran was the insider trying to throw Woobie under the bus. Although I don't like Fran, I really never thought she'd stoop so low that she would alter documents. I had always thought of her like another Mike Steele, obnoxious but ethical.

"But if Fran is behind the document tampering, that's something that could get her disbarred—both of them disbarred, if it can be proved they did it in cahoots. Why would they risk their careers like that?"

Willie reached over and thumped me on my forehead several times with an index finger. "Money, money, money—how many times do I have to say that to you?" Changing from a finger to his palm, he felt my forehead. "You have a slight fever, little mama."

Annoyed, I shook off his hand. My health was not the issue.

"It can't just be about money. Attorneys make good money, and who would pay them, especially her, to fool with documents? Silhouette wouldn't have any reason to do that." I gave it some thought before continuing. Willie was patient and let me think it through. "One of our partners told me that Silhouette is talking about dumping us and hiring Goldberg-Rawlings, Tim Weber's firm."

Willie gave it quick thought. "The mess with the case could be to make your firm look bad so that the decision would be easier. Weber and Walker could have been talking about that."

"And Fran is somehow tied in, making sure Woobie gets the axe?"

"Is she a partner?"

I shook my head. "No, a senior associate, but she's up for partnership. The decision should come down before the end of the year. That's what's so strange. By tanking Woobie, she's tanking her own future."

"Unless she thinks her future isn't with your firm."

"But to risk disbarment?" I shook my head. "And Walker could just fire us. He doesn't need to damage his company's own lawsuit to get rid of Woobie." I paused. "You found no link between Sweet Kiss and Fran Evans and/or Tim Weber?"

"None, but we've only just started looking into it. Maybe they're playing both sides of the fence."

"And what about Steele?" I gave Willie a quick rundown of what I saw and overhead in the parking lot.

"Excuse me, little mama, but I'm going to think on that while I use your facilities."

I pointed him in the right direction and got up to check on Henry. The poor little guy was sound asleep with his head on my kitchen table. Chocolate cookie crumbs surrounded his mouth and the milk was gone. I wondered about his mother and her relationship with Willie. About a year and a half ago Willie had invited me to go with him; to travel the world and live in luxury on his scam money. My relationship with Greg was up in the air then, but I still declined. And here we are again, Greg and I up in the air once more.

"Cute for a rug rat, isn't he," Willie whispered in my ear, his breath warm and close and smelling of beer.

"Is he yours?"

Willie looked into my eyes. "He's not some love child I reclaimed after my wife died, if that's what you're thinking."

I started to move Henry, but Willie stopped me. "Leave him be. One thing I've learned being around Henry is that he can sleep anywhere."

We adjourned to the living room and resettled on the sofa. We both sipped our beers in thoughtful reflection.

"About your boss," Willie said, breaking the silence. "My guess is these two sharks were setting him up to take the fall for the document tampering. With him out of the way, it would be easy to do. Also, I had all that personal information run on your boss and nothing came up."

"Nothing?"

"Just one charge for the Ojai Valley Inn for one night, but if he was a no-show at the hotel, that would be normal. As far as anything else, absolutely nothing—no checks have cleared, no credit cards used, no activity at all regarding his finances since the day you told me he left town, except for that one charge."

It was my turn to look into Willie's eyes. "You haven't told me the bad stuff yet, have you?"

"Good stuff, bad stuff, it's all the same."

I scrunched my brows at him again.

"No, little mama, I haven't even touched on the bad stuff." He tipped back his beer and drained the bottle, putting it empty on the coffee table when he was finished.

"I know this is going to go in one pretty ear and out the other, but I want you to stop looking into both the Oliver murder and this thing with your boss."

My mouth dropped open. "Then why did you give me all this information if only to tell me to stop? That doesn't make sense."

He took my hand and held it. "I gave it to you so you could give it to the authorities. Maybe someone like that Newport Beach cop who hangs around here."

I looked at him with surprise.

"Don't look so shocked, little mama. I know all about the good detective Frye. I also know your whoopee-on-wheels boyfriend isn't around as much these days. I'd give you some words of wisdom on that, but I wouldn't be entirely objective."

Feeling both astonished and annoyed, I just stared at him. He grinned at me.

"Anyway," he continued, "these photos and what you heard in the parking lot will help Frye do his job." Willie chuckled. "Not that I'm in the habit of helping the police, but right now I'm more interested in keeping you out of it."

I pulled my hand away. "Is there a man in my life not interested in keeping me out of it?"

Ignoring my question, Willie continued. "Did you ever make further contact with Let Mother Do It?"

"No. I found nothing on them when I did a business search, and when I tried calling again, the number was disconnected."

Willie seemed extremely relieved at the news and leaned back on the sofa. "Good."

"Why? What's the big deal about a cleaning company run by an old lady?"

Willie turned his head and stared at me a long time. "Let Mother Do It is a cleaning company, little mama, but not the kind you think." He took a deep breath. "They specialize in vermin eradication—of the human variety."

My addled brain was quickly connecting the dots, but my consciousness was erasing them as fast as it could, trying to shield me from the truth. "You mean—" I started to say, then stopped short, unable to get the words out.

Willie nodded and once again took my hand. "Let Mother Do It is a hit-man outfit, Odelia. You dug up hired killers, and they don't like that."

TWENTY-EIGHT

EVEN THOUGH I WAS already thinking about the possibility of a contract killer being involved, the news of my accomplishment brought on a fit of coughing, and the fit of coughing brought on gagging and vomiting. As I knelt on the floor of the guest bathroom, ridding my stomach of the beer and my earlier supper, Willie held my hair out of the way and caressed my forehead with a damp cloth.

Exhausted, I leaned my arm across the toilet seat and rested my head on it. Tears ran down my face. "I found that card at Steele's place. What does that mean? Is he dead?"

"We don't know if he's dead. And from what you overheard yesterday, if it pertains to Steele, he might still be alive."

"Steele's old cleaning lady said someone at the office referred Mother to him, gave him the card. Someone at the office connected Steele with the people who ... who ... " My voice trailed off.

"Generally, professional hit men don't have business cards. But in this case, I'd say it was used to reel him in, to set the trap."

Willie unrolled some toilet tissue and gave it to me so I could blow my nose. When I did, my head felt like it was going to explode.

"You still feel sick?"

I shook my head, which only increased the throbbing in my skull. He helped me up. After rinsing the cloth out, he wiped my face. I took the cloth from him and finished the job.

"Would you excuse me while I run upstairs and brush my teeth?"

"Go right ahead, little mama, take all the time you need."

I started to go but a thought made me turn in the doorway. "You have more to tell me, don't you?"

He nodded. "Yes, I do."

"Then tell it to me now. No sense cleaning myself up twice."

He put the lid down on the toilet and sat me on it. "My informants tell me that Let Mother Do It supplied the trigger man on the Donny Oliver murder."

"What?" I raised my voice, then remembered the child sleeping nearby, though if my coughing and vomiting hadn't wakened him, nothing would. "But I thought they were connected with Steele's disappearance."

"It seems they might be involved with both."

"What?" I cried again, this time in an exaggerated whisper.

I raked my hands through my hair until both palms cupped my skull, then I squeezed gently, hoping I could squeeze out both the pain and the information being given to me.

"How could this be, Willie? Was Mother running a two-for-one special? Did someone rack up some frequent killer miles? What?"

"Go upstairs and clean up." Willie once more raised me to my feet. "Then we'll discuss it—that is, if you're up to it."

When I came back down, my face was washed, my teeth brushed, and I was wearing fresh jammies and a robe. I had also taken a couple of Extra Strength Tylenol.

In my hand was a printout of one of the photos of Donny that Willie had purchased. After cleaning up, I had stuck the flash drive into my computer to see who was with Donny at the motel. At first, I didn't believe what I was seeing. Then I checked every single photo. Donny seemed to be having trysts with several women, but there was no doubt in my mind who the woman was in the photo in my hand. I knew then that the Tylenol would barely scratch the surface of my headache.

I found Willie in the kitchen making us some tea, but no Henry.

"Hope you don't mind me making myself at home," he said when he saw me, "but I thought you could use some tea. It will help you feel better." He had removed his pirate's shirt and sash and washed the makeup from his face. Standing in my kitchen in a tee shirt and jeans, he looked like the Willie I remembered.

"Thanks, that'll be great. Where's Henry?"

"On his way home. Enrique was waiting outside for us. I sent them both off."

"You're here with me without a bodyguard?"

"Little mama, it's not me who needs the bodyguard." He handed me my tea in a big white mug with kittens on it. His mug had a happy face. "Now drink up, and let's see what we know."

I held out the photo. "I know who this woman is," I said to him, my face grim.

"You don't seem too happy about that."

"I'm not. I'm in a complete meltdown of shock."

Willie studied the photo. "And?"

"And it's Johnette Morales, a friend from high school. Her husband was having an affair about a year or so ago with Donny's wife."

Willie gave a low whistle. "What tangled webs we weave."

"When were these photos taken?"

"Just a month or two ago, I believe. Why?"

I told Willie about Cindy and Victor, and about what Johnette had told me at the reunion about her suspicion that Victor was having an affair.

"You think this was payback or revenge sex?" he asked.

"Seems so, doesn't it?"

After pulling out a notepad and paper, I joined Willie at the kitchen table. Seamus, deciding Willie had been in the house way too long without his permission, came downstairs and sniffed him with great interest. Willie scratched the animal behind his ragged ear and was rewarded with a mild purr.

"He's a lot friendlier this time around."

"This time around, he's not being held hostage in a sack."

I wasn't sure where to begin with my notes, so I simply drew a line down the middle of the page. On the left, I put Donny Oliver's name; on the right, Steele's name. Under Donny's column, I listed the suspects I knew about: Cindy Oliver, Sally Kipman, Johnette Morales, Victor Morales, Tom Bledsoe, even me. Under Steele's column, I listed Fran Evans, Tim Weber, Tom Bledsoe, and Karen Meek.

Willie pointed to Steele's column. "You didn't put yourself down."

"Me? Why would I put my name down? I didn't have motive to get rid of him."

"From what I hear about this guy, everyone had motive to make him disappear, especially the ladies." He grinned at me.

"Be that as it may, I didn't get rid of my boss. Nor did I kill Donny."

"Still, you and this Bledsoe guy are the two common denominators."

I thought about that and wrote my name under Steele's column and circled both it and Tommy's name. "But," I said, thinking about Let Mother Do It and the type of business it is, "the same person doesn't have to be responsible for both. Two totally separate people could have hired them."

"True, and according to my sources, Mother is doing quite a booming business these days."

I looked at him with interest. "You're going to tell me everything you know about Let Mother Do It, aren't you?"

"Not sure. I'm worried that the more you know, the more likely you'll run off and play hero. My goal is to keep you from these killers."

"Killers? There's more than one? I thought hired assassins worked alone. Although I'm having a hard time imagining the old woman on the phone chasing people down with a gun or kidnapping someone as fit as Steele."

Willie looked at me, considering something for a moment. "Rumor, and it's only rumor, is that Let Mother Do It is a band of women."

"All women?"

He nodded. "That's the word on the street. Supposedly, they came on the scene about four or five years ago, just a single job now and then, but then word got out about their effectiveness and reasonable rates."

"Reasonable rates?" I was getting tired of parroting questions but couldn't help myself. "What are they, the Costco of murder and mayhem? Do they sell hits in large economy sizes like jars of dill pickles?"

"Laugh all you want, but I hear they're doing quite a business and operate with anywhere from ten to fifteen assassins. What's more, their clients are not from the traditional criminal community."

Taking a quick second, I thought about that newsflash. Let Mother Do It was bringing contract murder to the masses? What a concept.

"But if they are doing such a great business, why isn't there more on the news? There should be bodies strewn hither and yon."

Willie shrugged. "Not if the jobs are spread out geographically or if they're made to look like an accident or a botched robbery."

I held up a hand in the halt position. "Or a carjacking?"

"Sure, why not?"

"Tom Bledsoe's wife was killed in a carjacking a few years ago. They never found the person who did it." I underlined Tommy's name twice.

With a headache that had been ratcheted down a notch by the Tylenol, I tried to wrap my brain around what I was being told. It boggled my mind and made me want to whimper on behalf of humanity. A band of hit men—make that hit *women*—catering to everyday people, giving new meaning to "cleaning house" and "pest control."

"When I talked to Mother, she said they didn't advertise but that their business was all from referrals. Of course, at the time, I thought she was talking about housecleaning."

"They might actually be housekeepers, little mama." Willie smiled and drank some tea. "Housecleaning may be a front—a legitimate business to cover the criminal activities. Drug dealers do that all the time. It helps launder money. The government gets suspicious when people are living well with no visible means of support. Even I have legitimate business concerns—not under William Proctor, of course."

I raised an eyebrow at him before continuing. "But how do potential clients contact them for hits? Do they have a website? Advertise in the Penny Saver? Aren't past clients worried about handing out referrals?" I put down my pen and held my still-aching head in both hands. "I mean, say I wanted to bump someone off. How would I go about contacting them?"

"Oh, no, you don't, little mama." Willie wagged a finger at me. "This is exactly what I was afraid of. You are not to try to contact these crazy people. You lucked out when all they did was change their phone number. Probably a throwaway cell anyway."

Ignoring his warnings, I persisted. "But how do potential clients contact them?"

"You just never mind about that. Give this information to the police and walk away, preferably to Santa Fe or Madison or Hong Kong for a week or two or three until this blows over."

A yawn attacked me, and I was helpless to stop it.

"You're sick and exhausted, Odelia. Why don't you head on up to bed."

"What about you?"

"Don't worry about me. I'm going to hang out down here on your sofa."

"I have a guest room upstairs."

"I'm not here to sleep, and I'm not staying to make sure no one breaks in."

Willie reached under his shirt and pulled out a gun. He put it on the kitchen table.

"I'm staying to make sure you don't break out. I know you, little mama. As soon as I leave tonight, sick or not, you'll be out that door, stirring up trouble in the middle of the night."

I twitched my nose and stared at the gun. "Is that necessary?"

He chuckled. "Probably not for you, but I'm still a wanted man, remember?"

I wondered briefly if I should tell Willie that Mother had my name and where I worked, then decided against it. It would only worry him more, and I was worried enough for the two of us.

TWENTY-NINE

WHEN I CAME DOWNSTAIRS the next morning, I felt a lot better—not great, but better. Willie was gone, and a fresh pot of coffee was waiting for me. A clean mug sat next to my coffeemaker, on top of which balanced a sheet of paper torn from my notepad: *LM—1) the police; 2) disappear—in that order. Be good and be careful!* The words *be careful* were underlined and circled.

A band of hit women?

When I woke up this morning, that was the first thing that came to mind. For a brief moment, I thought I had dreamed the whole crazy idea—but I hadn't. Willie's informants had discovered that Donny had been killed by Let Mother Do It, a band of women who had turned contract killing into a booming cottage industry. Whatever happened to ladies earning extra money holding Tupperware parties or selling Mary Kay?

But the question remained: who had hired Let Mother Do It in the first place? No matter who held the gun, ultimately the real killer was the one who plopped down money for services rendered.

And did Let Mother Do It also kidnap Steele—and, if so, was he still alive? Generally, women were so resourceful and creative, who knows what else they could be into as a business venture. Maybe they also ran a kidnapping service on the side. You know, just for a little mad money.

Sitting down at the table with some toast and coffee, I pored over my notes from the night before. In less than twenty-four hours, Johnette Morales had floated to the top of the suspect list, fighting for space alongside Victor Morales and Cindy Oliver. Tom Bledsoe was a long shot, but you never know … especially with a contract killer in the mix and the suspicious eye I was now casting at his wife's death.

I turned my attention to Steele's side of the paper and focused on Fran and Tim. After about a half cup of coffee, my tired, mucus-sodden brain loosened, and I remembered that Tim Weber was meeting again with the woman in the car. He had said he'd see her Thursday—today—same time and place. That would mean just after three thirty in the parking garage.

Willie had been right. If he had not stayed, I would have been out the door last night as soon as I had printed those photos, pounding on Johnette's door, demanding answers. The night's rest had helped my cold and given me time to think. I still intended to get some answers from Johnette, but now I'd be doing it in a some-what reasonable state of mind in the light of day.

Halfway through my shower, I had an idea. Clutching a towel to my still-dripping body, I called Sally Kipman. After a couple of rings, Sally answered.

"I have some information," I told her without identifying myself. She hesitated, probably not sure who was calling at seven thirty in the morning.

"Is that you, Odelia? I was just going to call you." She sounded upset.

"Yes. I have information about Donny." She didn't respond. "Sally, what's wrong?"

"Something horrible has happened, Odelia. Cindy's mother, that nice Mrs. Poppin—she's been shot."

"What?" The news caused me to nearly drop the phone. "How did it happen? And when?"

"Poor Cindy's had to be given a tranquilizer, she's in such shock."

"But what happened?" I nearly shouted into the phone.

Sally paused before answering. I heard her sniff back tears. "Cindy's mother was shot last night by a trick-or-treater." She paused again. "Someone shot her when she opened up the door to pass out candy. She's in intensive care right now. It's pretty touch and go. I heard she's in a coma."

Suddenly I wanted to be sick, but this morning no one would be here to wipe my forehead. Cindy Oliver had lost a husband and almost a mother in less than two weeks. My mind felt like it had been zapped by a cattle prod. I fought back the nausea. "But who did it?"

"That's the thing, no one saw it. Cindy had taken the girls to a Halloween party at a local library while her parents stayed home to pass out candy. Her father never even heard the shot. Apparently, they used a silencer, and Mr. Poppin had the TV on pretty loud in the den. The oldest girl called Lucas this morning to tell him."

A silencer? I may not know much about the psyche of a murderer, but on TV, random killers do not use silencers. On TV, professionals use silencers. Immediately my shocked brain made the leap to Let Mother Do It. But why Mrs. Poppin? Then I had another thought. Maybe Mrs. Poppin wasn't the target. Maybe Cindy had been the intended victim. Maybe Let Mother Do It had been paid for a twofer, Mr. and Mrs. Oliver, but since Donny had gone to the reunion solo, they had to wait for another go at Cindy.

"Sally, I may have some information that might shed some light on everything. But you'd better sit down." I gave her a quick rundown of what I had learned the night before. When I was done, there was a very long pause.

"Wow," she finally said. "Are you sure your friend's information is correct?"

"Pretty sure, and so was he." I wrapped the towel around me and secured it. My wet skin was starting to feel chilly. Definitely not a good thing with my cold.

"Hate to say it, Odelia, but do you think maybe Johnette slipped a cog and hired this outfit to take out both Cindy and Donny?"

My stomach turned. I didn't want to think about sweet Johnette being a cold-blooded killer, but the evidence was gathering like dust bunnies under my bed in favor of that likelihood. Then I remembered the real reason I had called Sally and decided more than ever the timing was right.

"You up to playing Cagney to my Lacey today?"

THIRTY

A LITTLE BEFORE NINE, I was pulling up in front of Johnette's house. I had hoped that Sally would be able to come with me, but she had an important meeting scheduled at work this morning. However, she said her afternoon was cleared for takeoff. We agreed to meet for lunch at one o'clock. I expected to find Johnette home alone, with Victor already off to work, so I was surprised when Victor yanked open the door. He was dressed in jeans and a faded tee shirt and hadn't shaved or combed his hair. His eyes were dark and haggard.

"What's going on, Victor?"

"Johnette's not with you, by any chance?" He looked past me, perhaps half-expecting Johnette to be hiding, reading to pop out and yell *surprise*.

"No, I came here to talk to her."

He opened the door wider, and I walked in. In silence, I followed him once again to the cutesy-pie kitchen and sat at the kitchen table.

"You want some coffee? I just made some." He looked about to drop.

"Sit down, Victor. I'll get the coffee." I went to the cupboards and opened two before finding the mugs. I filled two and brought them to the table.

"Where's Johnette?"

He shook his head. "I don't know. I'm worried sick."

"Did you see the news this morning?" The Poppin shooting had been on the early morning news.

"Yes, I did. And Cindy called me."

"Do you think Johnette shot Mrs. Poppin? Maybe thinking she was Cindy?"

He shook his head. "I can't believe she'd do something like that. But …," his voice trailed off.

"But what, Victor?"

"I haven't seen Johnette since about eight last night. She was handing out candy, and I was watching TV. I remember her saying something about running out of candy and that she was going to the store for more. I didn't think anything about it until an hour later when she hadn't returned. I got up and noticed we still had plenty of candy. We hadn't run out at all."

I wrapped my hands around the warm mug. "She hasn't come home?"

Again, he shook his weary head. "I've been up all night, worried sick. I tried to call her cell phone but discovered she'd left it here. I even went out last night driving around, going between here and the store and up and down the streets throughout the city. Nothing."

"Did you call your boys?"

"No, not yet. I was going to wait until noon, in case she came back on her own. I didn't want to worry them."

"She's done this before, hasn't she, Victor?" I studied him.

He nodded. "Yes, a couple of times. Sometimes she'd be gone several hours or even a day. Once she took off for three days. I didn't want to put my boys through that again if she was just going to turn up as she'd done in the past."

"But when you heard the news about Cindy's mother, you began to worry that Johnette had something to do with it?"

"No! Johnette would never do anything like that. True, she's had problems, but she'd never hurt a fly. You know that, Odelia."

"I know that the Johnette I knew in school would never hurt anyone or anything intentionally, but we've all changed over the years. You said yourself the other day that Johnette had undergone treatment for serious depression."

"Once the depression set in," he said, tears welling, "she was never the same. She became moody and paranoid, swinging between zombie and hysteric. But I had hope. This past month, she was more like her old self, more like the lovely and sweet woman I married. Until this."

I took the photo of Donny and Johnette out of my bag and placed it on the table. "You had someone following Donny Oliver, didn't you?"

He looked at the photo and started crying in earnest, tears running down his stubbled cheeks. "Yes, I hired someone to follow and take photos of Donny. I was having it done so Cindy would have something to use against Donny. She always knew he had been cheating. I just never expected . . ."

"When were these taken?"

Grabbing a napkin from a holder on the table, he wiped his eyes and nose. "About two months ago." He looked at the photo, then up at me. "Where did you get this?"

"Seems your private snoop was planning on shaking you down for blackmail money after Donny's murder became public, but a friend of mine got the photos out of his hands."

Victor took a couple of sips of coffee and tried to pull himself together. "There were lots of pictures of Donny with other women, but as soon as I saw this one, I told the guy to stop."

"Did you ever discuss this with Johnette?"

"No. I just told Cindy I had photos that would help her get her divorce from Donny. I didn't tell either Johnette or Cindy about this particular photo." He lifted his face. "In fact, I'm not even sure Johnette knew about Cindy Oliver." He looked at me with a glimmer of hope in his eyes. "You said, Odelia, that she thought I was having an affair, but you didn't think she knew who it was with."

"She never mentioned a name to me."

I tumbled information around in my head, each thought hitting my brain like rolling, jagged rocks. Maybe the meeting with Donny wasn't about revenge sex, after all. Maybe Donny had contacted Johnette. Maybe he was the one who knew about the affair and decided to enlighten her. There was just this one photo of Johnette and Donny, and they didn't exactly look lovey-dovey in it. Either way, it still kept Johnette at the top of the suspect list. Maybe she paid someone to get rid of both of the Olivers. I didn't believe for a minute she did it herself, not unless they had a show on HGTV about making silencers.

I left Victor with the agreement that if he heard from Johnette, he would call me. Then I headed into the office for a few hours before meeting Sally.

I was shoveling through the mail and files on my desk when Carl Yates dropped by and closed the door. "Did you find out anything yesterday?"

"Yesterday I really was home sick. I have a cold."

"Yes, I can see that now." He leaned against the tall file cabinet next to the door, looking rather disappointed by my lack of news.

"However, I might have stumbled onto something. I'm just not totally sure yet."

"Mike's whereabouts?"

"No, still no idea about that, but I have a lead on what might have happened to him. I'm going to pursue it this afternoon, if you don't mind."

"By all means, Odelia." He stood straight and looked at me with great interest. "Is there something we should let the police know?"

Yeah, I thought, *there's a band of killer women on the loose. If they all go premenstrual at the same time, it'll cause worldwide havoc*. Instead, I slowly shook my head. "Not yet. I don't have that kind of evidence, just a lead."

Carl leaned forward, eyes locking onto mine. "Is there anything I should know about, Odelia?"

I hemmed and hawed, knowing my stalling was useless. Carl made a living out of getting to the bottom of things. He knew I was holding back something important, but I wasn't ready to tell him about Let Mother Do It. I was fairly sure he'd insist on calling the police, and I was worried that if the police got involved and Let Mother Do It had Steele, Steele would be toast for sure. They had killed Donny and were probably behind the attempt on Mrs. Poppin. I didn't like the idea of Steele being part of a trifecta. But knowing Carl, he'd keep us holed up in my tiny office until I gave in, so I threw him a bone—an important bone.

"Carl, how closely does Fran Evans work with Silhouette—you know, individually?"

"Why?"

I answered his question with a question. "Has she given any indication of not being happy here at the firm? Any rumblings about her looking for other employment?"

While he considered my questions, I reached into my tote bag and pulled out a photo from a manila folder. It was one of the photos of Fran and Tim Weber with Ben Walker. I handed it to Carl and gave him time to study it.

He held the photo in one hand and lightly shook it at me. "It's Fran with Ben Walker, the new CEO over at Silhouette."

"Do you know who the other guy is?" He shook his head, so I enlightened him. "That's Tim Weber, an attorney with Goldberg-Rawlings. Tim is also supposedly a close friend of Steele's."

"You think Fran had something to do with the documents and Mike's disappearance?" He asked the question dead-on, without a hint of surprise or shock.

"It's just speculation at this point, but I'm thinking that maybe Fran doctored or had someone doctor the Silhouette documents so that the firm would look bad."

I stopped, thinking I had to sneeze, but it was a false alarm.

"If the firm looked incompetent, it would be easier to convince them to go with Goldberg-Rawlings." I shrugged. "Maybe she was interviewing with Goldberg. Maybe she was going to leave and take the client with her, though why she would do that when she's just a few months away from partnership is beyond me."

Carl stared at the photo again and shook his head. His mouth was a tight slash across his flushed face. "She wasn't going to make partner, at least not this year. The partnership committee decided that she wasn't quite ready for the responsibility and suggested she wait one more year. She was told that just over a month ago."

All of a sudden, a new motive came into play. "Steele's on the partnership committee, isn't he?"

"He chairs it, Odelia."

Motives and theories were whirling around in my stuffy head like sugar in a cotton candy machine.

"Would being passed over for partner be motive enough to tank Steele and the firm?" I studied Carl, looking for answers. "I mean, if Fran tampered with the documents, that would be cause for disbarment, correct?"

Carl nodded. "Absolutely."

"Even with all the perks and status of partnership, would losing that be enough to risk your law license and even possibly wind up in jail?"

Carl started to say something, then stopped.

"What is it, Carl?"

Whatever Carl wanted to say, it was making him uncomfortable. Finally, he spit it out. "Did you know that Mike and Fran were having an affair? Or rather had one?"

I shrugged. "That was years ago, shortly after she came to the firm. You think she's been harboring ill feelings all this time? Isn't there a statute of limitations on the whole 'woman scorned' thing?"

He took a deep breath. "They did have a fling years ago. We all knew it. But few know that they started up again earlier this year."

The news just about knocked me off my chair. Steele had been running around with Fran Evans and I didn't know about it?

"I guess that makes me not very observant."

"Mike told me about it a few months ago. It had been very short-lived and already over, but under the circumstances he felt he should take himself off the partnership committee. I convinced him to stay, but we agreed that he would not vote on Fran's matter. We told the other partners it was because of the long-ago relationship, but I doubt we fooled anyone."

Steele had disqualified himself from voting on Fran's candidacy because of their prior relationship. I looked directly at Carl. "Now, does that sound like a man who would tamper with documents?"

He smiled. "No, it doesn't."

Again, Carl looked uncomfortable. "I shouldn't be telling you this, Odelia, but without Mike's support and influence, there was no way Fran was going to be offered a partnership this year or maybe even ever. And I think she knew it. I understand she got quite angry with Mike when he told her he had withdrawn from the vote."

Losing a prestigious partnership and being dumped by a boyfriend. The motive list had expanded, but was it enough? I thought back through the past few months, trying to establish a checklist of Steele's recent flings. I almost started laughing when the timing fell into place.

"Steele dumped Fran for that Swedish pro volleyball player, didn't he?"

Carl just stared at me with frank amusement.

Okay, now we were getting somewhere. No partnership. No wealthy, handsome boyfriend. Dumped for a double-D bikini-clad beach bunny who lasted no longer than a breath mint. That just might make a tightly wound sourpuss Stanford law grad go career postal. But still, to throw away all those years of school and work and risk disbarment? A person would have to be delusional to think she wouldn't get caught. But then, only a delusional woman would think she could tame Mike Steele.

I set my jaw and looked straight at Carl. "I honestly don't think Steele is missing because he was tampering with the documents. I think he's missing because he discovered what was going on."

"You mean kidnapped? By Fran Evans?"

I shrugged. "And maybe not just kidnapped."

Carl's mouth fell open, then he shut it like a trap. "Odelia, enough is enough. We have to go to the police."

"No, Carl, please. If Steele is still alive, police involvement might spook whoever has him, and he might end up dead."

"I don't know, Odelia. This is way out of our hands and your league. This is a helluva lot more involved than just asking a few questions. Let's just call the police and at least get Fran pulled in for questioning."

He had no idea how far this truly was out of my league, and I felt it better that he didn't. I'd worked with Carl a long time. I knew that if the words *professional killers* popped out of my mouth, he'd be on the phone to the police in less time than it takes me to scarf down a Thin Mint. Not to mention he might find a way to legally kidnap me for my own safety.

The mental cotton candy machine spun faster and faster, turning gray matter into pink, sticky fluff. I had to convince Carl to let me continue with the investigation on my own.

"Make you a deal, Carl?"

I was making things up as I went, hoping something worthwhile and convincing dribbled from my mouth as I talked. Who was I kidding? This wasn't a game show. This was Steele's life, maybe even my life, on the line, but my gut told me it wasn't time for the police to go barging in, at least not until we knew who all the players were. There was still the unknown woman in the car. There was still the location of Steele. There was still the question of how far Let Mother Do It was paid to go. And there was still the matter of Donny Oliver and, now, Carolyn Poppin.

Carl stared at me with expectation. He was a litigation attorney; negotiations were part of his stock in trade. Whatever I said next had to be convincing or my case was blown. I started by clearing my throat.

"Make you a deal," I said again. "Give me a couple of days. Like I said, I have some leads. I might be able to find out if Steele is alive and where he's located. That way, we can lead the police there instead of having them trample around blindly. If Steele's not alive, what will it matter?"

"I don't know, Odelia. Alive or not, checking into this may put you in serious danger, something I'm very worried about. I can't risk your life like that."

I sighed. "I'm going to do it anyway, Carl. I'd rather do it with your cooperation."

"And what about Fran and this Weber guy?"

Funny how things turn around. Now it wasn't him telling me what we were going to do, but me telling him. I rather liked it.

"Keep an eye on Fran, but don't let on you know about her meeting with Walker. A day or two won't matter." Then I remembered something. "Do you know what kind of car Fran drives?"

Curiosity crossed Carl's face. "Yes, as a matter of fact. She drives a new Lexus, a white one. Why?"

"You're sure it's not a Honda?"

Carl chuckled in spite of the gravity of the situation. "Fran Evans drive a Honda? That's rich. Why?" he asked again.

"Just one of the leads I'm working."

Carl got serious again. "Two days, Odelia. That's all you have—today and tomorrow. At five o'clock tomorrow, if you don't have answers, you and I will call the police together. In the meantime, I'd like to keep this photo."

"But Carl, that's not two days, that's only a day and a half. Since it's already Thursday, why not give me the weekend, too?"

He pulled down his glasses and glared at me over the top of them.

Granted, I'm not the brightest bulb on the tree, but I know when to fold in the presence of power over my employment.

"Okay, five tomorrow it is."

Carl opened my door, but before he left he turned to me. "By the way, how did you get this photo?"

I hesitated. I certainly couldn't tell him about Willie.

"Let's just say I have friends in low places."

THIRTY-ONE

RIGHT ON SCHEDULE, SALLY met me at one o'clock at Jerry's Famous Deli. Over lunch, I filled her in on all the details I'd learned from Willie, not just the highlights I had given her earlier, including the fact that Let Mother Do It may be involved in both Donny's murder and Steele's disappearing act—and now, possibly, the shooting of Carolyn Poppin. What started out to be two separate mysteries were now converging into one single investigation with side attractions. I also gave her a rundown on my talk with Victor.

Sally slathered dark mustard on her pastrami on rye. Her puffy eyes and somber speech demonstrated her concern over the escalation of the problems at hand, but her healthy appetite didn't seem diminished one whit. In addition to her sandwich, she had ordered fries, a salad, and a milk shake, and had even contemplated a wedge of pie. I looked it all over while I worked my way through a large bowl of matzo ball soup, which was going down like a warm hug.

"What can I say," said Sally, noting my inventory of her side of the table, "I eat when under stress."

"Usually me too, but somehow it all ends up looking different on me."

Sally gave me a small smile and poured a pond of ketchup next to her fries. "And they're all women, these killers?"

"That's what my source says. Though we still need to find out who hired them."

"Outside of the murder-for-hire common thread, do you really think that Donny and Mrs. Poppin are related to the disappearance of your boss?"

"I'm not sure. Steele had nothing in common with Donny. He didn't even know either of the Olivers, as far as I can tell." I thought about my neatly drawn columns on the notepad and found it hard to swallow for a minute. "The only thing Donny and Steele seem to have in common is Tommy Bledsoe." I took another spoonful of soup and forced it down. "And me."

Sally shot her focus up from her food and met my eyes. I didn't know if I had suddenly leapt to the top of her private suspect list or if it was a look of sympathy. Either way, the look lasted only an instant. Still, it was uncomfortable.

She picked up her sandwich, and just before she bit into it, said, "A band of hit women, huh? No matter what you think about their business, you have to give them a gold star for resourcefulness."

THE LAST TIME THE meeting between Tim Weber and the mystery woman took place, it was in the short-term parking area of the garage. Sally and I decided it would be best to do surveillance from two cars parked at different angles a few stalls apart. That way, no matter where the meeting took place, at least one of us might have a good shot at seeing and hearing something. We also both made sure our cell phones were fired up, and I was suddenly thrilled that I had listened to Greg and upgraded recently to a new one. It was very small and came with a camera and text messaging.

I moved my old Toyota from the tenant area to the short-term parking area by 2:20, parking it almost next to where the meeting took place last time. Sally was already parked in the guest area, and I told her to stay put since she was just a few parking spaces away. The way our cars were situated, we could see the remaining empty stalls from several angles without being too close.

I slunk down in the front seat of my Toyota, peeping over the bottom edge of the window. I had both of the back windows half open so I could hear better, but I left the driver's door window closed to give the car the appearance of being locked up. It was far from a comfortable position. Soon, a dark green PT Cruiser pulled in through the gate and nosed around for available parking. It turned into a space that was behind me and head-to-head with Sally's Jeep. Since Sally wasn't known to Tim, she got to sit upright. She played her radio and appeared to be paging through a newspaper, waiting for someone.

Before the PT Cruiser even turned off its motor, I received a text message on my vibrating cell phone: *???*

The driver got out. It was a man in his twenties. *No*, I texted back.

A few minutes later, as my back was protesting its pretzel position, I spotted Tim Weber coming into the garage. He paused and looked around, no doubt seeking his rendezvous partner. He hung back, loitering near the elevator. I texted Sally: *Elev.*

I C, came the return reply.

Tim Weber hung around, hands in his pockets, shifting from foot to foot. Every few seconds he'd glance at his watch. I couldn't tell if he was nervous or just impatient thinking about all the billable time he was wasting. A few minutes later, a dark gray Honda pulled into the garage and parked next to the PT Cruiser. This time I could see that it was an Accord, one of the hybrid models. Whoever drove it was at least energy conscious. The parking spot was perfect as I could watch from either my rear-view mirror or side mirror and could sit a bit more comfortably. Sally was parked facing it, one car over.

Bingo, I texted.

As soon as the Honda was parked, Tim sauntered over to it, taking his time, as if he had secret meetings in parking garages every day. He looked first left, then right, and even settled his glance on Sally for a fleeting moment before opening the car door and climbing in.

My cell phone vibrated again, but this time there was a photo being sent. Using her own cell phone's camera, Sally had managed to get a snapshot of the woman in the car. I studied the photo on the phone screen with surprise. It was Karen Meek.

I texted Sally back: *!!!* Then followed it with another longer message: *U folo her I him*.

K, was her response.

Karen and Tim sat in her car talking, for what seemed like a very long time. At least to my scrunched-up body it seemed like an eternity. I could hear voices drifting across to where I sat in my car, but couldn't make out any words. I texted Sally: *?*

Mad, came the reply. Another fuzzy photo soon followed, this one showing Karen gesturing with her hands, her face screwed in emotion. The photo caught just the side of Tim's face. He wasn't looking at Karen and certainly didn't appear to be smiling.

Shortly thereafter, Tim got out of Karen's car. Like before, he held the door open and spoke to her. This time I could hear.

"I told you I'd take care of it." His voice was almost a raised growl. After that, he slammed the door and stalked out of the garage.

Karen Meek sat in her car a few minutes before turning on the engine and pulling out of the parking spot. As she headed for the parking attendant, I received a call from Sally.

"I'll follow her," she said. Another nearby engine turned over, and I watched as Sally pulled out to follow Karen.

"Were you able to overhear anything?" I asked her. "All I heard was Tim saying he'd take care of something."

"I heard something about Monday and Walker. Mean anything to you?"

"Walker is the CEO of our candy client, the one whose documents are screwy."

"Well, supposedly, Walker is making some decision by Monday." She paused. "Also something getting out of hand ... not what they planned ... no turning back." Another pause. "I couldn't hear the exact words clearly, but it sounded like Tim was going to meet someone to pay them and end it ... 'get it over with' is how he put it." In the background, I heard the parking attendant tell Sally how much she owed.

"Odd thing is," I told her, "Karen Meek has nothing whatsoever to do with our client, or shouldn't have. She was one of the last people I expected to see in that car today."

"But she's Steele's ex."

"Yes, but she's not involved with our firm's work." It was my turn to pause. "But she is engaged to Tommy." I stopped to think about it. "You know, Tommy seems to be the only one who might have motives in both cases. Steele is standing in his way with regard to Family Bond, and maybe he's worried about Karen changing her mind. And he might still be holding a grudge against Donny."

"True, but what about Mrs. Poppin? Even if Cindy was the real target, why would Tommy have her killed? And what does he have to do with this Weber guy? There doesn't even appear to be a connection between them, except that they both know Karen."

"And again," I replied, "what does Karen have to do with Silhouette and Goldberg-Rawlings taking over their legal work?" Although my cold was getting better, my head was starting to ache once more, this time with cerebral overload.

"Keep in touch," I told Sally. "I'm going to try to shake Tim and see what falls from the tree."

We told each other to be careful and ended the call. I rolled up my back windows, locked my car, and started for the building. My plan was to try and have another meeting with Tim today. I didn't exactly know what about, but I wanted to see him and gauge his behavior. Then I planned on sticking to him somehow, someway, like glue.

As soon as I entered the foyer of the office building, I spotted my prey. He was coming out of the bank located in the lower level and heading for the elevators. I picked up my pace to meet him there, but not so fast as to look like I was stalking him.

"Hi, Tim," I said to him nonchalantly, as if I just noticed him this minute.

Lost in thought, it took him a second to place me. "Oh, hi, Odelia." He plastered what looked like a forced smile on his face, then changed it to a look of worry. "Any news on Mike? Anything at all?"

"No news on him, but some odd things have come up." That plainly got his attention.

The elevator came and we both got on it, along with two other people, one of who pushed a button for a few floors below Woobie. I turned to Tim. "You know, I've been meaning to call you. There are a few more questions I'd like to ask you, when you have the time."

"About those odd things you mentioned?"

"Yes. What time is good for you?"

He checked his watch when the other people got off the elevator. "Now's good, if it's okay with you."

I laughed. "My place or yours?" We arrived at Woobie's floor, and I held the door open, waiting for his answer.

"Do you mind coming up to my office? I have a call coming in soon."

I let the door shut without my getting off. "Of course not. Whatever is most convenient. I appreciate you taking the time for this."

"No problem. Anything to help Mike."

Right, I thought, *anything my big fat…*

"Excuse me?"

Stirred from my private thoughts, I looked up at Tim, puzzled.

"Excuse me," he repeated. "I didn't catch what you said, you were mumbling."

"Oh nothing, just thinking out loud, trying to remember everything I wanted to ask you." I smiled at him and mentally kicked myself.

The elevator sides were mirrored, and I watched him in the reflection. He stared up at the floor numbers as each one between the two firms was passed, his Adam's apple rising and falling as he swallowed several times. I didn't know if it was me making him nervous or his conversation with Karen Meek, or maybe both. Either way, he looked emotionally stretched. I hoped it was me causing his discomfort. It was kind of fun making an attorney nervous for a change. Usually, it's the other way around.

When we reached the floor housing Goldberg-Rawlings, Tim nodded hello to their receptionist, but before he could direct me back to his temporary office I asked to use the ladies' room. Tim told me just to go on back to his office when I was done.

The ladies' room was identical to the one on Woobie's floor. There were three regular stalls and one handicapped stall. I noted that two of the stalls were occupied as I slipped into the one closest to the sink area. Shortly after, the women in the other stalls made their way to the sink to wash their hands. I was lost in my own thoughts about how to approach Tim when I thought I heard his name over the splash of water. I held my breath.

"Which Tim's this?" I heard one woman ask. Her voice was youthful. "Tim Rice or Tim Weber?"

"Tim Weber," the other woman replied in a slightly deeper voice. Then there was a pause.

Worried they might think, and rightfully so, that I was eavesdropping, I fiddled with the toilet paper and shuffled my feet, acting like I was just minding my own business as I went about my business. Then I prayed they would continue. They did.

"Tim Weber," the second woman repeated. Her voice was lower but by now the water was off. "Judy in the LA office called me this morning. Tim's wife kicked him out."

"You're kidding," the other one said. "Isn't he married to some heiress or something like that?"

"Uh-huh. Judy said the separation was even in the paper, in the gossip column."

"Wow. Poor guy."

"Poor guy? Unless he has a prenup, he could make out like a bandit. If he has a prenup, he could be out on his ass with nothing. They don't have any kids."

"Maybe that's why he's been down here so much," commented the first woman. "Maybe he's relocating to Orange County."

There was a long pause. I stood up and started slowly straightening my clothing, but I kept my ears sharp.

"Okay, spill it," the first woman said. "You obviously know something else."

"Well." Another pause. "Judy said she heard Tim Weber is on probation with the firm."

The first woman openly gasped. "You're kidding!"

Before the woman with the loose lips could continue, I heard the restroom door open and someone walk in. The two women greeted the new woman but buttoned their lips with regard to Tim. A few seconds later, they left the bathroom, and the new woman entered the stall next to mine. Rats!

Tim was on the phone when I finally made my way back to his temporary digs. He waved me in and indicated the chair across from his desk. I sat down and placed my tote bag on the floor. I tried to casually study him. He had taken off his suit jacket, and since I didn't see it anywhere, I assumed he'd hung it on a hook behind the door. He soon finished his call and gave me his full attention.

"So what are these *odd* things you mentioned, Odelia?"

I had given some quick thought to how much I should say and what I should ask. Should I stroke the snake or give him a good, solid poke and see what happens? I decided to do a bit of both. If he didn't budge, maybe I could jab him with some of the personal information I'd just learned.

"You said the last time I was here that you and your wife thought Steele and Karen Meek might get back together."

"Yes, that's true."

"You didn't know that Karen is engaged to someone else? Tom Bledsoe, in fact, owner of Amazing Games Software."

"Really? No, I didn't know that. We haven't seen Karen in quite some time. Not since a ski trip we took together. Did Mike know?" While he spoke, I noted that he didn't look at me but busied himself shuffling papers on his desk. Even if I hadn't just seen him with Karen Meek, I would have thought he was lying from his lack of eye contact.

"According to Karen, she told him just before he disappeared."

Tim continued to shuffle. "You think maybe he disappeared because of that?"

"You mean skulked off somewhere to lick his broken-hearted wounds?" I shook my head. "I don't know about you, but that doesn't sound like the Mike Steele I know, especially considering he's been divorced from Karen for so long, but then you've been close friends a very long time. You probably know him a lot better than I do."

With those words, Tim looked up briefly, then back down at his paperwork. "I'm sorry, Odelia, it seems these papers aren't in order for my conference call, so unless you have something new to tell me about Mike, I'll have to cut this short."

Seems I was going to have to give the snake that good, hard jab sooner rather than later. "One more question, please, Tim?" Which meant I really wanted to ask him three or four more questions.

He looked at his watch. "Sure, a quick one."

As I started to say something, my phone vibrated. In the small, closed office it was easy to hear. Per the display, it was Sally. I ignored it and started to say something, but it kept vibrating, over and over. I looked up at Tim and saw that he was growing impatient with the delay.

"Just a minute, Tim," I said, holding up an index finger. "It's my boyfriend, and he's rather difficult to reach." Before Tim could say anything in the negative, I retrieved my phone and answered it. "Hi, honey. I'm kind of in the middle of something right now."

On the other end of the phone, Sally got straight to the point. "Johnette's in the hospital. She tried to commit suicide."

THIRTY-TWO

"Oh my gawd!" I stood up abruptly, almost knocking my chair backwards.

"What's the matter?" asked Tim, trying to hide his annoyance with fake concern.

Suddenly I remembered where I was and what I was doing when the call came through. Quickly, I collected myself.

"Sorry," I said to Tim. "It's my boyfriend's mother. She was in a car accident." Then to Sally on the phone, "Is she going to be okay?"

I listened as Sally assured me that Johnette would be fine. Then I said to her, "That's good news, honey. Tell your mother I'll come by the hospital as soon as I can get away from work."

From Sally's end came a "Huh?"

"I'll call you when I leave the office, probably in about an hour," I paused. "Love you, too."

After closing my cell phone, I sat back down and spent a few seconds composing myself. Things were getting out of hand.

"Is she going to be all right?"

I looked up and saw Tim peering at me with a mix of worry and frustration. He looked at his watch. Although I was quite flustered, I knew I wouldn't get another chance to question him like this. Things were closing in fast and furious with both situations. I had to think fast even if I sprang a mental cog doing so.

"Yes, thank you, Tim. Seems she had a flat and went off the road. The hospital's keeping her for observation."

"Well, that's good." Again with the watch. "I really must get back to work, Odelia. What was that last question you wanted to ask?"

"Yes, and I need to get to the hospital." I straightened my shoulders and surged forward. "By the way, are you a partner here at Goldberg?"

He looked surprised at my nosy question, but answered. "No, not yet, but I expect to be made one very shortly."

From probation to partner? Seemed highly unlikely to me. I flashed a smile at him. "Then early congratulations. I hope you get everything you deserve."

Tim Weber visibly relaxed upon hearing my best wishes. *Good*, I thought, *I want him nice and comfy and off guard when I ask the triple-point bonus question.*

"Guess I'm a little behind Mike in that regard." He leaned back in his chair and looked genuinely puzzled. "Is that the question you were dying to ask?"

"Actually, no, but it's related to the one I want to ask."

I steeled myself for the inevitable explosion and picked up my bag, ready for a hasty retreat.

"Is your making partner here at Goldberg contingent on you stealing the Silhouette account away from Wallace, Boer, Brown and Yates?"

"What?" Tim Weber flew forward, out of his chair, and slammed his hands down on the desk between us.

I stood up and eased back toward the door.

"I know you and Fran Evans met with Ben Walker on Sunday. Is Fran going to be made a Goldberg partner, too? Or is she staying behind at Woobie to continue serving our clients up to you on a silver platter?"

Tim said nothing, but the muscles on either side of his neck stood out thick and corded like the rope used to moor boats. For a minute, I thought I actually saw steam come out of his ears like it does in cartoons.

"What the hell are you talking about?"

He started to move from behind the desk, looking like he wanted to beat the crap out of me. I backed up closer to the door, thankful it was still normal business hours. Placing a hand on the doorknob, I turned it slightly. In my other hand, I had a tight grip on my tote bag. In an emergency, I figured it could be used as a weapon.

"You need to leave, Odelia, right now." His voice was the low growl I had heard him use with Karen Meek. "Before I decide to slap you with a slander suit."

"A partnership with Goldberg-Rawlings must be worth its weight in gold, especially since you're on probation." I rushed to get the words out before he decided to take a more physical approach to his threats. "In fact, such a partnership must be worth Mike Steele's weight in gold, wouldn't you think?"

Tim Weber literally got in my face. He approached me and leaned down, almost nose to nose. I could smell coffee on his breath.

"Out, now!" he shouted.

Without moving a smidgen, I looked him in the eye. "Careful. You wouldn't want everyone in your firm to know what I suspect." I opened the door.

"I'm warning you," he said with a lowered voice. He grabbed my arm and started to escort me out the door when a cell phone rang. Tim stopped and swore under his breath. The phone rang again. It was coming from his jacket on the back of the door. He looked at me and then toward the door.

"That must be the call you were waiting for," I told him, trying to be helpful.

The phone rang again. He dropped my arm and reached behind the door for it. He said hello and told the person to hold on. Covering the mouthpiece with one hand, he said to me, "Show your face here or anywhere near me again, and I'll have you arrested for trespassing and harassment, and don't think I won't."

I wiggled my fingers at him. "No need to show me out, I know the way."

He shut the door firmly in my face and took his call.

After buying a soda and a large fashion magazine from the little sundry store in the lobby of our building, I posted myself at one of the plastic picnic tables clustered near the parking garage. Being that it was late afternoon, it was too late for the lunch crowd and only a few smokers were scattered among the several tables. I chose an empty table partially hidden by a trash can. From here I could see everyone coming and going between the building and the garage. There was no other way for Tim to leave unless he was walking, and that was unlikely.

I had hoped that my questions would rattle him and make him angry, and they had. Now I was hoping that in his worked-up state, he would take off and lead me somewhere important. I didn't have a clue who had called him on his cell, but I was guessing that it had been a personal call. Office calls would generally come through the office phone, though not always. My questions might also cause him to make a few calls. If Tim Weber had nothing to hide, he would call Woobie and tell them to keep me on a leash. If I had hit home with the partnership thing, he might call Fran or Karen or even whoever has Steele. I still didn't understand Karen's involvement, and I wasn't worried about him calling Fran. If he did, she would have to do some fast talking if she wanted to implicate me in anything, and I knew Carl Yates had my back if she did try to stir up trouble.

Sally and I needed a breakthrough. We were never going to get close to Let Mother Do It unless someone led us there, and the clock was ticking. I had no doubt that Carl would hold me to my deadline. Right now, all we had was a sandwich cookie—a handful of suspects on one side, a handful of victims on the other, and a contract-killer crème center—and there was nothing sweet about it.

I was halfway through my soda when Tim Weber marched out of the building toward the parking garage. He didn't look left or right, just straight ahead as he aimed for the garage elevators. I watched as he punched the up button with impatience before finally taking the stairs. Wherever he was going, he was in a rush to get there. Quickly, I made my own way into the garage.

My car was still parked in short-term parking, so it would be easy to tail Tim as he came through the parking gate. There were two other gates, but they were solely for monthly permits. I was betting that if Tim was only in the Orange County Goldberg office a few times a month, they would give him parking validations, which could only be used at the main gate—the very gate I was watching like a hawk with my motor running.

My guess became reality when a few minutes later Tim Weber passed me, heading for the main gate. He was driving a black Mercedes SUV. I was glad of his automobile choice, because with the higher profile, the vehicle would be easier to track from behind.

Once out of the parking garage, Tim headed down MacArthur Boulevard and made his way onto the 55 Freeway heading north. I dialed Sally once we both settled into a middle lane.

"It's me," I announced. "Any more news on Johnette?"

"No, just that she's expected to make a full recovery. Victor tried calling you but couldn't find your number, so Cindy called me. Johnette was found in a motel room in Whittier, unconscious from alcohol and sleeping pills." She whistled. "Can you believe this?"

"What I don't want to believe is that Johnette is behind the two killings, but trying to kill herself makes it look like she's raising her hand in confession."

"I was thinking the same thing. Hard to believe any of them would be capable of this." Sally sighed deeply. "Well, at least Donny's murder is off our shoulders."

I hadn't thought of that, but Sally was right. The police would be swarming all over the connections between the Olivers and the Moraleses.

"Where are you now?" I asked her. "Heading for Santa Barbara?"

"No, after leaving her meeting with Tim, Karen made a beeline for San Marino."

"San Marino? Up near Pasadena?"

"Yep. She turned into a gated mini-mansion and even had the code for the gate."

"I'll bet that's Tom Bledsoe's house. I remember him telling me once in an e-mail that he lived in San Marino."

"I'd like to stay and see if she comes out with Tommy, but these streets are lousy with private patrol cars. If I don't move along soon, I'm sure they'll start asking questions."

"Okay, do what you think is best." While I talked, Tim made a move. "Hang on, Sally." I kept his vehicle in my sights as it made the transition to the 91 Freeway heading east, and I followed suit.

"Tim Weber is on the 91 heading toward Riverside," I said into my phone.

"Riverside? Wonder what's out that way?"

"Hopefully, Steele. I really rattled Tim's cage a little bit ago. I found out that his wife's dumped him and he's on probation at his firm, and I tweaked his nose with some of it. That's where I was when you called about Johnette and why I acted so bizarre." Pressing the gas, I edged my car a little closer to his. "I let him know I'm onto him. Soon after, he climbed into his SUV and took off like a bat out of hell."

"Odelia, be careful, and I mean very careful. I don't like the idea of you following Weber if he's leading you right into the hornet's nest." She paused. "In fact, why don't you call the police? Call Dev Frye, let him know where you are."

She had a good point, but I was still leery of police involvement and the effect it might have on Steele's survival.

"Because I'm afraid if Let Mother Do It has Steele, they will kill him as soon as the police try to take over. Sometimes the police aren't that subtle when it comes to surrounding buildings with hostages inside." Tim made a lane change, and I copied him from a few cars back. "If I can just be sure Steele's okay first, I'll feel better."

"I don't know, Odelia. I'm really very worried." She paused. "Uh-oh. Just as I feared. A patrol car just pulled up behind me and a rent-a-cop is getting out."

I heard someone say something to Sally in the background. She kept the phone on while she responded. It sounded like someone was asking her who she was and what she was doing. She told him she was lost and was calling a friend for directions.

"Tell him you're looking for the Huntington Library," I said loudly into the phone. A second later, I heard her ask for directions to the Huntington Library. There was some talk in the background.

"Okay, just got directions," she said to me. "I should be there in a few minutes." I heard her thank the person, followed by the sound of her car moving.

"Quick thinking, Odelia. I was stumped for something to tell him." She laughed. "Turns out that place is just a mile or so away."

"At least I didn't have to sacrifice Greg's mother this time." I watched as Tim pulled into the lane to his left to pass a slow-moving truck hauling gardening equipment. I accelerated and did the same, careful to still keep a few cars between us. "So what are your plans now?"

"Actually, I was thinking about pulling out the Thomas Guide and finding the quickest route to the 91."

"There's no reason to do that, Sally. Since you can't wait for Karen, I think you should go home. I'll call you later."

"No can do, Odelia. I can't go home and have a nice dinner with Jill, wondering if you're safe or not."

"I'll be fine. No sense in both of us wasting gas. He's probably just heading to some appointment."

"In Riverside, late in the afternoon—I doubt it." When I hesitated, she made a compelling argument. "Besides, Christine would never abandon Mary Beth for her gay lover."

"Christine Cagney was *not* a lesbian."

"How do you know?"

THIRTY-THREE

IN THE END, THE agreed-upon plan was for me to stay on Tim Weber's tail and for Sally to work her way to me through commuter traffic. We also agreed that I would text message her with changes in my direction, turns, roads, etc., so she could follow me—sort of a high-tech bread-crumb trail.

Up ahead, Tim was making another move. We were almost to the 15 Freeway interchange when he started moving over to make ready for the transition onto 15 south from 91. Once again, I followed. The 15 was moving steadily but not fast. As soon as we settled into a middle lane, I texted Sally the directions.

By moving into a middle lane, I took a guess that Tim was preparing to travel the 15 Freeway for several miles. He didn't appear to be frantic or aware of my presence, he just moved with the traffic. I took the time to reflect on what might be ahead and was suddenly glad Sally was following my trail. At least someone knew where I was heading, in case I ended up another missing link along with Steele.

I stared ahead, watching the Mercedes for any sign of sudden change of direction and wondering where and to what I was being led. Was Tim rendezvousing with the people who had Steele? Or was there yet another twist in this tale of greed and betrayal?

It hit me that I was calmly driving into deep shit, as both Carl and Sally were worried about. Thinking about facing Let Mother Do It sent chills up and down my spine. Maybe I should call Dev. This area wasn't his jurisdiction, but he certainly considered me part of his jurisdiction. What would he say if I told him about Let Mother Do It? Would he take me seriously? In spite of his early crankiness, I knew he would at least listen if I pressed him hard enough. But I couldn't tell him about Willie. Felon or not, Willie was my friend and was helping me.

What to do. What to do. What to do.

I was driving my old, reliable Toyota into the jaws of possible death and destruction, but I couldn't see how I could not. I clung to the hope that Steele was still alive, and I had to do whatever I could to find him, even if that meant following Tim Weber straight into Mother's hands.

Suddenly, I wanted to talk to the two people I loved the most— my father and Greg. Dad or Greg, which was it to be? I called my father. After letting it ring a dozen times without an answer, I called Greg.

Boomer, his right-hand man, answered the phone. I asked to speak to Greg. It took a few minutes before Greg came on the line. When he did, it was about the same time Tim Weber decided to make a lane change, moving one lane over to the right. I waited a few seconds before doing the same.

"Greg, I'm sorry. I have to go."

"Where are you?"

Here goes nothing, I thought, then plunged in feet first. "I'm on 15 heading south, following a friend of Steele's who may have something to do with his disappearance." I left out the part about contract killers.

"Tell me where you are *exactly*, Odelia." His tone was even but stern.

"I'm on 15 south, almost to Lake Elsinore. I'm following an attorney named Tim Weber who is in a black Mercedes SUV."

"I'm on my way."

"No, Greg, it's not necessary. Besides, it's rush hour, and I have no idea where my destination is. I'm just playing follow the leader, and Sally's a few miles behind me." I terminated the call.

The cell phone immediately vibrated. It was Greg. I ignored it. If I was heading into a black pit of danger, I wasn't dragging my beloved into it with me. It was bad enough that Sally was on her way.

Tim changed lanes again, and again I followed. There was only one car between us until another car changed lanes, making me two cars behind him. Then, out of nowhere, came a green motorcycle, just like the one I'd seen that day we'd visited Cindy. The motorcycle came up fast on my side and weaved in and out of traffic until it was ahead of Tim. Once there, the driver turned on his turn signal and made a right-hand turn arm gesture. Tim followed the motorcycle onto the exit ramp, and I turned on my blinker to do the same. One of the cars in front of me turned with us. The ramp was for Railroad Canyon Road. At the bottom of the ramp, all of us turned left. Railroad Canyon Road was small, and the intersection consisted only of freeway ramps and a traffic signal. I texted the info to Sally.

I was thankful for the car in front of me. I was also thankful Sally and I had taken her vehicle the day we went to see Cindy, just in case the motorcycle up ahead was the same one we saw that day. It looked to me like the rider on the bike was escorting Tim somewhere. With the area so sparsely populated, they would notice me for sure, so I tried to stay back as much as possible.

We followed the winding road past a couple of small housing developments until the area seemed almost deserted. The land on either side of the road was green and dense with trees and shrubs. Every now and then a driveway would open up between trees on one side or the other, and I could glimpse a house or other building set back from the road. Occasionally, a vehicle passed coming from the other direction. It occurred to me that if things got ugly, I could be killed and buried here quite easily. I quickly copied Greg with my last message to Sally just in case.

We had only gone a couple of miles when the motorcycle suddenly turned right into a gravel drive with a high, unkempt hedge on either side. Tim followed it. The car between us kept going and so did I, taking note of landmarks so I could find the driveway again. I looked for a place to turn around and found a small intersection about a quarter of a mile down the road. After waiting for an oncoming car to pass, I made a U-turn, but instead of heading back, I pulled the car over into a small turnout and thought about my next move.

Next move—who was I kidding? I didn't have a next move. I couldn't very well drive my car up that driveway like I was delivering a neighborhood Welcome Wagon basket. I had no idea what was on the other side of those hedges. I didn't even know if Steele was there or not. I texted Sally a cryptic message, hoping she understood from the gobbledygook that her destination was about two miles down the road, on the right, behind hedges.

Just as I finished my message to Sally, my phone vibrated. It was Greg again. This time I answered.

"Hi, I'm in a pickle."

"No shit, Sherlock." I could hear him, but there was a lot of static.

"I would prefer no shit, *sweetheart*."

"Where are you?" he asked again.

I gave him directions, but the static was louder. He responded, but I could hardly hear him. A second later, the call dropped. The reception must be bad out here. I tried calling him back, but the call kept failing. Finally, I sent him a quick text, hoping that might go through better than an actual call. CALL DEV was all it said. Almost immediately, my phone vibrated again. This time it was Dev. I looked at my phone's display. According to it, my message to Greg about calling Dev hadn't even gone through yet. The man must have ESP.

"Dev, that you?" The connection was a bit better but still not good.

"Stay put," he ordered.

"But—" was all I said before the call failed.

Staying put sounded like a grand idea—best I'd had all day, even if it wasn't *my* actual idea. But where could I stay put? I couldn't remain out in the open just a few hundred yards from where Tim turned in, and I wasn't about to leave without knowing if Steele was there. Maybe I could find a place to park that wasn't so notice-able. I put the car in gear and drove back the way I had come.

Just past the hidden drive, I spied a run-down shack set back a few yards from the road. It wasn't much more than a large lean-to, really—one of those small, wooden structures farmers set up to sell their fresh-picked vegetables to passing motorists. This one looked like it hadn't been used in years. The wood was weathered to various shades of gray, and the roof was half caved-in, with the rest hanging precariously. The ground in front was populated with scrub grass, weeds, and rough gravel.

No one was coming from the other direction. I checked to see if anyone was behind me, but there was not another car in sight. I pulled in and nosed my car around to the back, hoping there was enough clearance to hide it there. There was, but just barely. I turned off the engine and sat there, wondering how long it would take for the cavalry to show up.

I tried calling Sally, but the call kept failing. I tried calling both Greg and Dev, but again the calls failed. The sun was tucking itself in for the night, and soon it would be dark. From what I could see, Railroad Canyon Road didn't have a streetlight to its name.

After a short potty break between the shack and my car, I decided that staying put was not my strong suit, rationalizing that a lot could happen while I was sitting, twiddling my thumbs in a dark car. If this is where Let Mother Do It had Steele stashed, then Tim's arrival would sound the alarm, especially after our chat back in his office.

Sorry, Dev, I thought, *staying put is not an option.*

After giving my nose a good blow, I tucked the cell phone into my pants pocket, locked my tote bag in the trunk, and took a swig of water from the bottle I keep in the car. As a last act, I closed my eyes and said a short prayer that there wouldn't be any guard dogs across the way.

Poking my head out from behind the lean-to, I saw a pickup truck coming from the direction of the freeway. I pulled my head back and waited for it to pass before venturing out of my hiding spot and dashing across the road. Once on the other side, I disappeared into the protection of the high hedges where Tim and the green motorcycle had turned.

I was wearing the same outfit I'd worn to visit Cindy and was thankful I hadn't worn a skirt and heels. Still, as I made my way through the brush, my nubby hand-knit sweater wasn't doing so hot. I kept getting caught on branches like a human Velcro strip and had to keep stopping to pull myself free as I tiptoed from tree to shrub to bush to get closer to the house at the end of the long driveway.

There didn't appear to be any dogs on the premises, but I spotted Tim's SUV parked near the front of the house. Toward the back were two other vehicles—a white minivan and a dark green SUV. Next to them was the green motorcycle. The house itself was an old two-story home in need of new paint and some TLC. At the end of the driveway stood a large unattached garage and two smaller buildings—tool or gardening sheds maybe. In spite of sitting back from the road, all the drapes appeared closed. Lights were on in several rooms.

As I crept closer to the house, I kept my ears tuned for sounds of conversation and activity, but I heard nothing. Cooking smells drifted to me on the evening breeze. It was a hearty, beefy aroma like a stew or pot roast. It smelled yummy and made my mouth water. Once at the house, I pressed my body against its side and inched my way quietly toward the back where there was brighter light. I stopped under a window that was partially open. From here, the cooking smells were stronger and I could hear water running, making me think I might be under a kitchen window situated over a sink. I could hear voices, too, but not clearly over the splashing of the water. Soon the water stopped, and I strained to make out the conversation.

I heard Tim Weber's voice above the others—more high pitched than normal, like he was tense and anxious. He was arguing— almost pleading—trying to win a case before a jury not made up of his peers. The other voices weren't as clear or maybe not as stressed. After listening for another couple of minutes, I determined that the other voices were women, maybe two or three of them. One of the women seemed to be taking the lead. Her voice was a bit deeper than the others, and it didn't take me long to figure out that it might belong to the older woman I spoke to on the phone. It was very likely that this was Mother herself.

I needed to get closer to hear what they were saying, and I needed to find out where they had stashed Steele. If Steele was dead, I didn't think Tim Weber would be here in such an agitated state.

I edged closer to the end of the house, where I noticed another window open to the brisk evening air. Looking out past the house, there was just enough light for me to see that beyond the house the property dropped, not abruptly but down a small, steep hill. I was closer now to the garage and the two outbuildings and wondered if Steele was locked up in one of them. I looked all three over for traces of light from under a door crack but saw nothing. I went back to listening and tried to keep my knees from knocking.

The older woman was definitely in charge. In a comforting tone, she was trying to calm Tim down, telling him not to worry, that she would take care of everything.

"Don't you get it, old woman?" Tim said in a tone of angry frustration. "I don't want you to take care of anything. I want you to let him go."

Let him go? I stifled a sigh of relief. Steele must still be alive.

"Now, now, where are your manners? You don't come into my place of business shooting off your mouth and making demands." The woman's tone was still soothing even as she chastised him. "Do I come down to that fancy office of yours and tell you how to be a lawyer?"

"You've been paid for a full thirty days," Tim said. "You can keep the money, just let him go now. You can still make it look like he went on a bender or got in an accident and ended up with amnesia—whatever, just don't kill him. That wasn't part of the deal."

"Damn right we're keeping the money," I heard another female voice say. The voice sounded familiar, but I couldn't place it straight off.

"Calm down now," Mother chimed in. "The man is just upset because things got out of his control, and he doesn't like losing control. He's not used to it."

"Well, it's his fault we're in this mess," the other woman said. "And yours."

"*My* fault?" For the first time, I noticed anger in Mother's voice. "If you'll recall, young lady, it wasn't my idea to do this job. Kidnapping isn't what we do. We kill and we kill clean, no loose ends.

This job has as many loose ends as a fringed shawl." There was another pause, and I heard the sound of wood scraping on wood, followed by someone walking.

"I wasn't the one swayed by this man's money and promise of an easy job," I heard Mother say from a different direction. "No, it was the rest of you. I told you not to diversify. We had a good thing going. Built up a solid business with more than enough money coming in for all of us. It'll all be over if we don't do some mighty fast damage control."

"It was an easy job," Tim said. "All you had to do was grab Mike and hold him for four weeks, then release him without his knowing what happened and who did it. How did it get so screwed up?"

"You be still, Mr. Lawyer. Holding people against their will isn't easy, no matter how much money you throw at the problem." I could picture Mother scolding Tim Weber. "We only did it because a friend of yours is a good client and referred you. Now I'm regretting that decision every day."

There was more walking and more scraping on wood; must be a chair moving across the floor. I wanted to stretch up on my tiptoes and see if I could peek over the window ledge, but I didn't dare.

When Mother spoke again, it was from the other direction. "We should never have taken this job, especially on top of the other one. Now we're cleaning up our own mess instead of cleaning up other people's problems."

"The other job has nothing to do with me or Karen," I heard Tim say.

"Like hell it doesn't," Mother said. "If we hadn't snagged your annoying friend, the other job would have been done clean and simple, and we would have been back to normal, with a lot of quick cash and time to spend on our other clients." Mother made some unintelligible sounds of disgust. "We only took your job because your friend asked us to help out. He was so disappointed when someone else beat him to the punch on the Oliver hit, I couldn't bear to say no. Last time I'll have a soft heart, I'll tell you that."

"Bledsoe is not my friend," Tim said, almost spitting out the words. "I've never even met the guy."

Bledsoe! Tom Bledsoe had ordered a hit on Donny? Someone else had beat him to the punch? And it was Tommy who had referred Tim to Mother for the kidnapping? But who ordered the misfired hit on Cindy? Was Johnette still my top suspect in the Oliver matter? My mind was spinning faster than a Tilt-A-Whirl.

"Don't forget, Mother," the young woman said. "We were also promised a lot more work in the future. That's really why you agreed to go along with us on this."

There followed a long patch of silence.

Who was ordering the future work? Tom Bledsoe? Was he the good client Mother referred to? Had he ordered more killings than just possibly his wife's? He'd told me on the phone that he would consider a hit on Donny to be money well spent. What other "investments" did he plan on making—or had he made—and how did Karen figure into the mix? Question marks were floating around in my head like a moveable wallpaper pattern.

Finally Mother spoke. "Yes, that's true. We were promised a lot more work in return for the favor—enough work to keep us in business a long time."

There was another pause. I was going nuts under the window. I wanted Mother and the others to just spit it out, to tell me everything and hurry up about it.

"But now I'm thinking this Steele guy has to go. Too much heat coming down on everyone because of him. Too many people interested in finding him, like that damn Olivia or Ophelia or something."

"Odelia," the other woman corrected. "Her name is Odelia Grey."

"Whatever her name is, she isn't going to give up until she finds him. She already knows that Let Mother Do It is linked somehow to this guy, and someone in the shadows has been asking questions about us. We hear she's connected on both sides of the law."

At first surprised that she knew about Willie's inquiries, I quickly realized that if he had his informants in the criminal world, Mother would, too. It would be part of the day-to-day survival.

"And she's smart," the younger woman added. "Very smart and determined."

Hiding under the window, I didn't know whether to feel complimented or not, but I certainly felt frightened right down to my toenails, especially since the younger woman spoke like she knew me.

"Why don't we simply take her out?" another female voice asked. She had a slight accent—East Coast maybe. "It'd be easy enough. Just like the Poppin woman."

"You mean the Poppin woman's botched job." It was the young woman again, her voice laced with accusation.

"Hey, she turned at the last minute, and I didn't get a chance to pop her again."

"The Poppin woman?" It was Tim. "You were behind the shooting of that elderly woman last night?"

Mother laughed. "That elderly woman was a client, just like you, Mr. Weber. And just like you, she was having a bad case of buyer's remorse. Killing her was part of that damage control I was talking about—or should I say *trying* to kill her."

The third woman spoke up, anger in her voice. "I told you I'd take care of it. Trust me, the old gal won't ever come out of that coma."

Oh my gawd! Carolyn Poppin was the money behind the hit on Donny. Cindy Oliver's own sweet, kind mother. Suddenly I felt dizzy and chilled. Carolyn Poppin should have been baking brownies for her granddaughters, not looking for contract killers, no matter how mean and ugly her son-in-law was.

Then another horrible thought hit me, and if it hadn't hit Tim by now, it should have. Mother was doing damage control, taking care of clients with buyer's remorse. She said it herself. Something told me that Tim Weber's life expectancy now could be measured in minutes, not years, months, or even days.

"I say we kill both lawyers and this Odelia woman." It was the screw-up killer. "That should clean up this mess once and for all."

I'm pretty sure from my past studies of Shakespeare that when the Bard penned the words *kill all the lawyers*, he didn't include paralegals.

But then, it could have been in a footnote.

THIRTY-FOUR

WHILE I TRIED MY best not to retch from nerves, Tim Weber got his exercise doing a lot of backpedaling.

"There's no need to take that attitude," I heard him say. "I came down here to try to resolve these issues."

"Which we wouldn't have if you hadn't asked us to kidnap your friend," Mother reminded him. "If we had been hired to kill him outright, we wouldn't be having this discussion. You'd be a satisfied customer and we wouldn't be trying to cover our tracks."

"I was wrong, okay? I should never have done it. I just wanted him out of the way for a while, not dead." There was a pause. When Tim continued, his voice cracked with emotion. "Mike has always been there for me. He doesn't deserve this."

"My, my, what have we here, a lawyer with a conscience?" Mother's voice was laced with sarcasm "Not something you see every day."

"Please, release him. Do it tonight. Let me take him with me. I promise you: whatever consequences I face, I won't involve you."

"You bet your ass you won't." It was the kill-happy woman again.

With the sun down, the night was getting cooler by the minute. My body was chilled and my nose was running like a man trying to catch a bus. I pulled my sweater tighter around me and wondered if instead of more listening I should be inspecting the garage and outbuildings for Steele. After all, I now knew who was behind Donny's murder and Steele's kidnapping. The next order of business was to find Steele. With a big stroke of luck, I might be able to spring him and get down to the car without much fuss.

I didn't really believe that, but I had to at least make an effort to convince myself to take some action. Something told me that no matter how much Tim begged, he was never leaving here tonight with Mike Steele. And if that one crazy broad had her way, none of us would be leaving unless it was in the back of a hearse.

Now I was really worried. Sally and Greg, and possibly Dev, were all heading this way. I didn't want any more people in the line of fire. Dev at least was a professional, but Sally and Greg had no idea how to defend themselves against killers. I wondered if I should steal back to my car and wait for them, flag them down, and stop them from coming in closer contact with these nuts. But what about Steele? I couldn't just let them kill him off as collateral damage without taking some preventative action.

The people inside the house were still talking, each considering the pros and cons of doing away with the three of us. Like a true legal beagle, Tim continued to argue his case, his voice growing more desperate with each sentence. My nose at this point was now running a marathon. I dug into the pockets of my trousers, hoping to find some tissue, but only came up with the keys to my car and the cell phone. I wiped my nose on the back of my hand and tried to sniffle quietly while I poked in a message to send, but I was all thumbs. Hitting redial, I tried to call Greg, but the call kept failing. Frustrated, I jammed the phone back into my pocket and went back to trying to figure out what to do next.

A few seconds later, I knew the shit, or rather the snot, was about to hit the fan.

A sneeze started building deep inside my head. It rolled and rolled and rolled around in my sinus cavity, gathering strength like a pressure cooker about to explode. I desperately tried to quell it; I was willing to blow an eardrum, if necessary, rather than get caught spying on Mother and her gun-happy companions.

Pressing my fingers against both sides of my nose, I managed to let out a tiny poof of a sneeze without blowing the lid off my hiding spot. I bent down, hoping to stifle what little noise I was making, thankful the breeze was causing the trees in the yard to rustle. Looking down the driveway, I wondered if I could get far enough away to not be heard but knew any fast departure would make too much noise for even the trees to cover. Again I bent down in an effort to stifle smaller sneezes, hoping they would take some of the pressure out of my sinuses. Finally, I felt in the clear. The pressure subsided, and I was able to breathe with relief.

I straightened up and turned back, ready to start my inspection of the outbuildings. Instead, I found myself nose-to-nose with the muzzle of a gun. For a brief moment, I was sure I'd black out from raw fear. In all my worry about sneezing, I hadn't heard anyone sneak up on me. The weapon was at the end of an arm owned by a petite but sturdy woman wearing jeans, black Doc Martens, and a plain black sweatshirt. On her head was a black cap with the

Raiders logo. In the shadow of the house, I couldn't see her face under the cap. Waving the gun in the direction of the back of the house, she told me to get moving. From the voice, I determined it was the woman who wanted to kill me and everyone else on the planet.

And that's when the sneeze from hell broke loose, and the sneeze, and everything repulsive about it, hit her dead center in the chest.

I had to hand it to her, she never lost her concentration for an instant. Cool as a cucumber, she remained steady, and the gun remained trained on me. I, on the other hand, would have yelled *that's disgusting!* and done a dance of revulsion.

Again she waved the gun toward the back of the house. This time I obeyed and started walking ahead of her. At the back of the house was a short flight of concrete steps. On her instructions, I mounted them and entered a screened-in porch. Beyond that was an open door leading into the kitchen.

"Odelia!" Tim shouted with great surprise as soon as I entered the kitchen.

But the real surprise was mine. Seated at the table, doing her best to avoid my barefaced stare, was Rachel Keyo; no doubt the owner of the familiar voice I couldn't place. It also didn't take me long to notice that in the two weeks since she'd disappeared from her temp position at the firm, her swollen belly had become flat and trim.

"You!" I pointed at her. "You're part of this?"

Rachel scowled at me, then turned away, saying nothing.

"Well, well, look what Lisa dragged in." The comment came from a stocky older woman with short, gray hair standing at the stove. She was a few inches taller than me and a few pounds lighter, and she wore polyester pants and a sweater that said *Bingo Baby* on the front in rhinestones. She stirred something in a large pot as she spoke. "So you're Odelia Grey. I'm Mother. I believe we spoke on the phone."

I ignored her, keeping my attention on Rachel. "You must've been the one who referred Let Mother Do It to Steele." I hesitated. "But who planted you?" I was digging through my brain for that answer when the gun dug into my back. Then it came to me. Fran Evans had referred Rachel to our office. Fran had said a friend of hers highly recommended Rachel as a temp. It was all coming together.

"You're the one who changed the documents, aren't you?" I said to Rachel, making a guess that I knew I could defend. Rachel had the skills to expertly change the documents, and, as Steele's secretary, she had unlimited access to them. "You and Fran Evans changed the Silhouette documents, then helped Tim set up Steele's disappearance so he'd take the fall."

"Enough," Lisa barked, poking me harder with the gun. "Sit your fat ass down." As soon as I obeyed, she handed the gun to Rachel. "Keep an eye on her," she ordered, then made her way to the sink, where she took off her cap and proceeded to wash off the front of her sweatshirt.

Outside, I would have guessed Lisa to be about the same age as Rachel. But here in the kitchen, under the glare of the overhead light and with her cap off, I could see that her short, dark hair was laced with gray, and her makeup-free face bore fine lines around her mouth and eyes. The new age estimate was late thirties or early forties.

Saddled with the duty of holding the gun, Rachel now had to look at me.

"What did Mike Steele or I ever do to you?" I asked her.

She briefly cast her eyes down, then back up to meet mine. They were hard and sad at the same time, like an apology delivered with a backhand. "This isn't personal, this is business."

Why do people always say that just before they shaft you?

I slowly ran my eyes over Rachel's svelte body. "Did the baby come early?"

"There was no baby, you fool." She spit the words out.

Mother approached the table, wooden spoon in her hand. She was grinning. "After what we were told about that Mr. Steele, we couldn't take the chance of Rachel being side-tracked by charm. We didn't think he'd go after a pregnant lady, and we were right."

I stared up at Mother. "But why go through the ruse of the cleaning company if you had a plant in the office?"

"Who said the cleaning company isn't real?" Mother chuckled, and I remembered what Willie had said about a legitimate business covering for illegal business. "We had hoped to nab him at his home, but that didn't work out. He was never around when the cleaning crew was there. Would have made things much easier for us."

Tim sat there staring at me, his mouth open. Finally, he found his tongue. "How in the hell did you get here?"

Mother rapped him on the head with the spoon. "How do you think, lame brain? She followed you." She looked at Lisa. "Which means that you never noticed her when you were following him."

"Told you she was smart," chimed in Rachel.

Mother put the spoon down and wiped her hands on a nearby dishtowel. "Maybe you should come to work for me, Odelia, seeing as you're so sharp."

Oh boy, I thought, *I am being recruited by a professional killer.*

"Pay's great and the hours are flexible," she continued as if talking to a bunch of kids on career day.

Lisa approached the table, the front of her sweatshirt wet. "A minute ago we were discussing killing her, and now you're offering this dolt a job?"

"If there's a dolt at this table, it's not Odelia, it's this fool here." She indicated Tim, and everyone, including me, turned our eyes on him. He sat there, no longer huffing and puffing and intimidating as he had been in his office a few hours ago. Now he appeared shrunken and lost. His eyes, darting between each woman in the room, had the look of a rabbit trapped by a pack of hungry wolves. Finally, they settled on me.

"Tell them, Odelia, tell them to let Mike go. We'll take him home and never mention this to anyone, right?"

I turned to Mother. "Is Steele okay?"

"He's more than okay, he's a royal pain in the ass." Mother took the spoon and went back to her pot. "Humph, there were days I wanted to shoot him just on principle alone."

"Trust me, I know what you mean."

Mother chuckled and studied me. "Sure you don't want to work for me? We do a lot of good in this world."

"Good? Killing people is good?"

"Now, now, don't go getting all high and mighty with me. Some people are just too mean, greedy, and nasty to live, bringing more pain and suffering to this world than good. Take that Oliver guy, for instance. People merely pay us to clean up the two-legged vermin in their lives, just as they would pay a pest exterminator to get rid of the other kind." Mother stopped stirring and faced me, smiling. "I like to think we're doing our bit to clean up the world we live in—our own Keep America Beautiful program. We may kill people, but we have our standards. If we didn't, you wouldn't still be alive."

I swallowed hard and thought it best to move the conversation away from the topic of death, especially mine. Besides, if I could keep people talking, maybe I'd find out more about Steele's whereabouts and give Dev and the others time to find this place.

"Why?" I said to Tim. Again, everyone's eyes turned to him, this time in expectation. "Why would you have a close friend kidnapped and risk disbarment and jail, all for a partnership in a law firm? If that was why you did it."

Tim Weber looked only at me when he spoke. "I'm so sorry, Odelia. I was desperate. My wife left me, said I was a loser. It's tough being married to money."

"Yeah, right," Rachel scoffed.

Tim looked at all of us. "It is, especially for a man. I kept trying to make my own fortune, but the only thing I made was a mess. Got involved in a lot of deals that went sour. Ended up owing a lot of people money. People who'd think nothing of harming me or discrediting my wife and her family to make a point." He swallowed hard. "Finally, Roxanne said enough. She wasn't going to bail me out anymore. She paid off the last bunch of thugs and kicked me out."

"What about Goldberg-Rawlings?" I asked. "Rumor is you're on probation at the firm. Is that tied in to your bad business deals, too?"

"Partially. But mostly it's because I'm not a very good attorney. I'm not a rainmaker or brilliant like Mike. But I thought maybe if I landed a big client, it could change things for me at the firm. I had heard that the new CEO at Silhouette was looking for new representation and was thinking of going public with the company. Without Roxanne's money as a safety net, I was desperate to keep my job."

"And Fran?"

"We met a couple of years ago at another law firm. I knew she was pissed at Mike for dumping her and not helping her make partner."

"So she did it for revenge?"

"Mostly, yes. But she was also hoping that Walker would name her Silhouette's new general counsel. They don't have one, and it would be a natural move, with them going public soon and her familiarity with their work. Ben Walker was almost on board with it."

"But not quite, so you doctored documents and made Steele disappear to make it look like he was shady and Woobie incompetent, paving the way for Walker to make a decision."

Tim nodded.

I shook my head in wonder. "And you two really didn't think you'd get caught?"

Mother pointed her wooden spoon in his direction. "Like I said, he's a lame brain."

Tim ignored her. "When Mike disappeared in the middle of the fight with Sweet Kiss, Walker was adamant that Goldberg-Rawlings be their new counsel. The only thing that stopped it from happening was the longtime loyalty Silhouette's board felt toward your firm."

I thought about Carl and how haggard he had been looking. No doubt he had been working in high gear to keep the client. Everything was coming together. It was still a harebrained scheme with lots of holes, but desperate people do desperate and stupid things. And so do people blinded by their need for revenge.

"I saw those tampered documents." I glanced at Rachel, and she looked back with a cocky smile, all earlier traces of sadness gone. "They were pretty convincing. Had they been produced, it would have tilted the case in favor of Sweet Kiss, and no amount of loyalty would have saved Woobie. And Steele would have had a lot of explaining to do, especially since he held the originals." I sighed.

Tim Weber dropped his face into his hands. "It was a stupid, stupid mistake."

"No, Tim. A mistake is putting fabric softener in the dishwasher instead of soap. A mistake is debiting fifteen dollars from your checking account when it should have been fifty-one. Those are mistakes. This was planned and calculated, right down to planting Rachel in our office and a cleaning company in Steele's home weeks before you actually had him snatched. This wasn't a mistake, Tim. This was premeditated."

"Actually," Mother piped up from her spot by the stove, "it took us weeks to figure out how to grab him without witnesses. If we'd just been allowed to kill him," she said, looking at Tim in disgust, "it would have been over and done with a long time ago."

Mother and I were both harping on Tim, but for different reasons. I certainly hoped she didn't think I was on her team on this issue.

"But fortunately, or unfortunately, as the case may be," I continued, "Rachel supplied you with his travel information for that weekend. All you had to do was find a way to waylay him between Santa Barbara and Ojai, then plant his car at the airport. Is that how this went down?" I looked at Rachel, then at Mother.

Mother smiled. "Pretty much."

"And Karen Meek, how does she fit in? I mean, besides being engaged to Tom Bledsoe, who I'm guessing is the good client of Let Mother Do It who convinced Mother to take on this job." I looked at Tim. "Did you, Fran, and Karen split Mother's fee?"

"Hey, just how long were you standing outside, and how much did you hear?" Mother stood looking at me with a hand on one thick hip. Lisa and Rachel both narrowed their eyes.

Uh-oh. Where in the hell was Dev?

"A lot of what I know I learned long before getting here—like that Karen Meek wanted Steele out of the way so that she could put Tom Bledsoe on the board of Family Bond without his interference."

Tim shook his head. "Actually, Fran knew nothing about the kidnapping. That was just Karen and me."

I rolled my eyes.

"Truly, she didn't. I'm sure she suspected something when Mike disappeared, but she wasn't actually in on it. She did help plant Rachel, and she did coordinate the tampering of the documents, but she knows nothing about Mother or the kidnapping.

She thought Rachel was a friend of mine willing to help us out with the documents."

Tim looked down at the table. "But neither Karen nor I want Mike dead. That's Bledsoe's idea. Karen came to me and said Bledsoe wanted Mike gone permanently. That's why I'm here: to make sure that doesn't happen." He looked at Mother. "We didn't pay you to kill Mike Steele."

Lisa took the gun from Rachel and waved it around. "This whole thing is out of control. Let's just kill them and get out of here."

Mother approached the table, crossing her arms in front of her Bingo Baby slogan. "I think Lisa's right," she said in a calm, matter-of-fact voice. "This is out of control, and I don't see any way to resolve anything without killing all of you. You two know too much, and Mr. Steele is simply an inconvenience at this point."

Mother started laughing, giving off a deep cackle. "But I want you both to know first that little Ms. Meek isn't that meek at all."

Tim and I looked at each other, both with open mouths and wide eyes. The looks were not lost on Mother.

"That's right. Now that she's gotten a taste for our services, she's put in an order for the extermination of a particularly nasty bit of business—an abusive husband and father of one of her clients. Though I'm not sure we'll be able to handle it until all this fuss blows over."

"That was the promised new business, wasn't it?" I asked, my eyes still wide as saucers. "Family Bond is going to start rubbing out abusers—with your help."

Thinking back on some of the things Karen had said, it made sense. She had grown tired of trying to work within a broken system and was now going to embrace vigilante justice. Let Mother Do It would be her hired gun. In a sick way, both shared the same philosophy of the end justifying the means.

Mother clucked at me. "Now I know you heard too much. Pity, Odelia, I was really starting to like you."

Mother caught Lisa's eye and started to move back from the table. Just then my cell phone vibrated. What a time for the phone service to kick in.

"What was that?" asked Rachel.

I shrugged and looked around, hoping to put the focus on something else. The phone vibrated again, sending a soft hum into the still air of the room.

This time Lisa pointed the gun at my head and approached me. "It's coming from her," she announced to the others. Mother walked back to the table.

The phone vibrated a third time.

"Answer that," Mother ordered. "But be careful."

Keeping one hand flat on the table, I slowly slipped my other hand into my pocket and retrieved the phone. By the time I pulled it free, it had stopped ringing. I placed the phone on the table. A few seconds later, it started vibrating again. The display said private call. I looked at Mother. She nodded, indicating for me to answer it.

I flipped it open and held it to my mouth. "This really isn't a good time." I listened, surprised by the caller. "You're right, I am an idiot." As I listened some more, my eyes nearly popped out of my head. When the caller was through speaking to me, I held the phone out to Mother. "It's for you."

"What?" She stared at it with suspicion. "Who is it?"

"Someone who wants to talk to you."

Mother reached across the table and took the phone. "Who is this?" she demanded into the mouthpiece.

She listened a long time. "Uh-huh, and how do I know this isn't a bluff?"

She listened again before finally closing the phone and placing it on the table. Walking over to the stove, she turned it off and stood looking at the wall a moment. The rest of us didn't dare disturb her.

"Rachel," she finally said. "Get your ass into the minivan and get the hell out of here." Rachel started to protest. "Right now. No arguments. I'll explain later."

Obeying, Rachel got up from the chair. After grabbing a jacket and purse near the door, she headed outside and down the stairs.

"What's going on?" asked Lisa. "Who was that?"

"A favor for a favor," Mother answered simply before turning to stare at me. "You certainly do have interesting friends, Odelia. Anytime you want to change careers, you come see me. I'm serious about that."

She turned to Lisa. "Take her and lock her up with Mr. Steele. Then get your ass and that bike out of here as fast as possible. Don't take the main highway. Disappear until I contact you. It might be awhile."

"What's going on?" Lisa demanded again.

Mother started gathering up her own coat and things. "The police are on their way. The caller said he'll stall them, but in return for the head start, we can't harm her. If we do, he promised he'd hunt us down himself."

"But who was it?"

Mother looked at me when she answered Lisa. "Someone who knows all the wrong people for all the right reasons."

At Lisa's command, I stood up, and so did Tim

"Not so fast," Mother said to Tim. "The deal was only for Odelia and that Steele character."

"So I can go?" Tim Weber's voice was hopeful, but his eyes reflected his understanding.

Mother nodded to Lisa, and in a flash the gun pointed at me swung toward Tim, blasting him in the chest. I let out a shriek and fell to the floor at the exact time he did.

THIRTY-FIVE

LISA GRABBED MY ARM and tried to hoist me to my feet. Nauseous, I vomited on her Doc Martens. For a minute, I thought she was going to shoot me despite Mother's orders. Unable to get me up, she started kicking me, yelling for me to move. Slowly I got to my knees, then my feet, and staggered in the direction she pushed me. Mother unlocked a door just off an alcove and told us to hurry. As soon as I reached the door, I was shoved through it. Behind me, the door was closed and locked.

After standing still for a minute, I managed to squeak out, "Steele, you here?"

Nothing. Tears were running down my face, and I felt chilled to the bone, as if my very spine were made of ice. I shivered and called out a little bit louder, "Steele, are you here?"

"Grey?" came the familiar voice out of the darkness.

"Steele!" His name came out of me wrapped in a sloppy sob.

Still disoriented by the dark and in shock from the murder I'd just witnessed, I had no idea that I was standing on a small landing. In response to Steele's voice, I took a step and plunged down a wooden staircase feet first. Along the way, my left leg hit something; pain pierced through me like a hot iron. I landed at the bottom of the stairs in a broken lump.

"Grey!" Steele called out but didn't come to me. "Over here."

After shaking off some of my daze, I looked around and saw that light was coming from a small bathroom. Then a lamp was switched on. Blinking against the sudden glare, I finally saw him. The room was a small, windowless, partially finished family room with a TV against one paneled wall, a table with two folding chairs, and a sleep sofa that was pulled out and covered with rumpled blankets. The room was cold and damp.

Steele was standing a few feet away but didn't come closer. Through my haze, I took note that around his ankle was a chain length with the other end attached to a support post near the sofa bed. He had it stretched to its limit in an attempt to get to me.

"Are you okay?" he asked.

Steele was disheveled and dirty, wearing gray sweatpants and a stained gray sweatshirt. His beard had grown out and his hair was matted. But he looked healthy and, more importantly, unharmed and alive.

As I tried to move, the pain in my leg almost made me vomit again. "I think I broke my leg."

Again he tried to reach me and couldn't. I heard the chain scrape against the floor as he tried to stretch it like a rubber band. "Did I hear a gunshot?"

I didn't want to tell Steele that one of his best friends was dead any more than I wanted to tell him that same friend had set him up to be kidnapped. Instead of answering, I tried to crawl to him.

I managed to get myself sitting upright with my good leg straight out in front of me. Using both hands, I straightened my broken leg out next to the good one. The pain was so intense I thought I was going to pass out, but instead I took deep breaths, released a few muffled sobs, and waited it out as best I could.

I rolled onto my tummy and crawled toward Steele, doing my best not to jostle my bad leg any more than necessary. The pain was still bad, but I forced mind over matter.

As soon as I reached Steele, he helped get me up onto the sofa bed. Again, severe pain shot through my leg and up into my brain like an electrical shock. With his chain chinking behind him, Steele disappeared into the bathroom and returned with a wet cloth. He wiped my face gently with it. It was cool and felt good against my flushed face. I was getting used to men mopping me up.

"We have to get you help." He grabbed a nearby broom and started banging on the ceiling with it. "Hey," he yelled, his face looking upward. "We need some help down here. She's hurt."

"Stop it, Steele. There's no one up there to hear you."

He kept banging. "Has to be. They've never left me alone before."

"They're all gone, taken off, gotten the hell out of Dodge." He turned to me, puzzled. "They got wind that the police are on their way," I explained. "They shoved me in here and hit the road."

He put down the broom. "Guess we'll just sit tight until they get here." He sat in one of the folding chairs and raked both hands through his greasy hair. "How in the hell did you find me? In fact, where in the hell am I?"

"We're somewhere east of Lake Elsinore." I shifted to sit up. Pain vibrated in my leg, and I held my breath until it passed. Steele came over and helped by scrunching up a pillow and placing it behind me. "Thanks."

He gave me a weak smile and patted me on a shoulder. "Why am I not surprised?"

"Huh?"

"I should have realized that it would be you who'd find me and not the police."

"It's my job, Steele. Taking care of you is my job."

He studied me in silence before offering another weak smile.

"Steele, do you remember what happened? You know, on the day you were snatched?" I wanted to see how much he knew before I filled him in on all the gory details.

"I left Karen's. Karen is my ex-wife, by the way."

I nodded. "We've met."

He stared at me briefly before continuing. "Anyway, I left Santa Barbara and was heading to the Ojai Inn, traveling along Route 150, when I saw a van broken down along the side of the road." He paced as he talked, the chain snaking behind him. "The hood was up and an elderly woman was standing next to it, looking rather helpless."

"Short and stocky, with short, curly gray hair?"

"Yes, exactly. You know her?"

"Unfortunately."

When I didn't offer an explanation, he shrugged. "I pulled over to see if I could help, and the next thing I knew I was in the back of the van with a nasty headache and several angry women holding guns and wearing ski masks." He stopped and looked at me. "They held me down while one of them put something over my mouth and nose. Next thing I knew, I woke up here."

"Did they ever tell you why they were holding you?"

He shook his head. "Every time one of them came down with food they wore a ski mask, except for the older woman. She was the only one whose face I saw. She kept telling me it would be over before I knew it. I didn't know if she meant my captivity or my life."

I shuddered, remembering how close we'd come to the latter. Better Steele not know, at least not yet.

He sat down again in one of the folding chairs. "You know why I'm here, don't you?"

I nodded.

"And?"

"Maybe we should try to get out of here. This place is pretty hard to find, especially in the dark. Wouldn't want the police to miss their big chance to rescue us. Hate to spend the night here."

"You're babbling, Grey."

"I am?"

"Yes, and you always babble when you're nervous and/or avoiding something. So out with it."

Why did it have to be me to tell him the whole sordid story?

"I found you. I'll let someone else tell you what's been going on."

"Tell me now, Grey."

"Did you know that Greg and I broke up?"

"I'm sorry to hear that, truly." His eyes bore into me. "Now quit stalling." When I didn't say anything, he added, "Does it have anything to do with Silhouette?"

"It has everything to do with Silhouette. At least the part involving you."

"What do you mean by that?"

"It's a rather complicated story with a lot of players and as many motives."

Steele sighed. "Just before this happened, I discovered that someone at the office was altering documents in the Silhouette case. I have a feeling it was Fran Evans." He looked at me for comment, and I confirmed his suspicion with a nod. "Did Fran have me kidnapped?"

I shook my head. "Not technically, but it is connected."

"I'm all ears, Grey. We've got nothing else to do."

"Yes, we do. We can get out of here." With considerable pain, I shifted myself to the edge of the pull-out bed. "I'm not waiting here another minute. It's creepy and too difficult to see from the road."

I was also worried that the trigger-crazed Lisa would come back and finish the job, just for the fun of it. With my broken leg and Steele in chains, she'd be able to pick us off as easily as nailing Bambi at a petting zoo.

"What about me?" Steele picked up his chain and rattled it as though auditioning for the part of Jacob Marley in *A Christmas Carol*.

I looked around for something to break or cut the chain but saw nothing. The padlock fastening it looked sturdy.

"Can that post be moved or broken?"

"I've already tried it, Grey. It's a support post, probably holds up the floor above us."

"Anything to pick the lock?"

"There are two locks, one at the base of the post and another connecting the chain to my ankle." He held up a fork that was on the table. "I've tried using this, but the tines are too thick for both locks. We need a thin piece of wire of some kind."

I dug into my pocket and came out with my key ring. On it were my car keys and house keys, including the key to Greg's house.

"Steele, come over here so I can see the lock, and bring the fork."

"I told you it won't fit."

"You want to get out of here or not?" He didn't answer. "It's been awhile since they left. And who knows if the police are even looking in the right area?" I looked up at him. "Or, if you'd rather, I'll hobble up those steps alone."

Grudgingly, Steele came over to the bed, bringing a chair with him. He lifted his leg onto the chair so I could inspect the lock at his ankle. It was a standard padlock. I tried all the keys on my key chain just in case, on a fluke, one of them fit. None did. I tried the fork, but only succeeded in bending two of the tines.

"What now, MacGyver?"

I shook a few brain cells to see what rattled loose. What did seemed outrageous and out of the question, but I couldn't think of anything else.

"Turn around and face the wall," I told him.

"What?"

"You heard me. Face the wall and don't turn back around until I tell you."

Once Steele was turned, I stripped off my sweater and knit top. He started to turn to say something.

"Turn around and you're dead, Steele. Face the wall or rot here for all I care."

He chuckled. "Now there's the Grey I know and love."

With some difficulty, I managed to unhook my bra. It was an expensive black lacy number, but more importantly it was an underwire bra. The idea of cannibalizing it for its flat, thin wire appalled me, but sacrifices had to be made. Once off, I tore at the end of the wire casing with my teeth and the fork until I managed to rip a hole in the end and push out the wire. On the end of the underwire was a plastic tip to guard it from poking through and mangling the wearer. A little more work with my teeth, and the tip was off. Quickly, I put my bra back on and, with one boob drooping, redressed.

"Okay, you can turn around now."

"Where did that come from?" he asked, inspecting the curved wire. I said nothing but went straight to work on the padlock, poking the end of the wire into the keyhole and wiggling it around.

Steele laughed, finally realizing what the wire was and where it had come from. "Now I've seen everything."

"Just shut up and help by holding the lamp closer."

Steele picked up the lamp from the table next to the sofa and held it close to where I was working. The light helped a great deal but it was still frustrating. After a while, I stopped long enough to roll my aching neck and shoulders. The fall down the stairs was beginning to make itself known in more than my broken leg.

When I was a kid, one Christmas I picked a lock off a footlocker where my parents had hidden my gifts. The lock was similar to the one on Steele's chain, but back then I had the single-mindedness of a kid and a pair of sturdy tweezers. Now I was working with a bra wire and a broken leg. As a kid I had been successful. I prayed I still had the gift of a light touch.

I extracted the wire and inspected the end. It was getting bent. I turned it around and removed the plastic guard from the other end. After taking a few deep breaths, I went back to work.

"You want me to try?" asked Steele.

"Maybe in a little bit. Just hold the light steady and close."

More time passed. The police hadn't arrived, and the lock wasn't budging. I was about to give up and let Steele have a go when I felt and heard a faint click. I gently wiggled the wire a little more, trying to wedge it in farther. Another minute and the lock opened.

As I leaned back against the pillows to rest, Steele wasted no time in removing the chain from his leg.

"Now you," he said.

"What are you talking about?"

Steele retrieved the broom from where he'd dropped it. "We need to fix you up so you don't injure that leg any worse."

Lining up the broomstick against my leg, he eyeball-measured it and broke it over his knee. While I watched, he fashioned a splint from the broom and strips he tore from the bed sheets, immobilizing my broken leg.

Grabbing one of the ripped sheets, I blew my nose with it. "What? I have a cold," I explained when he shot me a look of disgust. Steele might be disheveled and dirty, but at his core he was still a fussbudget.

Once done, he put an arm around me and helped me up. I tried to throw an arm around his shoulders, but he was too tall for me. Instead, I wrapped an arm around his waist and hung on while we hobbled together in a clumsy three-legged race to the stairs. At the stairs, he took each one first and helped me hop up behind him. It was painful and tedious, but soon we were near the top.

Steele had me stay a few steps below the landing while he threw his shoulder against the door over and over until the lock finally gave. As soon as the door flew open, he helped me up the final few steps.

"The door's that way," I said, pointing toward the back door. Tim's body was on the floor near the kitchen table. On the table was my cell phone. I wanted to grab the phone but didn't want Steele to see Tim. My mission was to get us out the door.

We were almost out of the house when Steele, like Lot's wife, couldn't resist taking a last look and turned into a pillar of salt—or, in his case, into a pillar of horror. Abandoning me to balance myself against the doorjamb, he ran to Tim's body.

"Tim!" He shook the body and examined the hole in Tim's chest. He felt for a pulse. Finding none, he turned to me and bellowed. "What happened? Why is Tim here? Why is he dead?"

"We need to leave, Steele," I said, trying to keep my voice even. "I'll tell you once we're safe."

"No, I can't leave him here."

"You can't help him. You must help yourself."

"No!"

"Damn it, Steele. He's the one who had you kidnapped!"

A deadly hush, louder than a hundred screams, filled the room. Steele stared at me with unbelieving eyes. He turned his gaze upon his friend's body, then back to me, weighing what I said with the evidence before him. I nodded and looked down at the floor.

Slowly Steele got up from the floor and made his way back to me. His shoulders sagged, and his face was pale beneath the two-week growth. He was shaken to his core by the betrayal and the loss, and I knew he'd never be the same.

I hopped over to the table and grabbed my phone while Steele took his turn leaning against the doorjamb. Once I returned to him, we wrapped our arms around each other and made our way down the steps to the ground. From there we started our slow shuffle down the driveway. When we passed Tim's Mercedes SUV, Steele looked at it. In the faint glow of the porch light, I could see tears running down his face.

But something was out of kilter.

Before, in addition to Tim's vehicle, there had been the white minivan and the dark green SUV parked in the driveway, along with the motorcycle. The minivan, the green SUV, and the bike were now gone, no doubt halfway to who-knows-where. Now, just behind Tim's Mercedes was another Mercedes, a snazzy dark coupe. I didn't know who it belonged to, but one thing I did know, it certainly wasn't a police car.

I started limping faster, encouraging Steele with my body language to pick up the pace. He looked down at me. I glanced over at the coupe and then back at him with urgency. He read my concern and immediately moved faster, almost picking me up with each step. We were almost down the long drive. Just a few more steps and we would be at the road. A few more yards after that and we would reach my half-hidden car. A car drove by on the road but kept going. There was no sign of any police.

We were between the hedges guarding the entrance to the drive when a shadow came out of one of the bushes.

"Don't you two make a cute couple?" It was a man, slightly built, and holding a gun. I recognized the voice.

314

THIRTY-SIX

"YOUR PAID ASSASSINS ARE gone, Tommy. Flown the coop."

Steele looked down at me. "You know this guy?"

"Long story. I'll tell you later."

Tommy laughed. "Same old Odelia."

"What's this about, Bledsoe?" asked Steele. "What do you have to do with Silhouette?"

"Tommy wasn't behind your abduction, Steele. Karen and Tim were. Tommy just gave them the referral to your abductors."

Tom Bledsoe smiled at me. I hadn't seen him in over twenty-five years, but even in the dark, I could see that except for losing his hair, he hadn't changed much in appearance. The noticeable difference was his self-assurance. In school, he had been a timid bookworm, nervous and unsure of himself. Now he was a man in control, a multimillionaire business owner and a puppet-master.

"Karen came to me, saying Tim was going to blow the whistle on everything. Seems he had a bad case of the guilts. So I came down to make sure all the loose ends got tied up nice and neat.

Looks like I arrived too late. Also looks like they did a half-assed job." He raised the gun higher. "No Christmas bonuses for them this year."

"Mother got a call, Tommy, giving her a heads-up that the police were on their way. She and her gang took off, leaving us behind."

"That doesn't sound like Mother. She's very detail oriented. She'd never leave live witnesses behind without a good reason."

Steele stepped forward, moving me behind him. Pain shot through my leg. "Well, this time she did, Bledsoe."

Another car went by on the road just a few yards away. I held my breath, hoping it was the police, but it didn't stop or even slow down.

"There was a deal cut," I said, poking my head out from behind Steele. The two men looked at me with interest. "She got a call from someone. Our lives for hers and a head start on the police."

"Who called, Odelia?"

I wasn't about to let Tommy know I knew the caller's identity or that the call actually came in on my phone.

I shrugged. "Not sure, but she seemed to think it was a deal worth taking. In fact, the caller rattled her enough for them to scatter like roaches."

"So who does this SUV belong to?"

"Tim Weber," Steele told him in a low voice. "He's inside—dead."

"Well, at least I don't have to do all of her cleanup."

I started backing up, edging for the road a few feet away, and pulling Steele with me.

"This isn't necessary, Bledsoe," Steele said, backing up with me very slowly.

"Sure it is, Mike. You see, I really do love Karen, and I believe in her work. She and I have plans for Family Bond, and those plans include rather unorthodox methods. It would never do to have you on the board, nosing around. So when Karen told me that her friend Tim needed you out of the way for a bit, I figured why not take advantage of it for our own purposes. It seemed like a natural way for all of us to get what we wanted."

He laughed. "The only thing is, I never intended for Mother to release you. They, on the other hand, did. Very naïve on their part." Tommy looked at me. "And I never expected you to get involved, Odelia. Still can't believe you work for this clown."

Saying nothing, I backed up a little more, again trying to take Steele with me.

"Did you like my little gift to you, Odelia?"

I stopped dead in my tracks. "Gift?"

"Donny Oliver. Well, an almost gift. When I found out about the theme of the reunion, I just knew I had to reward you for all your kindnesses. Nice dramatic touch, don't you think? Unfortunately, someone had already paid Mother for a hit on him." He grinned. "Still, my heart was in the right place."

Steele glanced from me to Tommy and back to me. "Who's Donny Oliver?"

"I'll tell you later."

Tommy laughed again and took aim with his gun. "As much as I like you, Odelia, I'm afraid there won't be a later ... for either of you."

Just then, another vehicle approached. I could see the headlights lighting up the road ahead of it, but this time it didn't pass. Instead, it aimed for the driveway.

Steele flung me to the ground and threw himself at Tommy. I screamed as flames of pain scorched my broken leg. My cries mingled with the sounds of another scream, a gunshot, and a crash. Seconds later, all was silent, except for the sound of a running engine.

I lifted my head. A few feet away was another SUV, a Jeep Grand Cherokee. It had barreled into the driveway, taking with it part of the hedge, and crashed into the back of Tommy's car.

"Sally!" I screamed. "Sally!"

In the darkness, a man rose from the ground. In his hand was a gun. I shrank in fear until I realized the figure was tall. Steele ran to the driver's side of the Jeep. I tried to roll over and thought I was going to pass out from the pain.

"She's okay," Steele yelled. "Banged up, but okay."

I watched as he scurried back to where he'd left Tommy.

"Bledsoe's still alive, but just barely," he reported. "Stay put. I'm going to see if there's a phone in the house."

Stay put. It was the second time that night I'd been told that. What would have happened, or not happened, had I stayed put when Dev had ordered me to? Steele might be dead now. Certainly Tim Weber's fate would not have been different, and my leg wouldn't be shattered. But Steele was alive, and that had been my mission.

Biting back cries of pain, I dug out my cell phone. I tried calling Dev, but the call failed. I tried Greg, but again it failed. Where were all those network people you see following customers around on TV?

I kept punching speed-dial numbers, going back and forth between Greg and Dev, until by luck one of them started ringing.

"Where are you?" Greg's frantic voice demanded on the other end. I started sobbing but somehow managed to tell him.

THIRTY-SEVEN

THE STILLNESS AFTER THE crash seemed to last for hours, but in reality it was only a couple of minutes before we heard sirens heading our way. Steele went to the road to flag them down. My call to Greg got dropped, but he called back and got through, staying on until he arrived on the heels of the authorities, directly behind Dev's car.

Once the police got there, everything was kicked up several notches. People ran between me, Sally, and Steele, asking each of us questions about our identity, physical condition, and what we knew all at the same time; it was pandemonium backlit by flashing lights. The paramedics loaded Tommy onto a stretcher, stuffed him into an ambulance, and took off. Dev told me it didn't look good for him.

Soon Sally and I were also bundled into an ambulance and taken to the hospital. Greg never left my side once we got there. For a minute, the doctors and I thought he was going to insist on being in surgery with me, but Sally, who had only minor cuts and bruises from the accident, talked him into staying with her. It broke my heart to see his face as they wheeled me away from him.

Greg is right. He shouldn't marry a corpse magnet.

"You decent?"

I turned toward the voice and smiled, knowing who it was before I saw his face. I shifted myself in the hospital bed and smoothed the covers down. Dev came in and took the chair next to my bed.

"As decent as I'll ever be."

"I just saw Greg. He was heading out to get a bite to eat with Mike Steele."

"Now there's a duo you don't see every day." I laughed. "Actually, I enlisted Steele to get some food into Greg before he drops, but Greg had to agree to go to a decent restaurant."

Dev shook his head and gave a deep, gravelly chuckle. "Steele's not such a bad guy under all that Armani."

I thought about that and smiled. "I know, but that'll be our little secret. He'd die if the truth got out."

"Seems you and I have another little secret that shouldn't get out." He leaned forward, resting his arms on the bed railing, his face a foot away, his eyes locked onto mine.

"Willie?"

Dev nodded. "I got two hysterical calls about your shenanigans—one from Sally and one from Greg. Neither surprised me. But just before that I received a very concerned and calculating call. One I never expected to get."

I said nothing but studied the blanket where I was plucking at a loose thread.

"I didn't know you were still in contact with William Proctor."

321

"I'm not really. He just materializes from time to time, kind of like fog."

"Uh-huh, and this time he provided you with information about Let Mother Do It and told you to tell me. Which you did not. In fact, he told you to keep your big nose out of it, didn't he?"

"Maybe."

"In fact, it's my understanding that he told you to tell me about Mother and then disappear."

"Maybe."

"Odelia, Odelia." Dev shook his big blond head. "Just be thankful the men in your life know you so well."

I studied Dev's lined face. "Willie got you to hold up the police while he threatened Mother, didn't he?"

"Well, I don't exactly know what he said to the woman, but it worked. It was a risky plan, but we didn't have much choice. If the police had shown up, everyone in that house might have died. Those women would have killed you all without a second thought before going down themselves. It was a gamble we had to take."

I shuddered. "Have they been found?"

Again, a shake of his head. "The green motorcycle was found ditched, but no surprise there. But at least we have some good descriptions, thanks to you. There was suspicion that a gang of professional killers was operating in California, perhaps in all of the Northwest, but in all these years there's never been any hard evidence. Mother may seem homespun and folksy, but she's very smart."

A silence settled between us. I studied Dev's face, feeling bad that I had placed him in such a spot professionally and emotionally.

"I'm sorry, Dev." I paused. "About everything. I haven't been very fair to you."

Dev picked up one of my hands and held it gently. "I'm a big boy, Odelia. And I'm no fool. In my heart, I've always known that you and Greg belonged together."

Tears rolled down my face as I slipped my hand out of Dev's and cupped it against his warm cheek. He turned and kissed my palm.

THIRTY-EIGHT

My leg itched like hell. I slipped a letter opener I'd found on the desk between the cast and my skin and tried my best to worm it down far enough to reach the itch that was becoming as annoying as a colony of fire ants.

"Stop that," Zee ordered. "You can get an infection that way." She snatched the letter opener from my hands and stuck it in a desk drawer.

I was staying with the Washingtons in their downstairs guest-room/office. They had moved out the sofa bed that usually occupied the room and replaced it temporarily with a rented hospital bed. Not that I needed a hospital bed, but it did make it easier for me to maneuver and get comfortable with my heavy cast. I had also rented a wheelchair. It was a nice respite from trying to work with the crutches all the time. But the wheelchair would soon be history. How Greg manages to use one of these day in and day out and do all the incredible things he does, including sports, is even more amazing to me now. For the past three weeks, I've seen life from his level, and it has been an eye opener, believe me.

Seamus, ensconced on a cushion on the desk chair, meowed softly. In spite of his allergies, Seth had allowed Seamus to also move in temporarily. In fact, he had even suggested it. Zee, suffering from near-empty nest syndrome, was spoiling the surly cat more than I ever dreamed of doing or thought possible. It worried me a bit that when it was time to go, Seamus would not want to budge.

Thrilled that I had found Steele, solved the mystery of the altered documents, and managed to save Silhouette from jumping to Goldberg-Rawlings, the firm had given me four weeks off with pay. But even with their generosity, I was antsy to return to work and resume my normal life, or rather, new life. Tonight I was moving in with Greg—lock, stock, cat, and temporary wheelchair. When I did go back to work, I would be commuting from Seal Beach. It was a much longer commute but worth it. As soon as I was able, I would pack up my townhouse and rent it out.

Johnette Morales is in a private residential facility. Victor reports she is doing quite well and is expected to come home by Christmas. Sally and I are going to visit her next week.

She told police that she and Donny never had an affair, though that was her original intent in meeting him that time at the motel. She had discovered on her own about Cindy and Victor, but when push came to shove she couldn't go through with her plan of having payback sex with Donny. Halloween night she got it in her head to confront Cindy and had left the house bound for the Olivers' residence. On the way, she lost her gumption and instead picked up a bottle of vodka and some over-the-counter sleeping pills and headed for the same motel where she'd met Donny. The register at the motel showed Johnette checking in before Carolyn Poppin was shot.

Devastated by current events, Cindy Oliver packed up her girls and moved into her parents' home just outside of Seattle to help her father care for her mother, who was now partially paralyzed from a stroke she suffered soon after the shooting. I hadn't heard yet what the authorities planned to do about Mrs. Poppin and the murder charge, but I hoped they would leave her alone, deciding it would do no good to throw an elderly, disabled woman in prison.

Tommy Bledsoe died from the gunshot wound he received while struggling with Steele over the gun.

Both Fran and Karen were arrested on charges of conspiracy. I told the police everything I had learned while sitting at the kitchen table with Mother, including that Tim had said Fran had no part in the kidnapping. I don't know what will happen to them, but I do know that I will be expected to give testimony when the time comes.

Steele's back to working ten- and twelve-hour days. The few times I've seen him, he hasn't said a word about Tim Weber or Karen's betrayal. The Silhouette/Sweet Kiss matter was settled in favor of our client, and once again there is a parade of temporary secretaries going in and out of Steele's life. But Jolene McHugh and I have a surprise for Steele. Unbeknownst to him, we have located, interviewed, and hired a permanent new secretary for that spot. She starts a week from Monday, the same day I return. Her name is Jill Bernelli. That's right, Sally Kipman's Jill. Jill of the fabulous bundt cake. Jill the lesbian. Seems Jill worked as a legal secretary for many years, until two years ago when the firm she was working at dissolved.

I can't wait to see Steele's face.

Zee continued to fuss over me, fixing my hair and straightening my dress over my cast, until I thought I was going to roll over her foot out of desperation. But looking at her glowing face, I couldn't stay annoyed. She was hovering and fussing because she loves me, so she can hover and fuss all she likes.

"Odelia, honey, you ready?" It was Seth, standing at the door, looking so handsome in his tux. "People are waiting."

I nodded. It was shit or get off the pot time.

Zee handed me my bouquet and grabbed her own. She bent down and gave me a kiss on my cheek, and I saw that she was crying. She paused long enough to whisper in my ear. "You are so blessed."

And don't I know it.

Zee left, and Seth took command of the wheelchair, being careful that my gown wasn't in the way of the wheels. He wheeled me out of the room and through the house to the back patio, where a white runner had been placed going from the house to the pool area. At the end of the runner, an altar had been constructed with an arched trellis interwoven with flowers. Greg and I would be married on the exact spot where we met.

On either side of the runner were rented white chairs filled with the people we love. I saw Greg's parents in the front. Sitting obediently with them, Wainwright sported a jaunty white bow for the occasion. When he saw me, Wainwright let out a short, loud whine, causing everyone to laugh. I also spotted Kelsey and Joan, Dev, Boomer, Steele and Jolene, Jacob and Hannah Washington, even Carl Yates and his wife. They were all there, including my goofy stepmother, whom today I loved unconditionally. Even Willie had sent flowers along with a handwritten note that said: *No worries, little mama.*

At the end of the altar stood Zee, my matron of honor, wearing a dark blue simple gown, and Sally Kipman, wearing a silk pantsuit of the same color. Greg's brother was his best man, and Seth would join them as a groomsman.

And then there was Greg, sitting in his wheelchair, looking gorgeous in a tux. The man who loved me in spite of my faults and stubbornness. The man who decided it was better to love me and worry about me than to live without me. The man who told me if I continued sticking my nose into other people's business, then he intended to take out a lot of life insurance on me.

The man who proposed to me surrounded by murder, mayhem, and flashing police lights, and said he didn't care as long as he got to stay by my side forever.

As soon as Seth negotiated the chair onto the runner, the music started, and my father joined us. He beamed at me with tears in his eyes. Here was a man who was seldom out of droopy pants and old suspenders, but today he was in a tuxedo—just for me. He held out his arm and I took it, and with Seth pushing the wheelchair, my father walked me down the aisle.

As I sat in my wheelchair with my broken leg, next to Greg in his, I had a fleeting moment of fear as Pastor Hill recited the vows. Greg answered his with confidence and conviction. Then it was my turn.

"Odelia Patience Grey," I heard as if in a dream, "do you take Gregory William Stevens to be your wedded husband, to live together in marriage? Do you promise to love, comfort, honor, and keep him for better or worse, for richer or poorer, in sickness and in health, and forsaking all others, be faithful only to him so long as you both shall live?"

I paused and felt the people around me hold their breath. I studied Greg's face, both of us at eye level, both of us with tears of joy in our eyes.

"I do."

In the end, it wasn't the wedding of my dreams. But in the end, I married the man of my dreams, and isn't that what really matters?

No worries, little mama.

THE END

ABOUT THE AUTHOR

LIKE THE CHARACTER ODELIA Grey, Sue Ann Jaffarian is a middle-aged, plus-size paralegal. She lives in Los Angeles with her two cats, B and Raffi, and writes mysteries and general fiction, as well as short stories. In addition to writing, she is nationally sought after as a motivational and humorous speaker. Sue Ann is currently working on *The Ghost of Granny Apples*, the first book in a new series for Midnight Ink, as well as *Epitaph Envy*, the next book in the Odelia Grey series.

Visit Sue Ann on the Internet at:

WWW.SUEANNJAFFARIAN.COM

and

WWW.SUEANNJAFFARIAN.BLOGSPOT.COM